Hat with triple feather, doublet with twice-triple skirt, cloak which his interminable rapier lifts up behind, with pomp, like the insolent tail of a cock; prouder than all the Artabans that Gascony ever bred, he goes about in his stiff Punchinello ruff, airing a nose. . . . Ah, gentlemen, what a nose is that! (page 16)

His blade is half the shears of Fate! (page 16)

Face about, I say . . . or else, tell me why you are looking at my nose. (page 27)

Be it known to you that I am proud, proud of such an appendage! inasmuch as a great nose is properly the index of an affable, kindly, courteous man, witty, liberal, brave, such as I am! (page 28)

"It is a crag! . . . a peak! . . . a promontory! . . . A promontory, did I say? . . . It is a peninsula!" (page 29)

Of wit, O most pitiable of objects made by God, you never had a rudiment, and of letters, you have just those that are needed to spell "fool!" (page 30)

My foppery is of the inner man. (page 30)

I am without gloves? . . . a mighty matter! I only had one left, of a very ancient pair, and even that became a burden to me . . . I left it in somebody's face. (page 31)

My rapier prickles like a foot asleep! (page 31)

As I follow with my eyes some woman passing with some cavalier, I think how dear would I hold having to walk beside me, linked like that, slowly, in the soft moonlight, such a one! I kindle—I forget— and then . . . then suddenly I see the shadow of my profile upon the garden-wall! (page 38)

To displease is my pleasure. I love that one should hate me. Dear friend, if you but knew how much better a man walks under the exciting fire of hostile eyes, and how amused he may become over the spots on his doublet, spattered by Envy and Cowardice!   (page 70)

Eloquence I will lend you! . . . And you, to me, shall lend all-conquering physical charm . . . and between us we will compose a hero of romance!   (page 75)

Roxane shall not have disillusions! Tell me, shall we win her heart, we two as one? will you submit to feel, transmitted from my leather doublet into your doublet stitched with silk, the soul I wish to share?
(page 76)

You shall never find us—poets!—without epistles in our pockets to the Chlorises . . . of our imagining!   (page 76)

My heart always cowers behind the defence of my wit.   (page 93)

Your name is in my heart the golden clapper in a bell; and as I know no rest, Roxane, always the heart is shaken, and ever rings your name!
(page 94)

Terrible and jealous, is love . . . with all its mournful frenzy!
(page 94)

The madman is erudite.   (page 104)

I came to implore your pardon—as it is fitting, for we are both perhaps about to die!—your pardon for having done you the wrong, at first, in my shallowness, of loving you . . . for mere looking!
(page 132)

While I have stood below in darkness, others have climbed to gather the kiss and glory!   (page 158)

Thanks to you there has passed across my life the rustle of a woman's gown.   (page 158)

CYRANO DE BERGERAC

Edmond Rostand

*With an Introduction and Notes
by Peter Connor*

GEORGE STADE
CONSULTING EDITORIAL DIRECTOR

BARNES & NOBLE CLASSICS
NEW YORK

JB

BARNES & NOBLE CLASSICS

NEW YORK

Published by Barnes & Noble Books
122 Fifth Avenue
New York, NY 10011

www.barnesandnoble.com/classics

Rostand's *Cyrano de Bergerac* was first published in French in 1898.
Gertrude Hall's English translation appeared later that year.

Originally published in mass market format in 2004 by Barnes & Noble Classics
with new Introduction, Notes, Biography, Chronology, Inspired By,
Comments & Questions, and For Further Reading.
This trade paperback edition published in 2008.

Cyrano de Bergerac
ISBN-13: 978-1-59308-387-8
ISBN-10: 1-59308-387-4
LC Control Number 2007941533

Produced and published in conjunction with:
Fine Creative Media, Inc.
322 Eighth Avenue
New York, NY 10001

Michael J. Fine, President and Publisher

Printed in the United States of America
WCM

3 5 7 9 10 8 6 4

EDMOND ROSTAND

Edmond Rostand was born on May 1, 1868, in Marseille to wealthy, literary-minded parents. His father, an avid essayist, versifier, and translator of Catullus, instilled in young Edmond what would be a lifetime devotion to such literary masters as Miguel de Cervantes, William Shakespeare, and Victor Hugo. Indeed, although Rostand lived well into the beginning of the modern age, many scholars contend that he carried on the romantic tradition of Hugo and other writers.

Edmond completed his secondary education at the College Stanislas in Paris, where he showed his considerable literary talent, then studied law, which he never practiced. While hiking in the Pyrenees in 1888 he met his future wife, Rosemonde Gérard, an aspiring poet of moderate success. Rosemonde's family helped Rostand's early career immensely: He wrote his first play, a four-act vaudeville-style piece called *Le Gant rouge* (*The Red Glove*), with her half-brother, William Lee, and published his well-received first collection of verse, *Les Musardises*, with the help of Gérard's godfather, the poet Leconte de Lisle.

Cyrano de Bergerac premiered to a rapturous reception in 1897 and remains one of the great classics of nineteenth-century France. The flamboyant character Cyrano, rural hero and national champion, was a charismatic representative of the grandeur of France and helped a wounded nation recover from defeat in the Franco-Prussian War, the loss of Alsace-Lorraine, and a series of political and military scandals that included the Dreyfus Affair. Rostand achieved success with other notable productions—including *La Princesse lointaine* (*The Faraway Princess*) and *La Samaritaine* (*The Woman of Samaria*), both with the great actress Sarah Bernhardt in the leading role—but *Cyrano* remains the work for which Rostand is known. He spent most of his last twenty years in near-retirement at his home in the Pyrenees and died of Spanish flu in 1918.

TABLE OF CONTENTS

The World of
Edmond Rostand and
CYRANO DE BERGERAC

1619   Savinien de Cyrano, the real Cyrano de Bergerac, is born in Paris.

1640   While fighting for France in the Thirty Years War, de Bergerac receives a stab wound to the throat during the siege of the town of Arras in northern France and leaves the military.

1641   Cyrano begins studying at the Collège de Lisieux under the philosopher Pierre Gassendi, known for his libertine views.

1654   Two of Cyrano's plays, *La Mort d'Agrippine* (*The Death of Agrippine*) and *Le Pédant joué* (*The Pedant Imitated*), are published.

1655   Cyrano dies on July 28, possibly of injuries sustained when a scrap of wood falls from a building and strikes him on the head (some believe the accident was planned) or from complications of a venereal disease.

1657   Cyrano's *Histoire comique des états et empires de la lune* (*Comical History of the States and Empires of the Moon*) appears posthumously. In this and a companion volume, *Histoire comique des états et empires de la soleil* (*Comical History of the States and Empires of the Sun*), published in 1662, he satirizes contemporary society and the prevailing belief that Earth is the center of the universe.

1858   Cyrano's works are published for the first time since the seventeenth century.

1868   Edmond Rostand is born into a well-off family in Marseille on May 1.

1872   De Bergerac's tragedy *Le Mort d'Agrippine* is revived for one performance in Paris.

1878   Rostand begins his studies at the lycée of Marseille.

1884   The Rostands move to Paris, and Edmond continues his studies at the Collège Stanislas. Miguel de Cervantes, William Shakespeare, Victor Hugo, and Theodore de Banville are his literary heroes.

1887   The Académie de Marseille gives Rostand top honors for his entry in the essay contest "Deux romanciers de Provence: Honoré d'Urfé et Émile Zola" ("Two Provencal Romantic Writers: Honoré d'Urfé and Émile Zola").

1888   While on vacation in the Pyrenees, Rostand meets aspiring poet Rosemonde Gérard, goddaughter of the poet Leconte de Lisle, and falls in love.

1889   The Eiffel Tower is completed. Rostand's first play, a four-act, vaudeville-style piece called *Le Gant rouge* (*The Red Glove*), written with Gérard's half-brother, William Lee, premiers without success.

1890   Rostand and Gérard marry. Gérard helps Rostand publish his first collection of verse, *Les Musardises*, to critical praise.

1892   The Comédie-Française accepts Rostand's *Les Romanesques* (*The Romancers*), Rostand's first full-length play.

1894   *Les Romanesques* premiers at the Comédie-Française. An innocent Jewish army officer named Alfred Dreyfus is convicted of leaking French military secrets to Germany, beginning the disastrous Dreyfus Affair, which deeply divides France.

1895   Sarah Bernhardt stars in the premiere of *La Princesse lointaine* (*The Faraway Princess*), which Rostand wrote with the star in mind, but it closes before finishing its 35-performance contract. Bernhardt introduces Rostand to well-known actor Constant Coquelin, who asks Rostand to write him a part in his next play. The role and the play will be *Cyrano de Bergerac*.

1897   *La Samaritaine* (*The Woman of Samaria*), starring Bernhardt, premiers in April, and has a brief yet popular run. President François Grévy is forced to resign upon the revelation that his son-in-law, Daniel Wilson, has been selling membership in the

Legion d'Honneur. The Dreyfus Affair reaches its peak, rock-ing France, as Mathieu Dreyfus discovers that the army and government are suppressing evidence that would exonerate his brother, Alfred. In the midst of the turmoil *Cyrano de Berg-erac* premieres on December 28, to enormous success.

1898   Four days after the premiere of *Cyrano*, Rostand is created chevalier de la Légion d'Honneur and President Félix Faure attends a performance. Émile Zola publishes the immensely influential pro-Dreyfus article "J'accuse," which results in Zola's imprisonment. Despite Rostand's conservative back-ground, he sides quietly with the Dreyfus supporters, who in-clude Marcel Proust and Anatole France. *Cyrano* premieres simultaneously in Philadelphia and New York. The Paris Métro opens.

1899   A comic opera based on *Cyrano* opens in New York. The Cour de Cassation (French Supreme Court) orders a retrial for Dreyfus, who receives a presidential pardon.

1900   Rostand's *L'Aiglon* (*The Eaglet*), starring Bernhardt, premiers to moderate success. Rostand's health is declining, and he withdraws to Cambo-les-bains in the Pyrenees. He does not complete another play for ten years. Coquelin and Bernhardt perform *Cyrano* in New York.

1901   Rostand is elected to the Académie française, but his continu-ing poor health prevents him from making an acceptance ad-dress. He is created officier de la Légion d'Honneur. Coquelin and Bernhardt perform *Cyrano* in London. Henri Toulouse-Lautrec, who created a lithograph of Coquelin playing *Cyrano*, dies.

1902   Rostand receives a commission to travel to Hernani, Spain, to participate in festivities marking the centenary of Victor Hugo's birth. André Gide's *The Immoralist* appears. Zola dies.

1905   Rostand more or less retires to a residence he has built near Cambo-les-bains with his earnings from *Cyrano*. He will spend the rest of his life living in this house.

1910   *Chantecler*, an experimental drama based on stories of fabulist Jean de La Fontaine, premiers to disappointing reviews. The next year Rostand finishes most of his final play, *Le Dernière Nuit de Don Juan* (*The Last Night of Don Juan*), inspired by Miguel de Cervantes's novel *Don Quixote*, but does not release it.

1913   *Cyrano* has its thousandth performance in Paris. Marcel Proust publishes the first part of *À la recherche du temps perdu*.

1914   World War I begins.

1915   Rostand visits the trenches.

1916   *Le Vol de la Marseillaise* (*The Flight of the Marseillaise*), a collection of Rostand's World War I poetry, appears.

1918   Rostand falls victim to the Spanish flu and dies in Paris on December 2, six weeks after the end of World War I. His current partner, Mary Marquet, as well as Gérard and their two sons, Maurice, a novelist and critic, and Jean, a notable scientist and writer, survive him.

1922   *Le Dernière Nuit de Don Juan* premiers.

INTRODUCTION

A great deal of lore surrounds the premiere of *Cyrano de Bergerac* at the Théâtre de la Porte-Saint-Martin in Paris on December 28, 1897. That just before the curtain went up, Rostand fell at the feet of leading actor Constant Coquelin and exclaimed: "Forgive me! Oh, forgive me, my friend, for having dragged you into this disastrous adventure!" That he then donned a costume and slipped onstage during the first act, causing surprise and confusion among the actors. That the first act was greeted with bravos, the following ones with standing ovations, and the final scene with forty-two curtain calls, so many that at two o'clock in the morning the exhausted stage manager simply left the curtain open and went home to bed.

Much of this lore comes from an interview given by Rostand himself, as well as from an account of opening night by his wife, Rosemonde Gérard. Theater people, especially when they are also interested parties, can be relied upon to dramatize a little; it is indeed their prerogative. Still, by any account, *Cyrano de Bergerac* was an immense, indeed a phenomenal, success. At twenty-nine—the English critic Sir Max Beerbohm referred to him as "the talented boy-playwright"—Rostand became what we now know as an overnight sensation: Only Victor Hugo, and then only after a long career as a writer and statesman, had known the kind of fame and glory that Rostand achieved in a single night. Paris was in a collective swoon. The most caustic of theater critics—men who were paid to be nasty—hailed *Cyrano* as "the most beautiful dramatic poem to appear for half a century" (Emile Faguet in *Le Journal des débats*) and spoke of December 28 as "a date that will live in the annals of the theater" (Francisque Sarcey of *Le Temps*). The 29th started out pretty well, too: On that day the French Minister of Education nominated Rostand for the *Légion d'Honneur*, France's highest honor. Two days later, just in time for the New Year's honors list, the decree officially naming him a chevalier de la Légion d'Honneur had found its way onto the desk of Félix Faure, president of the Republic, who, having signed it, booked a loge at the Théâtre de la Porte-Saint-Martin for himself and his family. More laurels were to follow. Elected to the Académie des sciences morales et politiques in 1898, Rostand would surely have been elected also to the Académie française were its membership not fixed at seventy (someone has to die before a new member can be elected; Rostand had to wait until 1901). *Cyrano* was soon being performed in New York (at the Garden Theater in 1898), in Berlin (at the Deutsches Theater in 1898), in London (in French at the Lyceum in 1898, in English at Wyndham's Theatre in 1900). The play was translated into the major European languages: in 1898 into English (two versions), German, Dutch, Italian, Hungarian, and Polish (two versions); in 1899 into Spanish, Czech, and, once again, into Polish.

What accounts for the success of this play, a success that has lasted now for more than a century? This is a question that has vexed literary critics and rather annoyed the intelligentsia, who have been at pains to insist that the popular appeal of *Cyrano* has less to do with the intrinsic artistic merits of the play than with the historical and cultural context in which it was received. For once the euphoria of opening night had died down, other, less sympathetic voices began to be heard. Some, like Jules Romains, saw Rostand as one of a group of "eloquent and vulgar poets" peddling a "degraded form of romantic drama" to the middle classes. Rostand and his ilk, according to Romains, "deserve more than scorn: reprobation. They have lowered French taste, perverted the public, compromised our national dignity." André Ferdinand Hérold saw in *Cyrano* a fine exercise in "cacography" (Monsieur Rostand "knows a thousand ways to torture a line") and a "masterpiece of vulgarity" by one who has perfected "the art of writing badly."

Critics almost never like popular successes (if the vulgar public were able to identify good theater and literature on its own, critics would be left with nothing to do), but Rostand's case is of more than

passing interest because the divisiveness surrounding the reception of
Cyrano reflects a great cultural unease, a malaise in late-nineteenth-
century French society. *Cyrano* became an *affaire*, as the French say,
such that writers, critics, and even ordinary theatergoers had to be either for or against it. "Claudel or Rostand," said the novelist André
Gide, "you have to choose," meaning: One must either grapple with all
the harshness and the complexities of the modern world (Paul
Claudel, a contemporary of Rostand's, was a highly original playwright influenced by symbolism), or else remain in the idealized, fanciful place depicted by Rostand and incarnated by his valiant
soldier-poet Cyrano.

The Théâtre de la Porte-Saint-Martin's production of *Cyrano*
provoked a new round in the old French debate between the ancients
and the moderns, a debate that was intricately related to the raging
political issue of the day—namely, nationalism. Rostand, rightly or
wrongly, was associated with what Jehan Rictus, referring to the
right-wing royalist movement, called "a form of literary Boulangism."
He was perceived by many of his contemporaries as an old guard,
highly conservative figure. Rictus surely went too far—Rostand's
personal politics were quite liberal; he was a Dreyfusard and a friend
of the socialist Léon Blum. But from a literary point of view, it is un-
deniable that *Cyrano* breaks no new ground. Rostand, moreover, was
not bashful about his dislike for the changing times: "I wrote
Cyrano . . . with love, with pleasure, and also with the idea of fighting against the tendencies of the times, tendencies which, in truth, ir-
ritated me, revolted me."

While Rostand is not explicit about these "tendencies," it is not
hard to guess what he has in mind. The overall cultural mood in France
during the 1890s was gloomy, joyless, and resentful. In literature,
harsh forms of realism prevailed (especially Émile Zola's doctrine of
naturalism), alongside a Wagnerian-influenced decadence (as in the
works of Joris Karl Huysmans and Octave Mirbeau, for example); in
the theater, the psychological drama of Henrik Ibsen and Maurice
Maeterlinck played in theaters that seemed ever more open to

experimentation. Against this backdrop, Rostand's play, while it draws upon the melodramatic and vaudeville-style traditions of boulevard theater, represented something very different from what was on offer in Paris. Above all, it came as a welcome release from the often rebarbative, highly cerebral avant-garde art forms, offering by contrast an intellectually undemanding spectacle full of movement and pathos ("a fanfare of red pants," as one critic put it). "What happiness! What happiness!" wrote Francisque Sarcey. "We are at last to be rid of Scandinavian mists and overly minute psychological analyses, and of the deliberate brutalities of realist drama. Here is the joyous sun of Old Gaul which, after a long night, is rising over the horizon. This brings pleasure; it refreshes the blood!"

After Maeterlinck's "static drama," in which a clock chiming constitutes a major event, it must indeed have been refreshing to see Cyrano leap onto the stage and fight a duel while composing a ballad. But there are other reasons for the success of *Cyrano*. One explanation sometimes advanced appears paradoxical: In spite of its worldwide appeal (performed from Moscow to Tokyo to Reunion Island, the play has been adapted to fit the context of colonial India, translated into Scottish dialect, etc.), *Cyrano*'s appeal has a lot to do with its irreducible Frenchness. For Cyrano is a Gascon, and to the French theatergoer this evokes a particularly flattering image of French national identity. In the French imagination, the Gascon—the model is d'Artagnon in Alexandre Dumas' *Three Mousqueteers* (1844)—is proud, gallant, loyal, honest (the French expression "parole de Gascon" means something like "Scout's honor") and, above all, courageous. This last characteristic, which is related to Gascony's history—war was for centuries a way of life in this fiercely independent province—must have appealed to the French public in 1897: Still in mourning after a humiliating military defeat in 1870 in the Franco-Prussian War, mired in the sordid revelations of the Dreyfus Affair, the French were primed to welcome this vision of France in a sweeping cape, this story of French bravura, heroism, and panache.

Thus *Cyrano* was seen as a tonic for the neurasthenic French spirit ("sickly product of the North," to cite the words used to describe Christian in the play), and Rostand was seen as upholding the endangered values of old France (that President Faure took his family along to the play is indicative of the kind of values the play was thought to impart). Rostand, in fact, belongs if not to "Old Gaul" then at least to a fairly archaic France, different from the thoroughly industrialized and modern country described minutely in the novels of Émile Zola. The contrast between the two authors is stark and instructive (Rostand's first important piece of writing compared Zola, unfavorably, with the precious novelist Honoré d'Urfé). While Zola was down in the mines and sewers of Paris, taking notes on the daily life and *mœurs* of the French worker as though in a laboratory, Rostand was dreaming up *Cyrano* in his comfortable apartment in the rue Fortuny. In his living room stood a black-lacquered piano, a wedding gift to Rosemonde from the composer Jules Massenet, who had been the witness at the marriage; in the study hung two Fragonards; on the writing table the Countesse de Genlis, an ancestor of Rosemonde, had written love letters to the Duke of Orleans, etc., etc. Aspects of *Cyrano* bear the imprint of this association with the aristocracy. There is, for example, the obvious point that the subject of the play is a nobleman. There is the fact that Rostand chose to write in rhymed alexandrines (lines of twelve syllables that obey fairly rigid laws of prosody), an anachronism, to say the least, in an era that long ago had seen this tradition challenged by Charles Baudelaire (with his "prose poems") and Stéphane Mallarmé. The seventeenth-century setting of the play seems a deliberate avoidance and implicitly a rejection of everything contemporary, suggesting Rostand's nostalgia for a time when relations were more strictly and more hierarchically organized. The evils that Rostand chooses to fight are not the complicated social ills of alcoholism, unemployment, and destitution; in *Cyrano* enemies are easily identifiable (the bullies who threaten Lignière; the Prince of Spain in the siege of Arras; the inherent corruptness of the patronage system), and the absolutism of the response is accordingly simple.

*   *   *

There is some truth to the argument that *Cyrano de Bergerac* succeeded because it permitted a demoralized population to believe once again in the ideals of valor, courage, and sacrifice that recent experience had so severely challenged. At the same time, there is something inherently unsatisfying about such a line of reasoning. It seems a peculiarly negative way of assessing the worth and impact of a work of art, interesting enough from an extratextual perspective, but neglectful of the intrinsic merits of the play, which might also help explain the thralldom of spectators at the turn of the century and beyond. For a great deal of the aesthetic appeal of this play stems from within: from the ingenuity of its characterization (I refer to Cyrano, obviously, but also to Ragueneau, Cyrano's alter ego, in a sense), from the drama as well as the sheer unexpectedness of its plot (no one was expecting a play about a man with a big nose), from its thrilling dynamism (Rostand is superb at handling large-scale crowd scenes with lots of action; see the opening act). Moreover, in broad terms, *Cyrano* succeeds because it stages so well the tension between the earthly and the ethereal, between the base and the sublime, and because theatergoers recognize in it an intelligent balance of irony, realism, and fantasy. To go a step further, *Cyrano* stages the triumph of the ethereal over the earthly, of the sublime over the base. To put this in the language of the play, *Cyrano* is a staging of panache, without doubt the single most important word in the play and one we will examine here in some detail.

But first things first. As the title of the play suggests, *Cyrano de Bergerac* is very much about Cyrano, and Cyrano is a likable character. There is hardly a juicier role in the dramatic repertory: Cyrano is almost always on stage, and it is almost always Cyrano who does the talking (to such an extent that even when Christian is speaking, it is often in a sense still Cyrano). Rostand fully exploits the dramatic potential of a character whose physical and verbal assuredness "dominates the situation," to use a phrase Rostand applied to panache. If Cyrano's centrality to the play corresponds to Rostand's dramatic vision, it stems partly also from the circumstances of composition of the play. The part of Cyrano was written for one of the leading actors of the time, Constant Coquelin, whom Rostand had met through Sarah Bernhardt. Rostand got into the habit of showing Coquelin completed sections of the play as he went along. Some of the speeches scripted for other characters so pleased the star of the Paris stage that he claimed them for himself. The famous scene (act two, scene vii) in which Cyrano presents the cadets of Gascony, for example, was originally scripted for Carbon de Castel-Jaloux. (During rehearsals, when the actor playing Le Bret complained that he had very few lines, Coquelin responded: "But you have a fine role. I talk to you all the time.")

Theater that stages a hero allows for more immediate and arguably more gratifying forms of identification than the theater of ideas. Like the cadets in Carbon de Castel-Jaloux's company, the spectators of this play watch and listen to see what Cyrano will do and say next. Now everything Cyrano does and says is governed by what we could call an ethics of panache. Panache is Rostand's word, or at least a word he made his own; before him, no one had used it in quite the same sense. In its simplest and literal sense, panache refers to the feathered plume of a helmet or other type of military headgear. This is the meaning of the word as it appears in act four, scene iv, where Cyrano speaks of Henri IV, who urged his soldiers during the battle of Ivry to "rally around my white plume; you will always find it on the path of honor and glory" (cited in the Bair translation of *Cyrano*; see "For Further Reading"). But when Cyrano uses the word again at the end of the play—poignantly, it is his and the play's last word—it has acquired a metaphorical dimension, and suggests at once a commitment to valor, a certain elegance, self-esteem verging on pride, and also a certain . . . *je ne sais quoi*. Such vagueness is disappointing but also inevitable: Rostand himself warned against limiting the meaning of the word to a dictionary definition, as though to do so would be to imprison a sentiment the essence of which is to insist on absolute freedom from convention.

In his speech to the Académie française in 1903, Rostand described panache, rather mystically, as "nothing more than a grace." "It is not greatness," he said, "but something added on to greatness, and which moves above it." Panache is not just physical courage in the face of danger; it includes a verbal assertiveness in the face of possible death. "To joke in the face of danger is the supreme form of politeness," Rostand said. Hence panache is "the wit of bravura"—not bravura alone (which might be perfectly stupid), but the expression in language of that bravura and indeed language *as* an expression of bravura: "It is courage that so dominates a particular situation, that it finds just what to say."

Panache thus describes the remarkable alliance of physical courage and verbal acuity that Cyrano so dramatically displays in act one, scene iv, where he engages in a duel while simultaneously composing a ballad. There is fundamentally here no difference between the sword and the word. Nobility of action and elegance in language—this is the rather aristocratic ideal that Rostand wishes to resurrect. (To the extent that it is related to linguistic brilliance, panache, we might note in passing, is a literary-artistic ideal; Cyrano is in part a portrait of the artist, the one who struggles against the vulgarity of the world and the baseness of language, and who redeems it through a winning phrase.)

A code of ethics, dictating behavior and speech in given situations, panache is akin to the concept of honor in Golden Age Spain. Like honor, panache represents a law of conduct that must remain inviolate, "unblemished and unbent," and that not only explains the life of sacrifice that Cyrano has lived, but redeems that life. In a period of fin-de-siècle decadence, the audience at the Théâtre de la Porte-Saint-Martin might well have found seductive this new and rather dashing version of morality. There is evidence that Rostand envisioned Cyrano as a figure to be emulated. Invited back to his Paris secondary school, the Lycée Stanislas, he encouraged the pupils (in rhymed verse, of course) to aspire to the ideal of panache ("*empanachez-vous!*"). Cyrano's sacrifices, his refusal to be morally tainted or compromised (see his famous "No thank you!" speech in act two, scene viii; pp. 68–69) make for great theater but also seem to belong to a credo, or seek to impart a lesson. And Rostand indeed conceived of the theater as a privileged space in which the spirit of the people might be lifted up, morally elevated through a collective communion in common values. In his reception speech to the Académie française, Rostand said: "It is good that once in a while a people should once again hear the sound of its own enthusiasm. . . . It is really only now in the theater that souls, side by side, can feel like they have wings."

Panache is supposed to be that common value around which we can all rally. It defines Cyrano, who, to the exclusion of all else, is equal parts courage and wit. Yet as stirring as are Cyrano's perform-ances, in deed as in word, it is worthwhile examining the play to see just what panache—the clamor of language and the bluster of sword-play—might serve to occlude. What precisely must be sacrificed if the ideal of panache is to be always honored? In Cyrano's case, what is sac-rificed is nothing less than his sexuality. That Rostand wants us to un-derstand this seems evident from the blaring symbolism of the last line of the play, which contains a rhetorically remarkable use of the word panache:

> CYRANO: . . . Spite of your worst, something will still be left me to take whither I go . . . and to-night when I enter God's house, in saluting, broadly will I sweep the azure threshold with what despite of all I carry forth unblemished and unbent . . . [*He starts forward, with lifted sword*] . . . and that is . . . [*The sword falls from his hands, he staggers, drops in the arms of Le Bret and Ragueneau.*]
> ROXANE: . . . That is? . . .
> CYRANO: . . . My plume!

"*Mon panache*," in French: You don't need to be a Freudian to get the point.

And the point is this: The ideal in *Cyrano*—panache, sacrifice, wit, elegance—is shadowed at every moment by its opposite—the material, the down-to-earth, the body and its functions. For if *Cyrano* carries us aloft toward the difficult ideal of panache, much of the rest of the play is concerned with more earthy matters. At bottom—and this goes a long way to explaining the enduring appeal of the play— *Cyrano* is a reflection on two abiding and related preoccupations: food and sex. French preoccupations, or at least things the French like to think they know a lot about (it would be difficult to contest them on the former). In *Cyrano*, which the astute critic Patrick Besnier has called "an apology for and a gigantic reverie about food," references to a markedly French cuisine abound (see especially act two, scene i, and act four, scene vi): The Frenchness of the dishes here is somewhat lost in the present translation. Ragueneau is as French as Tartarin de Tarascon; he is a sort of national treasure whose role, among other things, involves assuring the high quality of French culinary productions ("You, sir, be so good as to lengthen this gravy,—it is too thick!" etc. [act two, scene i]).

The entirety of the second act ("The Cookshop of Poets") takes place in and around Ragueneau's kitchen, which is more than just a background for the meeting between Cyrano and Roxane. Rostand took every precaution to make sure the setting for act two seemed authentic; in particular, he deemed the fake foodstuffs unconvincing and sent a stagehand to the local butcher to buy the genuine article. Already in the first act the small but important role of the sweetmeat vendor allows Rostand to bring into play the theme of food. Simply by naming aloud the "goodies" she sells at her stand—oranges, milk, raspberry cordial, citron-wine, grapes, lacrima, macaroons—she participates in one of the great pleasures associated with food—talking about it—and anticipates the cornucopia of the "Cookshop of Poets" as well as the feast at the siege of Arras. She also makes explicit a connection in *Cyrano* between food and femininity.

At the end of act one, noting that Cyrano has had nothing to eat, she freely offers him her wares ("Help yourself!"). Cyrano's response is telling; consenting to eat only for fear that to refuse to do so might grieve the sweetmeat vendor, he takes a single grape, a glass of water, and half a macaroon. His abstemiousness with regard to the pleasures of the table extends symbolically to all pleasures of the flesh; a facet of his idealism, which leads him to prefer contemplation of the stars and the moon over more earthly and earthy delights, we will see as the play progresses that this tendency toward self-denial comes close to a philosophy of life—such that he manages to reach the end of the play and the end of his life without having conquered the object of his desire.

Cyrano's attitude toward the sweetmeat vendor thus foreshadows his attitude toward the body in general (it is not a zone of pleasure) and the fair sex in particular. More comfortable with the gallant word (such as, "despite my Gascon pride") or gesture ("*He kisses her hand*") than with the idea of accepting her "dainties," he settles for a mere "trifle," for which silliness he is lambasted by his friend Le Bret. Under the guise of gallantry, Cyrano has found a way to formalize a circumspection with regard to women, a hesitancy and perhaps a fear that we see at work also in his relation to Roxane. His relation to sex is purely rhetorical. Cyrano himself attributes his unease with women to fear of being laughed at. By his own admission, the distance he imposes between himself and women is a form of self-defense: "My heart always cowers behind the defence of my wit. I set forth to capture a star . . . and then, for dread of laughter, I stop and pick a flower . . . of rhetoric" (act three, scene vii; p. 93). It is a system of defense born of his physical deformity, of course, of his "ungainliness" and the rejection to which it exposes him, to the point that one can reasonably suspect that Cyrano dies a virgin.

In addition to the sexual symbolism of the last line (his plume remains intact, "unblemished and unbent"), Cyrano in the death scene makes the following assertion: "Woman's sweetness I had never known. My mother . . . thought me unflattering. I had no sister. Later, I shunned Love's cross-road in fear of mocking eyes" (act five, scene vi; p. 158). This key passage helps to explain what might seem an implausible element in the plot: Cyrano's choice of the precious, capricious, and rather empty-headed Roxane as his only beloved. For in Roxane, who is his cousin, Cyrano finds both the mother (the good, maternal mother) and the sister that he has never known. It is an arrangement—a pact, I would say—in which Roxane is a knowing and willing participant. For her "almost brother," as she calls him, Roxane fulfils both the maternal role ("So prettily, so cheeringly maternal!" says Cyrano in the same scene), bandaging his wounds, both real and psychological (act two, scene vi), and the role of a sister— that is, an intimate but nonsexual relation, an ideal of sublimated love celebrated in Romanticism (one thinks of William Wordsworth and his sister Dorothy).

The pact between the eloquent but ugly Cyrano and the handsome but dumb Christian thus seems designed to safeguard a much earlier pact signed between Cyrano and Roxane. "Eloquence I will lend you! . . . And you, to me, shall lend all-conquering physical charm . . . and between us we will compose a hero of romance!" (act two, scene x; p. 75). An unequal exchange, as Cyrano must know, for while it advances Christian's cause—it is he who gets "Roxane's Kiss" in act three—it leaves Cyrano where he was to start with—that is to say, arrested in an archaic, childhood relation to Roxane.

The sexual politics of *Cyrano* are thus more complicated than they might seem to be at first. Although it seems that in stepping aside Cyrano is sacrificing his own interests in order to further Roxane's happiness, we also get the sense that this pact is not a disagreeable arrangement for Cyrano. In order to avoid conscription into the King's army, it was once customary for those in a position to do so to "buy a man"—that is, to pay someone to go in their stead. Cyrano has managed something similar in the zone of sexual relations. Christian will serve as his sexual surrogate, which shelters him from the possibility of rejection but also more generally absolves him of the messy business of physical entanglements, while at the same time (this is the genius of the pact) allowing him to indulge in the flowery rhetorical exercises on safe ground. "Let us profit a little by this chance of talk-

ing softly together without seeing each other," says Cyrano in the balcony scene (p. ooo). Is this not his most ardent desire? To limit the ap-
petitive drive to language alone? No looking, no seeing, just talking.
Hence Cyrano ends up literally pushing Christian into the arms of
Roxane: "CYRANO [*pushing* CHRISTIAN]: Scale the balcony, you
donkey!" (act three, scene x; see p. 98).

The body (the donkey) is there in *Cyrano*, but it is oddly stifled,
reticent. To call Christian a donkey is a deft way of recalling his stu-
pidity and at the same time drawing attention to his animality (*"Monte
donc, animal!"* in French): Cyrano is the blithe spirit ("I am a shadow
merely . . ." act three, scene vii; p. 92), while Christian is the lusty
beast. Both of them in the end get what they want: Christian gets to
kiss Roxane, and Cyrano gets to pluck lots of rhetorical flowers while
keeping his precious plume unblemished.

In this reading of the play, Roxane appeals to Cyrano precisely
because she is a *précieuse*. Cyrano and Roxane share a disdain for ba-
nality, be it in language or in deed. Wit and courage—panache, in a
word—are Cyrano's weapons against everything that is ordinary,
dull, pedestrian, stupid (for example, Valvert in act one, scene iv);
both his sword and his word are sharp, dazzling, and unexpected, as
we see in the duel-ballad scene. Preciosity, which emerged in the
seventeenth century, thus in the time in which *Cyrano* is set, began as
a reaction against the vulgarity of the times, seeking through elegance and refinement (in dress, in language, in manners) to rise
above the common and the clichéd. Regrettably, it is remembered
today (largely on account of Molière's satire *Les Précieuses ridicules*)
more for its excesses and its extravagances than for the philosophy
behind the movement or the literary changes that resulted from it.
The salon of Madame de Rambouillet, the gathering place for a host
of talented writers (François de la Rochefoucauld, Madeleine de
Scudéry, Voiture, Paul Scarron, Jean-Louis Guez de Balzac) who
would not have disputed their allegiance to the *esprit précieux*, signif-
icantly influenced literary developments in France, notably by pop-
ularizing the pastoral novel and by establishing the letter as a

legitimate literary form (see *Cyrano*, edited by Aziza). In any case, *Cyrano* seems to belong to the tradition of preciosity not so much because Roxane is herself a *précieuse* (like Molière's characters, she is fairly ridiculous) but because Rostand's aesthetic philosophy turns on the precious premise that language counts for more than action. This is especially true in the realm of love. From a sexual point of view, *Cyrano* is a play in which nothing happens. The consummation of Christian and Roxane's marriage is artfully avoided thanks to a theatrical device (Christian is called to war on their wedding night and is killed at Arras minutes after Roxane shows up there), so we may presume that Roxane, like Cyrano, dies a virgin. *Cyrano* thus stages the power of rhetoric as an instrument of seduction, while skillfully avoiding the *passage à l'acte*.

So although *Cyrano de Bergerac* seems at first to adhere to traditional gender roles, staging burly Gascon soldiers against dainty precious women, these gender assignments become more complicated as the play progresses and we begin to sense that it is constructed around a hole: One way or another, all the principal characters miss the encounter with their apparent desire. In this heftily physical play (the antithesis of intellectual theater), the body is engaged in three ways: *militarily*, which includes dueling as an expression of the Gascon spirit; *gastronomically*, which includes the famine as well as the feast; and, especially, *discursively*, as in the way Cyrano's nose engenders language (poetry, puns, jokes), the need to detain de Guiche (act three, scene viii) provokes Cyrano's meditations on traveling to the moon, and the famine at the siege of Arras leads to all kinds of "meaty remarks." The body, like Cyrano, is "everything and nothing" (see the final scene): It is an engine of discourse (and so is "everything," the *sine qua non* of the play), and is also peculiarly absent, denied (it is "nothing"). It is never truly engaged erotically, except for the famous kiss (act three, "Roxane's Kiss"); even then, as we have pointed out, Christian has to be pushed into it ("Now I feel as if I ought not!"), and the kiss is interrupted almost before it has begun.

Is such prudery gallantry carried to its logical conclusion? Or is the true alliance—the explicit one in which no one is duped—that between Christian and Cyrano? "Will you complete me, and let me in exchange complete you?" says Cyrano to Christian, *"with rapture"* according to the scene indication (act two, scene x; see p. 76). Earlier in the same scene, Cyrano says of Christian: "It is true that he is handsome, the rascal." Which leads us to question Cyrano's motive for entering into the pact with Christian. Repressed homosexuality? Possibly. Or more generally a denial of the body (a mere extension of the extreme protectiveness of his nose)? The wonderful thing about Rostand's theater is that he does not ask us to decide. In the end, what we find in *Cyrano* is a group of characters whose alliances and pacts suggest unconscious arrangements with their own uncertain sexuality as much as strategic moves in a classical game of heterosexual seduction.

Cyrano de Bergerac is a work of the imagination; Rostand's admirers and even some of his critics agree that he has a flair for the picturesque detail, for colorful language and dress, for poetic inventiveness. But what of the historical Cyrano? Rostand knew of the real Cyrano—Savinien de Cyrano (1619–1655), later known as de Bergerac—from the testimony of Cyrano's faithful companion Henri Le Bret, whose preface to Cyrano's *Comical History of the States and Empires of the Moon* (1657) he read carefully, as well as from the portrait of Cyrano by the nineteenth-century writer Théophile Gautier, whose book *Les Grotesques* (*The Grotesque Ones*) was apparently Rostand's favorite in high school (see Ripert, *Edmond Rostand*, p. 78). Cyrano, along with Le Bret, had been a soldier in the regiment of Captain Carbon de Castel-Jaloux. This regiment was composed almost entirely of Gascons, and it was in his early days in the field that he distinguished himself as a duelist (if Le Bret is to be believed, Cyrano fought one a day, quickly acquiring a reputation as "the demon of bravura"). He participated in the campaigns of Champagne (he was wounded by a bullet during the siege of Mouzon) and Picardy

(1640). Like his fictional counterpart, he was present at the siege of Arras, where a blow from a sword wounded him in the throat. Unlike his fictional counterpart, he was a homosexual. Having left the army in 1641, he studied under the famous philosopher Pierre Gassendi and frequented free-thinking literary circles. In addition to the aforementioned *States and Empires of the Moon*, he wrote *Comical History of the States and Empires of the Sun*, also published posthumously (1662), and a play, *La Mort d'Agrippine* (*The Death of Agrippine*; 1654), which was performed at the Hôtel de Bourgogne but was closed down on account of some lines suggesting an atheistic worldview ("These gods that man made, and which did not make man"). His death in 1655 may have been due to an aggravation of an existing illness—he had been suffering from a venereal disease since 1645—or it may have been the result of an incident in which a beam of wood fell on his head (assassination has not been ruled out).

What did Rostand retain from his reading of Le Bret, of Gautier, and of Cyrano himself? A good number of things, many highly serviceable from a dramatic point of view—the quarrel with the actor Monfleury (act one, scene iv), the possibility that Cyrano might have known Molière (see act five, scene vi), his fanciful ideas for traveling to the moon (act three, scene xiii), the manner of his death, etc. And, of course, one other, very big thing: the nose. It was Gautier who, extrapolating on a passage in *States and Empires of the Moon*, insisted on the importance of the nose to Cyrano's physiognomy and to his psychology, and developed something of a philosophy around it: "Without the nose, according to Cyrano, there can be nothing of worth, no finesse, no passion, nothing of what truly makes man: The nose is the seat of the soul." In Rostand's play, the "tirade of the nose" in act one (pp. 29–30) is one of the most memorable moments in French theatrical history; many French people can recite at least some of it. It is important to point out, I think, just what an enormous risk Rostand took when he decided to create a play based on a man with a very large nose ("If it wasn't for the nose, he'd be a very handsome fellow," writes Gautier). The risk of farce could never be very far. Ripert mentions that a friend tried to prevail upon Madame Rostand to have her husband excise the nose scene, which would obviously have required on the part of Rostand some major rewriting but which would avoid "covering the play in ridicule" (pp. 75–76).

And it is important to note also that Rostand based most of the characters in this play on figures from Savinien de Cyrano's life and times: Christian (based on Christophe de Champagne, baron de Neuvillette, who married Madeleine Robineau—Roxane—and who died in the siege of Arras); De Guiche (Antoine de Gramont, Richelieu's nephew); Roxane (Madeleine Robineau, baronne de Neuvillette, Cyrano's cousin); Le Bret (himself); Ragueneau (Cyprien Ragueneau, pastry cook, then actor and poet, and candlesnuffer for Molière); as well as many of the smaller roles, including Castel-Jaloux, Lignière, Montfleury, Cuigy, Brissaille, even Mother Margaret of the Convent of the Sisters of the Cross (for details, see Besnier, pp. 427–433). There is in Rostand an almost manic concern for precision, both in terms of historical exactitude, which contributes to the overall verisimilitude of the settings, and in the scenic indications (both concerning the décor and the attitudes and movements of the actors), which are unusually detailed. Rostand cannot be so easily divorced from naturalism, it seems. But it is Rostand's blending of realism and fantasy that so seduces in this play, for he manages both to temper the harshness of naturalism and to avoid the emptiness of pure fantasy.

Cyrano de Bergerac carries the subtitle "Heroic Comedy" and Cyrano, of course, is its hero. The historical Cyrano was perhaps heroic in battle, but his life, which took many turns, ending in penury and possibly with his murder, was less than romantic. His writings went virtually unknown in his lifetime. Rosemonde Gérard, Rostand's wife, has something interesting to say about Cyrano and Rostand's attraction to him: "Cyrano had the touching grace to be a failure—and this is above all what must have seduced the poet, for could there exist anything more paradoxically poetic than to crown with such glory a failure?"

(Gérard, *Edmond Rostand*, p. 9). Her judgment of Savinien de Cyrano may seem harsh, but her insight into her husband's empathy for the great losers of the world (she cites a paean to the failed [*les ratés*] from Rostand's collection of verse *Les Musardises*: "I love you and want the world to know it . . ." etc.) seems astute. For surely Rostand felt failure even in (perhaps because of) the rush of the unimaginable success he knew.

Cyrano, after all, is a play about insecurity and vulnerability; we must assume that Rostand wrote out his own weaknesses. "We all have a nose, somewhere," quipped the actor Jacques Weber. Crowned in real life with a glory that few have known, he became increasingly unsure of himself and his writing. It cannot be mere coincidence that a writing block struck him precisely when he had to compose an acceptance speech upon his election to the Académie. "I have already written one word of it: *Gentlemen*," he wrote to a friend. The toast of Paris, he retired in 1905 to the provinces, where he wasted away days in idleness, playing in the garden with his two sons, beginning but rarely finishing new projects. Although he knew further critical successes in the theater, he resembles in this period of his career the Cyrano who (in act one, scene v; p. 36) "was wandering aimlessly; too many roads were open . . . too many resolves, too complex, allowed of being taken."

Edmond Rostand died in Paris during the epidemic of Spanish flu in 1918. Of the many assessments of *Cyrano de Bergerac* and its creator, the most judicious is no doubt that of Leon Blum, the socialist thinker and literary critic who was later to become president of the Republic. Perhaps necessarily, it is also the most circumspect, for to judge Rostand—to imagine that we can easily classify him according to the existing protocols of literary criticism—might be simply foolish. "We should not have for Monsieur Rostand a scorn that would be all too unjust and facile," wrote Blum (quoted in de Margerie, *Edmond Rostand*, p. 199). "But nor should we say that he is a poet of genius. He is not a great poet, he is a great . . .—we would need to find a new word to describe such a unique concoction. But he is nonetheless something great."

PETER CONNOR is Associate Professor of French and Comparative Literature at Barnard College, Columbia University. He is the author of *Georges Bataille and the Mysticism of Sin* (Johns Hopkins University Press, 2000). He has translated Bataille's *The Tears of Eros* (City Lights Press, 1989), as well as many works in the area of contemporary French philosophy, including *The Inoperative Community*, by Jean-Luc Nancy (Minnesota University Press, 1991).

CYRANO DE BERGERAC

A HEROIC COMEDY
IN FIVE ACTS

DRAMATIS PERSONÆ

CYRANO DE BERGERAC
CHRISTIAN DE NEUVILLETTE
COMTE DE GUICHE
RAGUENEAU
LE BRET
CAPTAIN CARBON DE CASTEL-JALOUX
LIGNIÈRE
DE VALVERT
MONTFLEURY
BELLEROSE
JODELET
CUIGY
BRISSAILLE
A BORE
A MOUSQUETAIRE
OTHER MOUSQUETAIRE
A SPANISH OFFICER
A LIGHT-CAVALRY MAN
A DOORKEEPER
A BURGHER
HIS SON
A PICKPOCKET
A SPECTATOR
A WATCHMAN
BERTRANDOU THE FIFER
A CAPUCHIN
TWO MUSICIANS
SEVEN CADETS
THREE MARQUISES
POETS
PASTRYCOOKS

ROXANE
SISTER MARTHA

LISE
THE SWEETMEAT VENDER
MOTHER MARGARET
THE DUENNA
SISTER CLAIRE
AN ACTRESS
A SOUBRETTE
A FLOWER-GIRL
PAGES

The crowd, bourgeois, marquises, mousquetaires, pickpockets, pastrycooks, poets, Gascony Cadets, players, fiddlers, pages, children, Spanish soldiers, spectators, précieuses, actresses, bourgeoises, nuns, etc.

CYRANO DE BERGERAC

ACT ONE

A Play at the Hôtel de Bourgogne*

The great hall of the Hôtel de Bourgogne, in 1640. A sort of tennis-court arranged and decorated for theatrical performances.

The hall is a long rectangle, seen obliquely, so that one side of it constitutes the background, which runs from the position of the front wing at the right, to the line of the furthest wing at the left, and forms an angle with the stage, which is equally seen obliquely.

This stage is furnished, on both sides, along the wings, with benches. The drop-curtain is composed of two tapestry hangings, which can be drawn apart. Above a Harlequin cloak, the royal escutcheon. Broad steps lead from the raised platform of the stage into the house. On either side of these steps, the musicians' seats. A row of candles fills the office of footlights.

Two galleries run along the side; the lower one is divided into boxes. No seats in the pit, which is the stage proper. At the back of the pit, that is to say, at the right, in the front, a few seats raised like steps, one above the other; and, under a stairway which leads to the upper seats, and of which the lower end only is visible, a stand decked with small candelabra, jars full of flowers, flagons and glasses, dishes heaped with sweetmeats, etc.

In the centre of the background, under the box-tier, the entrance to the theatre, large door which half opens to let in the spectators. On the panels of this door, and in several corners, and above the sweetmeat stand, red playbills, announcing LA CLORISE.†

---

*The oldest stage in Paris, built in 1548 in the former palace of the Dukes of Burgundy.

†Pastoral play by Balthazar Baro (1585–1650), staged at the Hôtel de Bourgogne in 1631.

At the rise of the curtain, the house is nearly dark, and still empty. The chandeliers are let down in the middle of the pit, until time to light them.

SCENE I

The audience, arriving gradually. Cavaliers, burghers, lackeys, pages, the fiddlers, etc.
A tumult of voices is heard beyond the door; enter brusquely a CAVALIER.

DOORKEEPER [*running in after him*]   Not so fast! Your fifteen pence!

CAVALIER   I come in admission free!

DOORKEEPER   And why?

CAVALIER   I belong to the king's light cavalry!

DOORKEEPER [*to another* CAVALIER *who has entered*]   You?

SECOND CAVALIER   I do not pay!

DOORKEEPER   But . . .

SECOND CAVALIER   I belong to the mousquetaires!

FIRST CAVALIER [*to the* SECOND]   It does not begin before two. The floor is empty. Let us have a bout with foils. [*They fence with foils they have brought.*]

A LACKEY [*entering*]   Pst! . . . Flanquin!

OTHER LACKEY [*arrived a moment before*]   Champagne? . . .

FIRST LACKEY [*taking a pack of cards from his doublet and showing it to* SECOND LACKEY]   Cards. Dice. [*Sits down on the floor.*] Let us have a game.

SECOND LACKEY [*sitting down likewise*]   You rascal, willingly!

FIRST LACKEY [*taking from his pocket a bit of candle which he lights and sticks on the floor*]   I prigged an eyeful of my master's light!

ONE OF THE WATCH [*to a flower-girl, who comes forward*]   It is pleasant getting here before the lights. [*Puts his arm around her waist.*]

ONE OF THE FENCERS [*taking a thrust*]   Hit!

ONE OF THE GAMBLERS　Clubs!

THE WATCHMAN [*pursuing the girl*]　A kiss!

THE FLOWER-GIRL [*repulsing him*]　We shall be seen!

THE WATCHMAN [*drawing her into a dark corner*]　No, we shall not!

A MAN [*sitting down on the floor with others who have brought provisions*] By coming early, you get a comfortable chance to eat.

A BURGHER [*leading his son*]　This should be a good place, my boy. Let us stay here.

ONE OF THE GAMBLERS　Ace wins!

A MAN [*taking a bottle from under his cloak and sitting down*]　A proper toper, toping Burgundy, [*drinks*] I say should tope it in Burgundy House!*

THE BURGHER [*to his son*]　Might one not suppose we had stumbled into some house of evil fame? [*Points with his cane at the drunkard.*] Guzzlers! . . . [*In breaking guard one of the fencers jostles him.*] Brawlers! . . . [*He falls between the gamblers.*] Gamesters! . . .

THE WATCHMAN [*behind him, still teasing the flower-girl*]　A kiss!

THE BURGHER [*dragging his son precipitately away.*]　Bless my soul! . . . And to reflect that in this very house, my son, were given the plays of the great Rotrou!

THE YOUTH　And those of the great Corneille!†

[*A band of PAGES holding hands rush in performing a farandole and singing.*]

PAGES　Tra la la la la la la la! . . .

DOORKEEPER [*severely to the PAGES*]　Look, now! . . . you pages, you! none of your tricks!

FIRST PAGE [*with wounded dignity.*]　Sir! . . . this want of confidence . . . [*As soon as the doorkeeper has turned away, briskly to the SECOND PAGE.*] Have you a string about you?

---

*Heavy drinker.

†Jean de Routrou (1609–1650) and Pierre Corneille (1606–1684), playwrights and great rivals; Corneille is considered to have written some of the greatest tragedies in the French language, including *Le Cid*.

SECOND PAGE   With a fish-hook at the end!

FIRST PAGE   We will sit up there and angle for wigs!

A PICKPOCKET [*surrounded by a number of individuals of dubious appearance.*]   Come, now, my little hopefuls, and learn your A B C's of trade. Being as you're not used to hooking . . .

SECOND PAGE [*shouting to other* PAGES *who have already taken seats in the upper gallery*]   Ho! . . . Did you bring any pea-shooters?

THIRD PAGE [*from above*]   Yes! . . . And pease! . . . [*shoots down a volley of pease*]

THE YOUTH [*to his father*]   What are we going to see?

THE BURGHER   Clorise.

THE YOUTH   By whom?

THE BURGHER   By Balthazar Baro. Ah, what a play it is! . . . [*Goes toward the back on his son's arm.*]

PICKPOCKET [*to his disciples*]   Particularly the lace-ruffles at the knees, . . . you're to snip off carefully!

A SPECTATOR [*to another, pointing toward an upper seat*]   Look! On the first night of the Cid, I was perched up there!

PICKPOCKET [*with pantomimic suggestion of spiriting away*]   Watches . . .

THE BURGHER [*coming forward again with his son*]   The actors you are about to see, my son, are among the most illustrious . . .

PICKPOCKET [*with show of subtracting with furtive little tugs*]   Pocket-handkerchiefs . . .

THE BURGHER   Montfleury . . .

SOMEBODY [*shouting from the upper gallery*]   Make haste, and light the chandeliers!

THE BURGHER   Bellerose, l'Épy, the Beaupré, Jodelet . . .*

A PAGE [*in the pit*]   Ah! . . . Here comes the goody-seller!

THE SWEETMEAT VENDER [*appearing behind the stand*]   Oranges . . . Milk . . . Raspberry cordial . . . citron-wine . . . [*Hubbub at the door.*]

---

*All famous actors at the Hôtel de Bourgogne.

FALSETTO VOICE [*outside*]   Make room, ruffians!

ONE OF THE LACKEYS [*astonished*]   The marquises . . . in the pit!

OTHER LACKEY   Oh, for an instant only!

Enter a band of foppish YOUNG MARQUISES.

ONE OF THE MARQUISES [*looking around the half-empty house*] What? . . . We happen in like so many linen-drapers? Without disturbing anybody? treading on any feet? . . . Too bad! too bad! too bad! [*He finds himself near several other gentlemen, come in a moment before.*] Cuigy, Brissaille! [*Effusive embraces*]

CUIGY   We are of the faithful indeed. We are here before the lights.

THE MARQUIS   Ah, do not speak of it! . . . It has put me in such a humor!

OTHER MARQUIS   Be comforted, marquis . . . here comes the candle-lighter!

THE AUDIENCE [*greeting the arrival of the candle-lighter*]   Ah! . . . [*Many gather around the chandeliers while they are being lighted. A few have taken seats in the galleries. LIGNIÈRE enters, arm in arm with CHRISTIAN DE NEUVILLETTE. LIGNIÈRE, in somewhat disordered apparel, appearance of gentlemanly drunkard. CHRISTIAN, becomingly dressed, but in clothes of a slightly obsolete elegance.*]

SCENE II

The Same, with Christian and Lignière, then Ragueneau and Le Bret

CUIGY   Lignière!

BRISSAILLE [*laughing*]   Not tipsy yet?

LIGNIÈRE [*low to CHRISTIAN*]   Shall I present you? [CHRISTIAN nods assent.] Baron de Neuvillette . . . [*Exchange of bows*]

THE AUDIENCE [*cheering the ascent of the first lighted chandelier*] Ah! . . .

CUIGY [*to BRISSAILLE, looking at CHRISTIAN*]   A charming head . . . charming!

FIRST MARQUIS [*who has overheard*]   Pooh! . . .

LIGNIÈRE [*presenting* CHRISTIAN]   Messieurs de Cuigy . . . de Brissaille . . .

CHRISTIAN [*bowing*]   Delighted! . . .

FIRST MARQUIS [*to* SECOND]   He is a pretty fellow enough, but is dressed in the fashion of some other year!

LIGNIÈRE [*to* CUIGY]   Monsieur is lately arrived from Touraine.

CHRISTIAN   Yes, I have been in Paris not over twenty days. I enter the Guards to-morrow, the Cadets.

FIRST MARQUIS [*looking at those who appear in the boxes*]   There comes the présidente Aubry!

SWEETMEAT VENDER   Oranges! Milk!

THE FIDDLERS [*tuning*]   La . . . la . . .

CUIGY [*to* CHRISTIAN, *indicating the house which is filling*]   A good house! . . .

CHRISTIAN   Yes, crowded.

FIRST MARQUIS   The whole of fashion!

[*They give the names of the women, as, very brilliantly attired, these enter the boxes. Exchange of bows and smiles.*]

SECOND MARQUIS   Mesdames de Guéménée . . .

CUIGY   De Bois-Dauphin . . .

FIRST MARQUIS   Whom . . . time was! . . . we loved! . . .

BRISSAILLE   . . . de Chavigny . . .*

SECOND MARQUIS   Who still plays havoc with our hearts!

LIGNIÈRE   *Tiens*! Monsieur de Corneille has come back from Rouen!

THE YOUTH [*to his father*]   The Academy is present?†

THE BURGHER   Yes . . . I perceive more than one member of it. Yonder are Boudu, Boissat and Cureau . . . Porchères, Colomby,

---

*Important social figures who personified a style of behavior known as "preciosity" that emphasized delicacy and refinement.

†L'Académie française, the body of distinguished French writers created by Cardinal Richelieu in 1635.

Bourzeys, Bourdon, Arbaut . . . All names of which not one will be forgotten. What a beautiful thought it is!*

FIRST MARQUIS   Attention! Our précieuses are coming into their seats . . . Barthénoide, Urimédonte, Cassandace, Félixérie . . .†

SECOND MARQUIS   Ah, how exquisite are their surnames! . . . Marquis, can you tell them off, all of them?

FIRST MARQUIS   I can tell them off, all of them, Marquis!

LIGNIÈRE [*drawing* CHRISTIAN *aside*]   Dear fellow, I came in here to be of use to you. The lady does not come. I revert to my vice!

CHRISTIAN [*imploring*]   No! No! . . . You who turn into ditties Town and Court, stay by me: you will be able to tell me for whom it is I am dying of love!

THE LEADER OF THE VIOLINS [*rapping on his desk with his bow*]   Gentlemen! . . . [*He raises his bow.*]

SWEETMEAT VENDER   Macaroons . . . Citronade . . .

[*The fiddles begin playing.*]

CHRISTIAN   I fear . . . oh, I fear to find that she is fanciful and intricate! I dare not speak to her, for I am of a simple wit. The language written and spoken in these days bewilders and baffles me. I am a plain soldier . . . shy, to boot.—She is always at the right, there, the end: the empty box.

LIGNIÈRE [*with show of leaving*]   I am going.

CHRISTIAN [*still attempting to detain him*]   Oh, no! . . . Stay, I beseech you!

LIGNIÈRE   I cannot. D'Assoucy‡ is expecting me at the pot-house. Here is a mortal drought!

SWEETMEAT VENDER [*passing before him with a tray*]   Orangeade? . . .

---

*Names of members of l'Académie française.

†Typically precious names taken from Antoine Baudeau de Somaize's *Dictionnaire des Précieuses* (1660).

‡Poet and friend of Cyrano de Bergerac, whose writings he edited; D'Assoucy's real name was Charles Coypeau (1605–1677).

LIGNIÈRE   Ugh!

SWEETMEAT VENDER   Milk? . . .

LIGNIÈRE   Pah! . . .

SWEETMEAT VENDER   Lacrima?* . . .

LIGNIÈRE   Stop! [*To* CHRISTIAN] I will tarry a bit. . . . Let us see
this lacrima? [*Sits down at the sweetmeat stand. The* VENDER *pours
him a glass of lacrima*]

[*Shouts among the audience at the entrance of a little, merry-faced, roly-
poly man.*]

AUDIENCE   Ah, Ragueneau! . . .

LIGNIÈRE [*to* CHRISTIAN]   Ragueneau, who keeps the great cookshop.

RAGUENEAU [*attired like a pastrycook in his Sunday best, coming quickly
toward* LIGNIÈRE]   Monsieur, have you seen Monsieur de
Cyrano?

LIGNIÈRE [*presenting* RAGUENEAU *to* CHRISTIAN]   The pastrycook of poets and of players!

RAGUENEAU [*abashed*]   Too much honor. . . .

LIGNIÈRE   No modesty! . . . Mecænas! . . .†

RAGUENEAU   It is true, those gentlemen are among my customers . . .

LIGNIÈRE   Debitors! . . . A considerable poet himself. . . .

RAGUENEAU   It has been said! . . .

LIGNIÈRE   Daft on poetry! . . .

RAGUENEAU   It is true that for an ode . . .

LIGNIÈRE   You are willing to give at any time a tart!

RAGUENEAU   . . . let. A tart-let.

LIGNIÈRE   Kind soul, he tries to cheapen his charitable acts! And
for a triolet‡ were you not known to give . . . ?

---

*Sweet wine made in the Pyrenees.

†First century B.C. minister under Roman emperor Augustus and great patron and
protector of men of letters, especially of Horace and Virgil.

‡Poem of eight lines.

RAGUENEAU   Rolls. Just rolls.

LIGNIÈRE [*severely*]   Buttered! . . . And the play, you are fond of the play?

RAGUENEAU   It is with me a passion!

LIGNIÈRE   And you settle for your entrance fee with a pastry currency. Come now, among ourselves, what did you have to give today for admittance here?

RAGUENEAU   Four custards . . . eighteen lady-fingers. [*He looks all around*] Monsieur de Cyrano is not here. I wonder at it.

LIGNIÈRE   And why?

RAGUENEAU   Montfleury is billed to play.

LIGNIÈRE   So it is, indeed. That ton of man will to-day entrance us in the part of Phœdo . . . Phœdo!* . . . But what is that to Cyrano?

RAGUENEAU   Have you not heard? He interdicted Montfleury, whom he has taken in aversion, from appearing for one month upon the stage.

LIGNIÈRE [*who is at his fourth glass*]   Well?

RAGUENEAU   Montfleury is billed to play.

CUIGY [*who has drawn near with his companions*]   He cannot be prevented.

RAGUENIEAU   He cannot? . . . Well, I am here to see!

FIRST MARQUIS   What is this Cyrano?

CUIGY   A crack-brain!

SECOND MARQUIS   Of quality?

CUIGY   Enough for daily uses. He is a cadet in the Guards. [*Pointing out a gentleman who is coming and going about the pit, as if in search of somebody*] But his friend Le Bret can tell you. [*Calling*] Le Bret! . . . [*LE BRET comes toward them*]. You are looking for Bergerac?

LE BRET   Yes. I am uneasy.

CUIGY   Is it not a fact that he is a most uncommon fellow?

---

*A character in the play *La Clorise* (see note on p. 7), whose name recalls *Phaedo*, Plato's discourse on the immortality of the soul.

LE BRET [*affectionately*]   The most exquisite being he is that walks beneath the moon!

RAGUENEAU   Poet!

CUIGY   Swordsman!

BRISSAILLE   Physicist!

LE BRET   Musician!

LIGNIÈRE   And what an extraordinary aspect he presents!

RAGUENEAU   I will not go so far as to say that I believe our grave Philippe de Champaigne* will leave us a portrait of him; but, the bizarre, excessive, whimsical fellow that he is would certainly have furnished the late Jacques Callot with a type of madcap fighter for one of his masques.† Hat with triple feather, doublet with twice-triple skirt, cloak which his interminable rapier lifts up behind, with pomp, like the insolent tail of a cock; prouder than all the Artabans that Gascony ever bred,‡ he goes about in his stiff Punchinello ruff, airing a nose. . . . Ah, gentlemen, what a nose is that! One cannot look upon such a specimen of the nasigera without exclaiming, "No! truly, the man exaggerates," . . . After that, one smiles, one says: "He will take it off." . . . But Monsieur de Bergerac never takes it off at all.

LE BRET [*shaking his head*]   He wears it always . . . and cuts down whoever breathes a syllable in comment.

RAGUENEAU [*proudly*]   His blade is half the shears of Fate!

FIRST MARQUIS [*shrugging his shoulders*]   He will not come!

RAGUENEAU   He will. I wager you a chicken à la Ragueneau.

---

*Philippe de Champaigne (1602–1674), painter of great political figures (he painted Cardinal Richelieu) and religious scenes.

†Jacques Callot (1592–1635), an engraver famous for the accuracy of his works as well as for a series of masques representing traditional characters of the Italian form of comedy known as commedia dell'arte.

‡The reference is to a historical character in *Cléopâtre* (1647), a play by Gautier des Costes, sieur de La Calprenède (1609–1663).

FIRST MARQUIS [*laughing*]   Very well!

[*Murmur of admiration in the house. ROXANE has appeared in her box. She takes a seat in the front, her duenna at the back. CHRISTIAN, engaged in paying the sweetmeat vender, does not look.*]

SECOND MARQUIS [*uttering a series of small squeals*]   Ah, gentlemen, she is horrifically enticing!

FIRST MARQUIS   A strawberry set in a peach, and smiling!

SECOND MARQUIS   So fresh, that being near her, one might catch cold in his heart!

CHRISTIAN [*looks up, sees ROXANE, and, agitated, seizes LIGNIÈRE by the arm*]   That is she!

LIGNIÈRE [*looking*]   Ah, that is she! . . .

CHRISTIAN   Yes. Tell me at once. . . . Oh, I am afraid! . . .

LIGNIÈRE [*sipping his wine slowly*]   Magdeleine Robin, surnamed Roxane. Subtle. Euphuistic.

CHRISTIAN   Alack-a-day!

LIGNIÈRE   Unmarried. An orphan. A cousin of Cyrano's . . . the one of whom they were talking.

[*While he is speaking, a richly dressed nobleman, wearing the order of the Holy Ghost on a blue ribbon across his breast,* enters ROXANE's box, and, without taking a seat, talks with her a moment.*]

CHRISTIAN [*starting*]   That man? . . .

LIGNIÈRE [*who is beginning to be tipsy, winking*]   Hé! Hé! Comte de Guiche. Enamored of her. But married to the niece of Armand de Richelieu. Wishes to manage a match between Roxane and certain sorry lord, one Monsieur de Valvert, vicomte and . . . easy. She does not subscribe to his views, but De Guiche is powerful: he can persecute to some purpose a simple commoner. But I have duly set forth his shady machinations in a song which . . . Ho! he must bear me a grudge! The end was wicked . . . Listen! . . . [*He rises, staggering, and lifting his glass, is about to sing.*]

---

*Reference to the famous *cordon bleu*, the insignia of the Ordre du Saint-Esprit, France's oldest chivalric order.

CHRISTIAN   No. Good-evening.

LIGNIÈRE   You are going? . . .

CHRISTIAN   To find Monsieur de Valvert.

LIGNIÈRE   Have a care. You are the one who will get killed. [*Indicating* ROXANE *by a glance.*] Stay. Some one is looking . . .

CHRISTIAN   It is true . . .

[*He remains absorbed in the contemplation of* ROXANE. *The pickpockets, seeing his abstracted air, draw nearer to him.*]

LIGNIÈRE   Ah, you are going to stay. Well, I am going. I am thirsty! And I am looked for . . . at all the public-houses! [*Exit unsteadily.*]

LE BRET [*who has made the circuit of the house, returning toward* RAGUENEAU, *in a tone of relief*]   Cyrano is not here.

RAGUENEAU   And yet . . .

LE BRET   I will trust to Fortune he has not seen the announcement.

THE AUDIENCE   Begin! Begin!

SCENE III

The same, except for Lignière; De Guiche, Valvert, then Montfleury

ONE OF THE MARQUISES [*watching* DE GUICHE, *who comes from* ROXANE'*s box, and crosses the pit, surrounded by obsequious satellites, among whom the* VICOMTE DE VALVERT]   Always a court about him, De Guiche!

OTHER MARQUIS   Pf! . . . Another Gascon!

FIRST MARQUIS   A Gascon, of the cold and supple sort. That sort succeeds. Believe me, it will be best to offer him our duty.

[*They approach DE GUICHE.*]

SECOND MARQUIS   These admirable ribbons! What color, Comte de Guiche? Should you call it Kiss-me-Sweet or . . . Expiring Fawn?

DE GUICHE   This shade is called Sick Spaniard.

FIRST MARQUIS   Appropriately called, for shortly, thanks to your valor, the Spaniard will be sick indeed, in Flanders!*

DE GUICHE   I am going upon the stage. Are you coming? [*He walks toward the stage, followed by all the marquises and men of quality. He turns and calls.*] Valvert, come!

CHRISTIAN [*who has been listening and watching them, starts on hearing that name*]   The vicomte! . . . Ah, in his face . . . in his face I will fling my . . . [*He puts his hand to his pocket and finds the pickpocket's hand. He turns.*] Hein?

PICKPOCKET   Aï!

CHRISTIAN [*without letting him go*]   I was looking for a glove.

PICKPOCKET [*with an abject smile*]   And you found a hand. [*In a different tone, low and rapid.*] Let me go . . . I will tell you a secret.

CHRISTIAN [*without releasing him*]   Well?

PICKPOCKET   Lignière who has just left you . . .

CHRISTIAN [*as above*]   Yes? . . .

PICKPOCKET   Has not an hour to live. A song he made annoyed one of the great, and a hundred men—I am one of them—will be posted to-night . . .

CHRISTIAN   A hundred? . . . By whom?

PICKPOCKET   Honor . . .

CHRISTIAN [*shrugging his shoulders*]   Oh! . . .

PICKPOCKET [*with great dignity*]   Among rogues!

CHRISTIAN   Where will they be posted?

PICKPOCKET   At the Porte de Nesle, on his way home. Inform him.

CHRISTIAN [*letting him go*]   But where can I find him?

PICKPOCKET   Go to all the taverns: the Golden Vat, the Pine-Apple, the Belt and Bosom, the Twin Torches, the Three Funnels, and in each one leave a scrap of writing warning him.

CHRISTIAN   Yes. I will run! . . . Ah, the blackguards! A hundred

---

*The French, at war with the Spanish since 1622, were campaigning to retake Flanders from their control.

against one! . . . [*Looks lovingly toward* ROXANE.] Leave her! . . . [*Furiously, looking toward* VALVERT.] And him! . . . But Lignière must be prevented. [*Exit running.*]

[*DE GUICHE, the MARQUISES, all the gentry have disappeared behind the curtain, to place themselves on the stage-seats. The pit is crowded. There is not an empty seat in the boxes or the gallery.*]

THE AUDIENCE   Begin!

A BURGHER [*whose wig goes sailing off at the end of a string held by one of the pages in the upper gallery*]   My wig!

SCREAMS OF DELIGHT   He is bald! . . . The pages! . . . Well done! . . . Ha, ha, ha!

THE BURGHER [*furious, shaking his fist*]   Imp of Satan! . . .

[*Laughter and screams, beginning very loud and decreasing suddenly. Dead silence.*]

LE BRET [*astonished*]   This sudden hush? . . . [*One of the spectators whispers in his ear.*] Ah?

THE SPECTATOR   I have it from a reliable quarter.

RUNNING MURMURS   Hush! . . . Has he come? No! . . . Yes, he has! . . . In the box with the grating. . . . The cardinal! . . . the cardinal! . . . the cardinal! . . .*

ONE OF THE PAGES   What a shame! . . . Now we shall have to behave!

[*Knocking on the stage. Complete stillness. Pause.*]

VOICE OF ONE OF THE MARQUISES [*breaking the deep silence, behind the curtain.*]   Snuff that candle!

OTHER MARQUIS [*thrusting his head out between the curtains.*]   A chair! [*A chair is passed from hand to hand, above the heads. The marquis takes it and disappears, after kissing his hand repeatedly toward the boxes.*]

A SPECTATOR   Silence!

[*Once more, the three knocks. The curtain opens. Tableau. The marquises*

---

*Reference to Cardinal Richelieu (1585–1642), powerful prime minister of France who sometimes attended the theater incognito.

seated at the sides, * *in attitudes of languid haughtiness. The stage-setting is the faint-colored blueish sort usual in a pastoral. Four small crystal candelabra light the stage. The violins play softly.]*

LE BRET [*to* RAGUENEAU, *under breath*] Is Montfleury the first to appear?

RAGUENEAU [*likewise under breath*] Yes. The opening lines are his.

LE BRET Cyrano is not here.

RAGUENEAU I have lost my wager.

LE BRET Let us be thankful. Let us be thankful.

> *[A bagpipe is heard. MONTFLEURY appears upon the stage, enormous, in a conventional shepherd's costume, with a rose-wreathed hat set jauntily on the side of his head, breathing into a be-ribboned bag pipe.]*

THE PIT [*applauding*] Bravo, Montfleury! Montfleury!

MONTFLEURY [*after bowing, proceeds to play the part of* PHŒDO]
Happy the man who, freed from Fashion's fickle sway,
In exile self-prescribed whiles peaceful hours away;
Who when Zephyrus sighs amid the answering trees. . . .

A VOICE [*from the middle of the pit*] Rogue! Did I not forbid you for one month?

> *[Consternation. Every one looks around. Murmurs.]*

VARIOUS VOICES Hein? What? What is the matter?

> *[Many in the boxes rise to see]*

CUIGY It is he!

LE BRET [*alarmed*] Cyrano!

THE VOICE King of the Obese! Incontinently vanish! . . .

THE WHOLE AUDIENCE [*indignant.*] Oh! . . .

MONTFLEURY But . . .

THE VOICE You stop to muse upon the matter?

SEVERAL VOICES [*from the pit and the boxes.*] Hush! . . .
Enough! . . . Proceed, Montfleury . . . Fear nothing!

---

*In the seventeenth and eighteenth centuries, nobility (usually minor nobility) often sat on the stage, at its sides.

MONTFLEURY [*in an unsteady voice*]   Happy the man who freed from Fashion's f——— . . .

THE VOICE [*more threatening than before*]   How is this? Shall I be constrained, Man of the Monster Belly, to enforce my regulation . . . regularly?

[*An arm holding a cane leaps above the level of the heads.*]

MONTFLEURY [*in a voice growing fainter and fainter*]

Happy the man . . .

[*The cane is wildly flourished.*]

THE VOICE   Leave the stage!

THE PIT   Oh! . . .

MONTFLEURY [*choking*]

Happy the man who freed . . .

CYRANO [*appears above the audience, standing upon a chair, his arms folded on his chest, his hat at a combative angle, his moustache on end, his nose terrifying*]

Ah! I shall lose my temper!

[*Sensation at sight of him*]

SCENE IV

The same, with Cyrano, then Bellerose and Jodelet

MONTFLEURY [*to the* MARQUISES]   Messieurs, I appeal to you!

ONE OF THE MARQUISES [*languidly*]   But go ahead! . . . Play!

CYRANO   Fat man, if you attempt it, I will dust the paint off you with this!

THE MARQUIS   Enough!

CYRANO   Let every little lordling keep silence in his seat, or I will ruffle his ribbons with my cane!

ALL THE MARQUISES [*rising*]   This is too much! . . . Montfleury. . . .

CYRANO   Let Montfleury go home, or stay, and, having cut his ears off, I will disembowel him!

A VOICE   But . . .

CYRANO   Let him go home, I said!

OTHER VOICE   But after all . . .

CYRANO   It is not yet done? [*With show of turning up his sleeves.*] Very
well, upon that stage, as on a platter trimmed with green, you
shall see me carve that mount of brawn. . . .

MONTFLEURY [*calling up his whole dignity*]   Monsieur, you cast in-
dignity, in my person, upon the Muse!

CYRANO [*very civilly*]   Monsieur, if that lady, with whom you have
naught to do, had the pleasure of beholding you . . . just as you
stand, there, like a decorated pot! . . . she could not live, I do
protest, but she hurled her buskin at you!

THE PIT   Montfleury! . . . Montfleury! . . . Give us Baro's piece!

CYRANO [*to those shouting around him*]   I beg you will show some regard for my scabbard: it is ready to give up the sword! [*The space
around him widens.*]

THE CROWD [*backing away*]   Hey . . . softly, there!

CYRANO [*to* MONTFLEURY]   Go off!

THE CROWD [*closing again, and grumbling*]   Oh! . . . Oh!

CYRANO [*turning suddenly*]   Has somebody objections? [*The crowd
again pushes away from him.*]

A VOICE [*at the back, singing.*]

> Monsieur de Cyrano, one sees,
> Inclines to be tyrannical;
> In spite of that tyrannicle
> We shall see La Clorise!

THE WHOLE AUDIENCE [*catching up the tune*]   La Clorise! La
Clorise!

CYRANO   Let me hear that song again, and I will do you all to death
with my stick!

A BURGHER   Samson come back! . . .

CYRANO   Lend me your jaw, good man!

A LADY [*in one of the boxes*]   This is unheard of!

A MAN   It is scandalous!

A BURGHER   It is irritating, to say no more.

A PAGE   What fun it is!

THE PIT   Ksss! . . . Montfleury! . . . Cyrano! . . .

CYRANO   Be still! . . .

THE PIT [*in uproar*]   Hee-haw! . . . Baaaaah! . . . Bow- wow! . . . Cockadoodledoooooo!

CYRANO   I will . . .

A PAGE   Meeeow!

CYRANO   I order you to hold your tongues! . . . I dare the floor collectively to utter another sound! . . . I challenge you, one and all! . . . I will take down your names . . . Step forward, budding heroes! Each in his turn. You shall be given numbers. Come, which one of you will open the joust with me? You, monsieur? No! You? No! The first that offers is promised all the mortuary honors due the brave. Let all who wish to die hold up their hands! [*Silence.*] It is modesty that makes you shrink from the sight of my naked sword? Not a name? Not a hand?—Very good. Then I proceed. [*Turning toward the stage where* MONTFLEURY *is waiting in terror*] As I was saying, it is my wish to see the stage cured of this tumor. Otherwise . . . [*Claps hand to his sword.*] the lancet!

MONTFLEURY   I . . .

CYRANO [*gets down from his chair, and sits in the space that has become vacant around him, with the ease of one at home*]   Thrice will I clap my hands, O plenilune!* At the third clap . . . eclipse!

THE PIT [*diverted*]   Ah! . . .

CYRANO [*clapping his hands*]   One! . . .

MONTFLEURY   I . . .

A VOICE [*from one of the boxes*]   Do not go! . . .

THE PIT   He will stay! . . . He will go! . . .

---

*That is, full moon; a reference to Montfleury's famous rotundity.

MONTFLEURY   Messieurs, I feel . . .

CYRANO   Two! . . .

MONTFLEURY   I feel it will perhaps be wiser . . .

CYRANO   Three! . . .

[*MONTFLEURY disappears, as if through a trap-door. Storm of laughter, hissing, catcalls.*]

THE HOUSE   Hoo! . . . Hoo! . . . Milk-sop! . . . Come back! . . .

CYRANO [*beaming, leans back in his chair and crosses his legs*]   Let him come back, if he dare!

A BURGHER   The spokesman of the company!

[*BELLEROSE comes forward on the stage and bows*]

THE BOXES   Ah, there comes Bellerose!

BELLEROSE [*with elegant bearing and diction*]   Noble ladies and gentlemen . . .

THE PIT   No! No! Jodelet! . . . We want Jodelet! . . .

JODELET [*comes forward, speaks through his nose*]   Pack of swine!

THE PIT   That is right! . . . Well said! . . . Bravo!

JODELET   Don't bravo me! . . . The portly tragedian, whose paunch is your delight, felt sick! . . .

THE PIT   He is a poltroon! . . .

JODELET   He was obliged to leave . . .

THE PIT   Let him come back!

SOME   No!

OTHERS   Yes! . . .

A YOUTH [*to CYRANO*]   But, when all is said, monsieur, what good grounds have you for hating Montfleury?

CYRANO [*amiably, sitting as before*]   Young gosling, I have two, whereof each, singly, would be ample. Primo: He is an execrable actor, who bellows, and with grunts that would disgrace a water-carrier launches the verse that should go forth as if on pinions! . . . Secundo: is my secret.

THE OLD BURGHER [*behind CYRANO*]   But without compunction you deprive us of hearing La Clorise. I am determined . . .

CYRANO [*turning his chair around so as to face the old gentleman;*

respectfully]   Venerable mule, old Baro's verses being what they are, I do it without compunction, as you say.

THE PRÉCIEUSES [*in the boxes*]   Ha! . . . Ho! . . . Our own Baro! . . . My dear, did you hear that? How can such a thing be said? . . . Ha! . . . Ho! . . .

CYRANO [*turning his chair so as to face the boxes; gallantly*]   Beautiful creatures, do you bloom and shine, be ministers of dreams, your smiles our anodyne. Inspire poets, but poems . . . spare to judge!

BELLEROSE   But the money which must be given back at the door!

CYRANO [*turning his chair to face the stage*]   Bellerose, you have said the only intelligent thing that has, as yet, been said! Far from me to wrong by so much as a fringe the worshipful mantle of Thespis. . . . [*He rises and flings a bag upon the stage.*] Catch! . . . and keep quiet!

THE HOUSE [*dazzled*]   Ah! . . . Oh! . . .

JODELET [*nimbly picking up the bag, weighing it with his hand*]   For such a price, you are authorized, monsieur, to come and stop the performance every day!

THE HOUSE   Hoo! . . . Hoo! . . .

JODELET   Should we be hooted in a body! . . .

BELLEROSE   The house must be evacuated!

JODELET   Evacuate it!

[*The audience begins to leave; CYRANO looking on with a satisfied air. The crowd, however, becoming interested in the following scene, the exodus is suspended. The women in the boxes who were already standing and had put on their wraps, stop to listen and end by resuming their seats.*]

LE BRET [*to CYRANO*]   What you have done . . . is mad!

A BORE   Montfleury! . . . the eminent actor! . . . What a scandal! . . . But the Duc de Candale is his patron! . . . Have you a patron, you?

CYRANO   No!

THE BORE   You have not.

CYRANO   No!

THE BORE   What? You are not protected by some great nobleman under the cover of whose name. . . .

CYRANO [*exasperated*]   No, I have told you twice. Must I say the same thing thrice? No, I have no protector . . . [*hand on sword*] but this will do.

THE BORE   Then, of course, you will leave town.

CYRANO   That will depend.

THE BORE   But the Duc de Candale has a long arm . . .

CYRANO   Not so long as mine . . . [*pointing to his sword*] pieced out with this!

THE BORE   But you cannot have the presumption . . .

CYRANO   I can, yes.

THE BORE   But . . .

CYRANO   And now . . . face about!

THE BORE   But . . .

CYRANO   Face about, I say . . . or else, tell me why you are looking at my nose.

THE BORE [*bewildered*]   I . . .

CYRANO [*advancing upon him*]   In what is it unusual?

THE BORE [*backing*]   Your worship is mistaken.

CYRANO [*same business as above*]   Is it flabby and pendulous, like a proboscis?

THE BORE   I never said . . .

CYRANO   Or hooked like a hawk's beak?

THE BORE   I . . .

CYRANO   Do you discern a mole upon the tip?

THE BORE   But . . .

CYRANO   Or is a fly disporting himself thereon? What is there wonderful about it?

THE BORE   Oh . . .

CYRANO   Is it a freak of nature?

THE BORE   But I had refrained from casting so much as a glance at it!

CYRANO   And why, I pray, should you not look at it?

THE BORE   I had . . .

CYRANO   So it disgusts you?

THE BORE   Sir . . .

CYRANO   Its color strikes you as unwholesome?

THE BORE   Sir . . .

CYRANO   Its shape, unfortunate?

THE BORE   But far from it!

CYRANO   Then wherefore that depreciating air? . . . Perhaps monsieur thinks it a shade too large?

THE BORE   Indeed not. No, indeed. I think it small . . . small,—I should have said, minute!

CYRANO   What? How? Charge me with such a ridiculous defect? Small, my nose? Ho! . . .

THE BORE   Heavens!

CYRANO   Enormous, my nose! . . . Contemptible stutterer, snubnosed and flat-headed, be it known to you that I am proud, proud of such an appendage! inasmuch as a great nose is properly the index of an affable, kindly, courteous man, witty, liberal, brave, such as I am! and such as you are for evermore precluded from supposing yourself, deplorable rogue! For the inglorious surface my hand encounters above your ruff, is no less devoid—[*Strikes him*]

THE BORE   Aï! aï! . . .

CYRANO   Of pride, alacrity and sweep, of perception and of gift, of heavenly spark, of sumptuousness, to sum up all, of NOSE, than that [*turns him around by the shoulders and suits the action to the word*], which stops my boot below your spine!

THE BORE [*running off*]   Help! The watch! . . .*

CYRANO   Warning to the idle who might find entertainment in my organ of smell. . . . And if the facetious fellow be of birth, my custom is, before I let him go, to chasten him, in front, and higher up, with steel, and not with hide!

---

*The personnel of a seventeenth-century theater included a guard charged with keeping order.

DE GUICHE [*who has stepped down from the stage with the marquises*]
     He is becoming tiresome!

VALVERT [*shrugging his shoulders*]   It is empty bluster!

DE GUICHE   Will no one take him up?

VALVERT   No one? . . . Wait! I will have one of those shots at him!
     [*He approaches* CYRANO *who is watching him, and stops in front of
     him, in an attitude of silly swagger.*] Your . . . your nose is . . .
     errr . . . Your nose . . . is very large!

CYRANO [*gravely*]   Very.

VALVERT [*laughs*]   Ha! . . .

CYRANO [*imperturbable*]   Is that all?

VALVERT   But . . .

CYRANO   Ah, no, young man, that is not enough! You might have
     said, dear me, there are a thousand things . . . varying the
     tone . . . For instance . . . here you are:—Aggressive: "I, mon-
     sieur, if I had such a nose, nothing would serve but I must cut it
     off!" Amicable: "It must be in your way while drinking; you ought
     to have a special beaker made!" Descriptive: "It is a crag! . . . a
     peak! . . . a promontory! . . . A promontory, did I say? . . . It is a
     peninsula!" Inquisitive: "What may the office be of that oblong re-
     ceptacle? Is it an inkhorn or a scissor-case?" Mincing: "Do you so
     dote on birds, you have, fond as a father, been at pains to fit the
     little darlings with a roost?" Blunt: "Tell me, monsieur, you, when
     you smoke, is it possible you blow the vapor through your nose
     without a neighbor crying "The chimney is afire?" Anxious: "Go
     with caution, I beseech, lest your head, dragged over by that
     weight, should drag you over!" Tender: "Have a little sun-shade
     made for it! It might get freckled!" Learned: "None but the beast,
     monsieur, mentioned by Aristophanes, the hippocampelephanto-
     camelos, can have borne beneath his forehead so much cartilage
     and bone!" Off-hand: "What, comrade, is that sort of peg in style?
     Capital to hang one's hat upon!" Emphatic: "No wind can hope, O
     lordly nose, to give the whole of you a cold, but the Nor-Wester!"
     Dramatic: "It is the Red Sea when it bleeds!" Admiring: "What a

sign for a perfumer's shop!" Lyrical: "Art thou a Triton, and is that thy conch?" Simple: "A monument! When is admission free?" Deferent: "Suffer, monsieur, that I should pay you my respects: that is what I call possessing a house of your own!" Rustic: "Hi, boys! Call that a nose? Ye don't gull me! It's either a prize carrot or else a stunted gourd!" Military: "Level against the cavalry!" Practical: "Will you put it up for raffle? Indubitably, sir, it will be the feature of the game!" And finally in parody of weeping Pyramus: "Behold, behold the nose that traitorously destroyed the beauty of its master! and is blushing for the same!"—That, my dear sir, or something not unlike, is what you would have said to me, had you the smallest leaven of letters or of wit; but of wit, O most pitiable of objects made by God, you never had a rudiment, and of letters, you have just those that are needed to spell "fool!"—But, had it been otherwise, and had you been possessed of the fertile fancy requisite to shower upon me, here, in this noble company, that volley of sprightly pleasantries, still should you not have delivered yourself of so much as a quarter of the tenth part of the beginning of the first. . . . For I let off these good things at myself, and with sufficient zest, but do not suffer another to let them off at me!

DE GUICHE [*attempting to lead away the amazed vicomte*]   Let be, vicomte!

VALVERT   That insufferable haughty bearing! . . . A clodhopper without . . . without so much as gloves . . . who goes abroad without points . . . or bow-knots! . . .

CYRANO   My foppery is of the inner man. I do not trick myself out like a popinjay, but I am more fastidious, if I am not so showy. I would not sally forth, by any chance, not washed quite clean of an affront; my conscience foggy about the eye, my honor crumpled, my nicety black-rimmed. I walk with all upon me furbished bright. I plume myself with independence and straightforwardness. It is not a handsome figure, it is my soul, I hold erect as in a brace. I go decked with exploits in place of ribbon bows. I taper to a point my wit like a moustache. And at my passage through the crowd true sayings ring like spurs!

VALVERT   But, sir . . .

CYRANO   I am without gloves? . . . a mighty matter! I only had one left, of a very ancient pair, and even that became a burden to me . . . I left it in somebody's face.

VALVERT   Villain, clod-poll, flat-foot, refuse of the earth!

CYRANO [*taking off his hat and bowing as if the* VICOMTE *had been introducing himself*]   Ah? . . . And mine, Cyrano-Savinien-Hercule of Bergerac!

VALVERT [*exasperated*]   Buffoon!

CYRANO [*giving a sudden cry, as if seized with a cramp*]   Aï! . . .

VALVERT [*who had started toward the back, turning*]   What is he saying now?

CYRANO [*screwing his face as if in pain*]   It must have leave to stir . . . it has a cramp! It is bad for it to be kept still so long!

VALVERT   What is the matter?

CYRANO   My rapier prickles like a foot asleep!

VALVERT [*drawing*]   So be it!

CYRANO   I shall give you a charming little hurt!

VALVERT [*contemptuous*]   A poet!

CYRANO   Yes, a poet, . . . and to such an extent, that while we fence, I will, hop! extempore, compose you a ballade!

VALVERT   A ballade?

CYRANO   I fear you do not know what that is.

VALVERT   But . . .

CYRANO [*as if saying a lesson*]   The ballade is composed of three stanzas of eight lines each . . .

VALVERT [*stamps with his feet*]   Oh! . . .

CYRANO [*continuing*]   And an envoi* of four.

---

*Final stanza of a ballad.

VALVERT   You . . .

CYRANO   I will with the same breath fight you and compose one.
And at the last line, I will hit you.

VALVERT   Indeed you will not!

CYRANO   No? . . . [Declaiming]
Ballade of the duel which in Burgundy House
Monsieur de Bergerac fought with a jackanapes.

VALVERT   And what is that, if you please?

CYRANO   That is the title.

THE AUDIENCE [at the highest pitch of excitement]   Make room! . . .
Good sport! . . . Stand aside! . . . Keep still! . . .
[Tableau. A ring, in the pit, of the interested; the MARQUISES and OFFI-
CERS scattered among the BURGHERS and COMMON PEOPLE. The
PAGES have climbed on the shoulders of various ones, the better to see. All
the women are standing in the boxes. At the right, DE GUICHE and his
attendant gentlemen. At the left, LE BRET, RAGUENEAU, CUIGY, etc.]

CYRANO [closing his eyes a second]   Wait. I am settling upon the
rhymes. There. I have them. [In declaiming, he suits the action to the
word.]

Of my broad felt made lighter,
I cast my mantle broad,
And stand, poet and fighter,
To do and to record.
I bow, I draw my sword . . .
En garde! with steel and wit
I play you at first abord . . .
At the last line, I hit!

[They begin fencing.]

You should have been politer;
Where had you best be gored?
The left side or the right—ah?

Or next your azure cord?
Or where the spleen is stored?
Or in the stomach pit?
Come we to quick accord . . .
At the last line, I hit!

You falter, you turn whiter?
You do so to afford
Your foe a rhyme in "iter"? . . .
You thrust at me—I ward—
And balance is restored.
Laridon!* Look to your spit! . . .
No, you shall not be floored
Before my cue to hit!

[He announces solemnly.]
ENVOI

Prince, call upon the Lord! . . .
I skirmish . . . feint a bit . . .
I lunge! . . . I keep my word!

[The VICOMTE staggers; CYRANO bows.]
At the last line, I hit!
[Acclamations. Applause from the boxes. Flowers and handkerchiefs are thrown. The OFFICERS surround and congratulate CYRANO. RAGUE- NEAU dances with delight. LE BRET is tearfully joyous and at the same time highly troubled. The friends of the VICOMTE support him off the stage.]
THE CROWD [*in a long shout*]   Ah! . . .
A LIGHT-CAVALRY MAN   Superb!

---

*Name of an ill-bred dog in a fable (book VIII, fable 24) by the French poet Jean de La Fontaine (1621–1695).

A WOMAN   Sweet!

RAGUENEAU   Astounding!

A MARQUIS   Novel!

LE BRET   Insensate!

THE CROWD [*pressing around* CYRANO]   Congratulations! . . .
Well done! . . . Bravo! . . .

A WOMAN'S VOICE   He is a hero!

A MOUSQUETAIRE [*striding swiftly toward* CYRANO, *with outstretched
hand*]   Monsieur, will you allow me? It was quite, quite excel-
lently done, and I think I know whereof I speak. But, as a fact,
I expressed my mind before, by making a huge noise. . . . [*He
retires.*]

CYRANO [*to* CUIGY]   Who may the gentleman be?

CUIGY   D'Artagnan.*

LE BRET [*to* CYRANO, *taking his arm*]   Come, I wish to talk with
you.

CYRANO   Wait till the crowd has thinned. [*To* BELLEROSE]. I may
remain?

BELLEROSE [*deferentially*]   Why, certainly! . . .
[*Shouts are heard outside.*]

JODELET [*after looking*]   They are hooting Montfleury.

BELLEROSE [*solemnly*]   Sic transit!† . . . [*In a different tone, to the
doorkeeper and the candle snuffer.*] Sweep and close. Leave the
lights. We shall come back, after eating, to rehearse a new
farce for to-morrow. [*Exeunt* JODELET *and* BELLEROSE, *after
bowing very low to* CYRANO.]

THE DOORKEEPER [*to* CYRANO]   Monsieur will not be going to
dinner?

CYRANO   I? . . . No.
[*The doorkeeper withdraws.*]

LE BRET [*to* CYRANO]   And this, because? . . .

---

*One of the heroes of Alexandre Dumas's *The Three Musketeers*.
†Thus passes worldly glory (Latin).

CYRANO [*proudly*]   Because . . . [*in a different tone, having seen that the doorkeeper is too far to overhear*] I have not a penny!

LE BRET [*making the motion of flinging a bag*]   How is this? The bag of crowns. . . .

CYRANO   Monthly remittance, thou lastedst but a day!

LE BRET   And to keep you the remainder of the month? . . .

CYRANO   Nothing is left!

LE BRET   But then, flinging that bag, what a child's prank!

CYRANO   But what a gesture! . . .

THE SWEETMEAT VENDER [*coughing behind her little counter*] Hm! . . . [*CYRANO and* LE BRET *turn toward her. She comes timidly forward.*] Monsieur, to know you have not eaten . . . makes my heart ache. [*Pointing to the sweetmeat-stand.*] I have there all that is needed. . . . [*impulsively*] Help yourself!

CYRANO [*taking off his hat*]   Dear child, despite my Gascon pride, which forbids that I should profit at your hand by the most inconsiderable of dainties, I fear too much lest a denial should grieve you: I will accept therefore . . . [*He goes to the stand and selects*] Oh, a trifle! . . . A grape off this . . . [*She proffers the bunch, he takes a single grape.*] No . . . one! This glass of water . . . [*She starts to pour wine into it, he stops her.*] No . . . clear! And half a macaroon. [*He breaks in two the macaroon, and returns half.*]

LE BRET   This comes near being silly!

SWEETMEAT VENDER   Oh, you will take something more! . . .

CYRANO   Yes. Your hand to kiss. [*He kisses the hand she holds out to him, as if it were that of a princess.*]

SWEETMEAT VENDER   Monsieur, I thank you. [*Curtseys.*] Good evening! [*Exit.*]

SCENE V

Cyrano, Le Bret, then the Doorkeeper

CYRANO [*to* LE BRET]   I am listening. [*He establishes himself before the stand, sets the macaroon before him,*] Dinner! [*does the same with the glass of water*], Drink! [*and with the grape*] Dessert! [*He sits down.*] La! let me begin! I was as hungry as a wolf! [*Eating.*] You were saying?

LE BRET   That if you listen to none but those great boobies and swashbucklers your judgment will become wholly perverted. Inquire, will you, of the sensible, concerning the effect produced to-day by your prowesses.

CYRANO [*finishing his macaroon*]   Enormous!

LE BRET   The cardinal . . .

CYRANO [*beaming*]   He was there, the cardinal?

LE BRET   Must have found what you did. . . .

CYRANO   To a degree, original.

LE BRET   Still . . .

CYRANO   He is a poet. It cannot be distasteful to him wholly that one should deal confusion to a fellow-poet's play.

LE BRET   But, seriously, you make too many enemies!

CYRANO [*biting into the grape*]   How many, thereabouts, should you think I made to-night?

LE BRET   Eight and forty. Not mentioning the women.

CYRANO   Come, tell them over!

LE BRET   Montfleury, the old merchant, De Guiche, the Vicomte, Baro, the whole Academy . . .

CYRANO   Enough! You steep me in bliss!

LE BRET   But whither will the road you follow lead you? What can your object be?

CYRANO   I was wandering aimlessly; too many roads were open . . . too many resolves, too complex, allowed of being taken. I took . . .

LE BRET   Which?

CYRANO By far the simplest of them all. I decided to be, in every matter, always, admirable!

LE BRET [*shrugging his shoulders*] That will do.——But tell me, will you not, the motive——look, the true one!——of your dislike to Montfleury.

CYRANO [*rising*] That old Silenus,* who has not seen his knees this many a year, still believes himself a delicate desperate danger to the fair. And as he struts and burrs upon the stage, makes sheep's-eyes at them with his moist frog's-eyes. And I have hated him . . . oh, properly! . . . since the night he was so daring as to cast his glance on her . . . her, who——Oh, I thought I saw a slug crawl over a flower!

LE BRET [*amazed*] Hey? What? Is it possible? . . .

CYRANO [*with a bitter laugh*] That I should love? [*In a different tone, seriously.*] I love.

LE BRET And may one know? . . . You never told me . . .

CYRANO Whom I love? . . . Come, think a little. The dream of being beloved, even by the beautiless, is made, to me, an empty dream indeed by this good nose, my forerunner ever by a quarter of an hour. Hence, whom should I love? . . . It seems superfluous to tell you! . . . I love . . . it was inevitable! . . . the most beautiful that breathes!

LE BRET The most beautiful? . . .

CYRANO No less, in the whole world! And the most resplendent, and the most delicate of wit, and among the golden-haired . . . [*with overwhelming despair*] Still the superlative!

LE BRET Dear me, what is this fair one?

CYRANO All unawares, a deadly snare, exquisite without concern to be so. A snare of nature's own, a musk-rose, in which ambush Love lies low. Who has seen her smile remembers the ineffable! There is not a thing so common but she turns it into

---

*In Greek mythology, a satyr-like creature and follower of Dionysus, the wine god.

prettiness; and in the merest nod or beck she can make mani-
fest all the attributes of a goddess. No, Venus! you cannot step
into your iridescent shell, nor, Dian, you, walk through the
blossoming groves, as she steps into her chair and walks in
Paris!

LE BRET   Sapristi! I understand! It is clear!

CYRANO   It is pellucid.

LE BRET   Magdeleine Robin, your cousin?

CYRANO   Yes, Roxane.

LE BRET   But, what could be better? You love her? Tell her so! You
covered yourself with glory in her sight a moment since.

CYRANO   Look well at me, dear friend, and tell me how much
hope you think can be justly entertained with this protuberance.
Oh, I foster no illusions! . . . Sometimes, indeed, yes, in the vio-
let dusk, I yield, even I! to a dreamy mood. I penetrate some garden that lies sweetening the hour. With my poor great devil of a
nose I sniff the April. . . . And as I follow with my eyes some
woman passing with some cavalier, I think how dear would I hold
having to walk beside me, linked like that, slowly, in the soft
moonlight, such a one! I kindle—I forget—and then . . . then
suddenly I see the shadow of my profile upon the garden-wall!

LE BRET [*touched.*]   My friend . . .

CYRANO   Friend, I experience a bad half hour sometimes, in feeling so unsightly . . . and alone.

LE BRET [*in quick sympathy, taking his hand*]   You weep?

CYRANO   Ah, God forbid! That? Never! No, that would be unsightly to excess! That a tear should course the whole length of
this nose! Never, so long as I am accountable, shall the divine
loveliness of tears be implicated with so much gross ugliness!
Mark me well, nothing is so holy as are tears, nothing! and never
shall it be that, rousing mirth through me, a single one of them
shall seem ridiculous!

LE BRET   Come, do not despond! Love is a lottery.

CYRANO [*shaking his head*]   No! I love Cleopatra: do I resemble Cæsar? I worship Berenice: do I put you in mind of Titus?*

LE BRET   But your courage . . . and your wit!—The little girl who but a moment ago bestowed on you that very modest meal, her eyes, you must have seen as much, did not exactly hate you!

CYRANO [*impressed*]   That is true!

LE BRET   You see? So, then!—But Roxane herself, in following your duel, went lily-pale.

CYRANO   Lily-pale? . . .

LE BRET   Her mind, her heart as well, are struck with wonder! Be bold, speak to her, in order that she may . . .

CYRANO   Laugh in my face! . . . No, there is but one thing upon earth I fear. . . . It is that.

THE DOORKEEPER [*admitting the* DUENNA† *to* CYRANO]   Monsieur, you are inquired for.

CYRANO [*seeing the duenna*]   Ah, my God! . . . her duenna!

SCENE VI

Cyrano, Le Bret, the Duenna

THE DUENNA [*with a great curtsey*]   Somebody wishes to know of her valorous cousin where one may, in private, see him.

CYRANO [*upset*]   See me?

THE DUENNA [*with curtsey*]   See you. There are things for your ear.

CYRANO   There are . . . ?

THE DUENNA [*other curtsey*]   Things.

CYRANO [*staggering*]   Ah, my God! . . .

---

*Reference to Pierre Corneille's *Tite et Bérénice* (1670), the story of Titus, who succeeded his father Vespasian as Roman emperor from A.D. 79–81.

†A sort of governess or chaperone, often advanced in years, responsible for overseeing the conduct of a young woman.

THE DUENNA   Somebody intends, tomorrow, at the earliest roses of the dawn, to hear Mass at Saint Roch.

CYRANO [*upholds himself by leaning on* LE BRET]   Ah, my God!

THE DUENNA   That over, where might one step in a moment, have a little talk?

CYRANO [*losing his senses*]   Where? . . . I . . . But . . . Ah, my God!

THE DUENNA   Expedition, if you please.

CYRANO   I am casting about . . .

THE DUENNA   Where?

CYRANO   At . . . at . . . at Ragueneau's . . . the pastrycook's.

THE DUENNA   He lodges?

CYRANO   In . . . In Rue . . . Ah, my God! my God! . . . St. Honoré.

THE DUENNA [*retiring*]   We will be there. Do not fail. At seven.

CYRANO   I will not fail.

[Exit DUENNA.]

SCENE VII

Cyrano, Le Bret, then the Actors and Actresses, Cuigy, Brissaille, Lignière, the Doorkeeper, the Fiddlers

CYRANO [*falling on* LE BRET*'s neck*]   To me . . . from her . . . a meeting!

LE BRET   Well, your gloom is dispelled?

CYRANO   Ah, to whatever end it may be, she is aware of my existence!

LE BRET   And now you will be calm?

CYRANO [*beside himself*]   Now, I shall be fulminating and frenetical! I want an army all complete to put to rout! I have ten hearts and twenty arms . . . I cannot now be suited with felling dwarfs to earth. . . . [*At the top of his lungs.*] Giants are what I want!

[During the last lines, on the stage at the back, shadowy shapes of players

have been moving about. The rehearsal has begun; the fiddlers have re-sumed their places.]

A VOICE [*from the stage*]   Hey! Psst! Over there! A little lower. We are trying to rehearse!

CYRANO [*laughing*]   We are going! [*He goes toward the back.*]
[*Through the street door, enter CUIGY, BRISSAILLE, several OFFICERS supporting LIGNIÈRE in a state of complete intoxication.*]

CUIGY   Cyrano!

CYRANO   What is this?

CUIGY   A *turdus vinaticus** we are bringing you.

CYRANO [*recognizing him*]   Lignière! Hey, what has happened to you?

CUIGY   He is looking for you.

BRISSAILLE   He cannot go home.

CYRANO   Why?

LIGNIÈRE [*in a thick voice, showing him a bit of crumpled paper.*] This note bids me beware . . . A hundred men against me . . . on account of lampoon. . . . Grave danger threatening me. . . . Porte de Nesle . . . must pass it to get home. Let me come and sleep under your roof.

CYRANO   A hundred, did you say?—You shall sleep at home!

LIGNIÈRE [*frightened*]   But . . .

CYRANO [*in a terrible voice, pointing to the lighted lantern which the DOORKEEPER stands swinging as he listens to this scene*]   Take that lantern [LIGNIÈRE *hurriedly takes it*] and walk! . . . I swear to tuck you in your bed to-night myself. [*To the OFFICERS.*] You, follow at a distance. You may look on!

CUIGY   But a hundred men . . .

CYRANO   Are not one man too many for my mood to-night!
[*The players, in their several costumes, have stepped down from the stage and come nearer.*]

LE BRET   But why take under your especial care . . .

---

*Humorous formation based on the Latin *turdus* (meaning "thrush") and *vinaticus* (suggesting "drunk").

CYRANO   Still Le Bret is not satisfied!

LE BRET   That most commonplace of sots?

CYRANO [*slapping* LIGNIÈRE *on the shoulder*]   Because this sot, this cask of muscatel, this hogshead of rosolio,* did once upon a time a wholly pretty thing. On leaving Mass, having seen her whom he loved take holy-water, as the rite prescribes, he, whom the sight of water puts to flight, ran to the holy-water bowl, and stooping over, drank it dry. . . .

AN ACTRESS [*in the costume of soubrette*]   *Tiens*, that was nice!

CYRANO   Was it not, soubrette?

THE SOUBRETTE [*to the others*]   But why are they, a hundred, all against one poor poet?

CYRANO   Let us start! [*To the* OFFICERS.] And you, gentlemen, when you see me attack, whatever you may suppose to be my danger, do not stir to second me!

ANOTHER OF THE ACTRESSES [*jumping from the stage*]   Oh, I will not miss seeing this!

CYRANO   Come!

ANOTHER ACTRESS [*likewise jumping from the stage, to an elderly actor*]   Cassandre, will you not come?

CYRANO   Come, all of you! the Doctor, Isabel, Leander, all! and you shall lend, charming fantastic swarm, an air of Italian farce to the Spanish drama in view. Yes, you shall be a tinkling heard above a roar, like bells about a tambourine!

ALL THE WOMEN [*in great glee*]   Bravo! . . . Hurry! . . . A mantle! . . . A hood!

JODELET   Let us go!

CYRANO [*to the fiddlers*]   You will favor us with a tune, messieurs the violinists!

[*The fiddlers fall into the train. The lighted candles which furnished the footlights are seized and distributed. The procession becomes a torchlight procession.*]

---

*Sweet Italian liqueur made of roses and orange flowers.

CYRANO   Bravo! Officers, beauty in fancy dress, and, twenty steps ahead . . . [*he takes the position he describes*]. I, by myself, under the feather stuck, with her own hand, by Glory, in my hat! Proud as a Scipio trebly Nasica!*——It is understood? Formal interdiction to interfere with me!——We are ready? One! Two! Three! Door-keeper, open the door!

[*The DOORKEEPER opens wide the folding door. A picturesque corner of Old Paris appears, bathed in moonlight.*]

CYRANO   Ah! . . . Paris floats in dim nocturnal mist. . . . The sloping blueish roofs are washed with moonlight. . . . A setting, exquisite indeed, offers itself for the scene about to be en-acted. . . . Yonder, under silvery vapor wreathes, like a mysteri-ous magic mirror, glimmers the Seine. . . . And you shall see what you shall see!

ALL   To the Porte de Nesle!

CYRANO [*standing on the threshold*]   To the Porte de Nesle! [*Before crossing it, he turns to the* SOUBRETTE.] Were you not asking, mademoiselle, why upon that solitary rhymster a hundred men were set? [*He draws his sword, and tranquilly*] Because it was well known he is a friend of mine! [*Exit.*]

[*To the sound of the violins, by the flickering light of the candles, the pro-cession——LIGNIÈRE staggering at the head, the ACTRESSES arm in arm with the OFFICERS, the players capering behind,——follows out into the night. Curtain.*]

---

*Literally, "having a pointed nose" (Italian); nickname of the Roman family Scipio.

ACT TWO

The Cookshop of Poets

RAGUENEAU'S shop, vast kitchen at the corner of Rue St. Honore and Rue de l'Arbre-Sec, which can be seen at the back, through the glass door, gray in the early dawn.

At the left, in front, a counter overhung by a wrought iron canopy from which geese, ducks, white peacocks are hanging. In large china jars, tall nosegays composed of the simpler flowers, mainly sunflowers. On the same side, in the middle distance, an enormous fireplace, in front of which, between huge andirons, each of which supports a small iron pot, roasting meats drip into appropriate pans.

At the right, door in the front wing. In the middle distance, a staircase leading to a loft, the interior of which is seen through open shutters; a spread table lighted by a small Flemish candelabrum, shows it to be an eating-room. A wooden gallery continuing the stairway, suggests other similar rooms to which it may lead.

In the center of the shop, an iron hoop—which can be lowered by means of a rope,—to which large roasts are hooked.

In the shadow, under the stairway, ovens are glowing. Copper molds and saucepans are shining; spits turning, hams swinging, pastry pyramids showing fair. It is the early beginning of the workday. Bustling of hurried scullions, portly cooks and young cook's-assistants; swarming of caps decorated with hen feathers and guinea-fowl wings. Wicker crates and broad sheets of tin are brought in loaded with brioches and tarts.

There are tables covered with meats and cakes; others, surrounded by chairs, await customers. In a corner, a smaller table, littered with papers. At the rise of the curtain,

RAGUENEAU *is discovered seated at this table, writing with an inspired air, and counting upon his fingers.*

SCENE I

FIRST PASTRYCOOK [*bringing in a tall molded pudding*]   Nougat of fruit!

SECOND PASTRYCOOK [*bringing in the dish he names*]   Custard!

THIRD PASTRYCOOK [*bringing in a fowl roasted in its feathers*] Peacock!

FOURTH PASTRYCOOK [*bringing in a tray of cakes*]   Mince-pies!

FIFTH PASTRYCOOK [*bringing in a deep earthen dish*]   Beef stew!

RAGUENEAU [*laying down his pen, and looking up*]   Daybreak already plates with silver the copper pans! Time, Ragueneau, to smother within thee the singing divinity! The hour of the lute will come anon—now is that of the ladle! [*He rises, speaking to one of the cooks.*] You, sir, be so good as to lengthen this gravy,—it is too thick!

THE COOK   How much?

RAGUENEAU   Three feet. [*Goes further.*]

THE COOK   What does he mean?

FIRST PASTRYCOOK   Let me have the tart!

SECOND PASTRYCOOK   The dumpling!

RAGUENEAU [*standing before the fireplace*]   Spread thy wings, Muse, and fly further, that thy lovely eyes may not be reddened at the sordid kitchen fire! [*To one of the cooks, pointing at some small loaves of bread.*] You have improperly placed the cleft in those loaves; the cæsura belongs in the middle,—between the hemistichs!* [*To another of the COOKS, pointing at an unfinished pasty.*] This pastry palace requires a roof! [*To a young cook's-apprentice, who, seated upon the floor, is putting fowls on a spit.*] And you, on that long spit,

---

*The caesura is the natural pause in a line of poetry; hemistich is the term for each of the two equal halves of the line.

arrange, my son, in pleasing alternation, the modest pullet and
the splendid turkey-cock,—even as our wise Malherbe* alter-
nated of old the greater with the lesser lines, and so with roasted
fowls compose a poem!

ANOTHER APPRENTICE [*coming forward with a platter covered by a
napkin*]   Master, in your honor, see what I have baked. . . . I
hope you are pleased with it!

RAGUENEAU [*ecstatic*]   A lyre!

THE APPRENTICE   Of pie-crust!

RAGUENEAU [*touched*]   With candied fruits!

THE APPRENTICE   And the strings, see,—of spun sugar!

RAGUENEAU [*giving him money*]   Go, drink my health! [*Catching
sight of LISE who is entering.*] Hush! My wife! . . . Move on, and
hide that money. [*To LISE, showing her the lyre, with a constrained air.*]
Fine, is it not?

LISE   Ridiculous! [*She sets a pile of wrapping-paper on the counter.*]

RAGUENEAU   Paper bags? Good. Thanks. [*He examines them.*] Heavens! My beloved books! The masterpieces of my friends,—dis-
membered,—torn!—to fashion paper bags for penny pies!—Ah,
the abominable case is re-enacted of Orpheus and the Mænads!†

LISE [*drily*]   And have I not an unquestionable right to make what use
I can of the sole payment ever got from your paltry scribblers of
uneven lines?

RAGUENEAU   Pismire!‡ Forbear to insult those divine, melodious
crickets!

LISE   Before frequenting that low crew, my friend, you did not use
to call me a Mænad,—no, nor yet a pismire!

---

*François Malherbe, French poet (1555–1628) whose theoretical writings con-
tributed much to French classicism.

†In Greek myth, the poet and musician Orpheus was devoured by the Maenads, fe-
male devotees of Dionysus, the wine god; they were also known as Bacchantes, after
Bacchus, as the Romans called Dionysus.

‡Term of obloquy; antecedent of today's "pissant."

RAGUENEAU   Put poems to such a use!

LISE   To that use and no other!

RAGUENEAU   If with poems you do this, I should like to know, Madame, what you do with prose!

SCENE II

The Same

[Two children have come into the shop.]

RAGUENEAU   What can I do for you, little ones?

FIRST CHILD   Three patties.

RAGUENEAU *[waiting on them]*   There you are! Beautifully browned, and piping hot.

SECOND CHILD   Please, will you wrap them for us?

RAGUENEAU *[starting, aside]*   There goes one of my bags! *[To the children.]* You want them wrapped, do you? *[He takes one of the paper bags, and as he is about to put in the patties, reads.]* "No otherwise, Ulysses, from Penelope departing. . . ." Not this one! *[He lays it aside and takes another. At the moment of putting in the patties, he reads.]* "Phœbus of the aureate locks . . ." Not that one! *[Same business.]*

LISE *[out of patience]*   Well, what are you waiting for?

RAGUENEAU   Here we are. Here we are. Here we are. *[He takes a third bag and resigns himself.]* The sonnet to Phyllis! . . . It is hard, all the same.

LISE   It is lucky you made up your mind. *[Shrugging her shoulders.]* Nicodemus!* *[She climbs on a chair and arranges dishes on a sideboard.]*

RAGUENEAU *[taking advantage of her back being turned, calls back the children who had already reached the door]* Psst! . . . Children! Give me back the sonnet to Phyllis, and you shall have six patties

---

*Name of a silly person.

instead of three! [*The children give back the paper bag, joyfully take the patties and exeunt.* RAGUENEAU *smoothes out the crumpled paper and reads declaiming.*] *"Phyllis!"* . . . Upon that charming name, a grease-spot! . . . *"Phyllis!"* . . .
[*Enter brusquely* CYRANO.]

SCENE III

Cyrano, Lise, Ragueneau, then the Mousquetaire

CYRANO   What time is it?

RAGUENEAU [*bowing with eager deference*]   Six o'clock.

CYRANO [*with emotion*]   In an hour! [*He comes and goes in the shop.*]

RAGUENEAU [*following him*]   Bravo! I too was witness. . . .

CYRANO   Of what?

RAGUENEAU   Your fight.

CYRANO   Which?

RAGUENEAU   At the Hôtel de Bourgogne.

CYRANO [*with disdain*]   Ah, the duel!

RAGUENEAU [*admiringly*]   Yes,—the duel in rhyme.

LISE   He can talk of nothing else.

CYRANO   Let him! . . . It does no harm.

RAGUENEAU [*thrusting with a spit he has seized*]   *"At the last line, I hit!" "At the last line I hit!"*—How fine that is! [*With growing enthusiasm.*] *"At the last line, I—*

CYRANO   What time, Ragueneau?

RAGUENEAU [*remaining fixed in the attitude of thrusting, while he looks at the clock*]   Five minutes past six.—*"I hit!"* [*He recovers from his duelling posture.*] Oh, to be able to make a ballade!

LISE [*to* CYRANO, *who in passing her counter has absentmindedly shaken hands with her*]   What ails your hand?

CYRANO   Nothing. A scratch.

RAGUENEAU   You have been exposed to some danger?

CYRANO   None whatever.

LISE [*shaking her finger at him*]   I fear that is a fib!

CYRANO   From the swelling of my nose? The fib in that case must have been good-sized. . . . [*In a different tone.*] I am expecting some one. You will leave us alone in here.

RAGUENEAU   But how can I contrive it? My poets shortly will be coming . . .

LISE [*ironically*]   For breakfast!

CYRANO   When I sign to you, you will clear the place of them.—What time is it?

RAGUENEAU   It is ten minutes past six.

CYRANO [*seating himself nervously at* RAGUENEAU's *table and helping himself to paper*]   A pen?

RAGUENEAU [*taking one from behind his ear, and offering it*]   A swan's quill.

A MOUSQUETAIRE [*with enormous moustachios, enters; in a stentorian voice*]   Good-morning!

[*LISE goes hurriedly to him, toward the back.*]

CYRANO [*turning*]   What is it?

RAGUENEAU   A friend of my wife's,—a warrior,—terrible, from his own report.

CYRANO [*taking up the pen again, and waving* RAGUENEAU *away*] Hush! . . . [*To himself.*] Write to her, . . . fold the letter, . . . hand it to her, . . . and make my escape. . . . [*Throwing down the pen.*] Coward! . . . But may I perish if I have the courage to speak to her, . . . to say a single word. . . . [*To* RAGUENEAU.] What time is it?

RAGUENEAU   A quarter past six.

CYRANO [*beating his breast*]   A single word of all I carry here! . . . Whereas in writing . . . [*He takes up the pen again.*] Come, let us write it then, in very deed, the love-letter I have written in thought so many times, I have but to lay my soul beside my paper, and copy! [*He writes.*]

SCENE IV

Ragueneau, Lise, the Mousquetaire, Cyrano, writing at the little table; the Poets, dressed in black, their stocking sagging and covered in mud

[*Beyond the glass-door, shadowy lank hesitating shabby forms are seen moving. Enter the poets, clad in black, with hanging hose, sadly mud-splashed.*]

LISE [*coming forward, to* RAGUENEAU]   Here they come, your scarecrows!

FIRST POET [*entering, to* RAGUENEAU]   Brother in art! . . .

SECOND POET [*shaking both* RAGUENEAU's *hands*]   Dear fellow-bard. . . .

THIRD POET   Eagle of pastrycooks, [*sniffs the air*], your eyrie smells divine!

FOURTH POET   Phœbus* turned baker!

FIFTH POET   Apollo† master-cook!

RAGUENEAU [*surrounded, embraced, shaken by the hand*]   How at his ease a man feels at once with them!

FIRST POET   The reason we are late, is the crowd at the Porte de Nesle!

SECOND POET   Eight ugly ruffians, ripped open with the sword, lie weltering on the pavement.

CYRANO [*raising his head a second*]   Eight? I thought there were only seven. [*Goes on with his letter.*]

RAGUENEAU [*to* CYRANO]   Do you happen to know who is the hero of this event?

CYRANO [*negligently*]   I? . . . No.

LISE [*to the* MOUSQUETAIRE]   Do you?

---

*Reference to Phoebus Apollo, god of the sun in Greek mythology.

†In this case, the reference is to Apollo as a god associated with such civilized arts as poetry and music.

THE MOUSQUETAIRE [*turning up the ends of his moustache*]
Possibly!

CYRANO [*writing; from time to time he is heard murmuring a word or two,*]
. . . "*I love you . . .*"

FIRST POET   A single man, we were told, put a whole gang to
flight!

SECOND POET   Oh, it was a rare sight! The ground was littered
with pikes, and cudgels . . .

CYRANO [*writing*]   "*Your eyes . . .*"

THIRD POET   Hats were strewn as far as the Goldsmiths' square!

FIRST POET   Sapristi! He must have been a madman of mettle. . . .

CYRANO [*as above*]   ". . . *your lips . . .*"

FIRST POET   An infuriate giant, the doer of that deed!

CYRANO [*same business*]   ". . . *but when I see you, I come near to swooning with a tender dread . . .*"

SECOND POET [*snapping up a tart*]   What have you lately written,
Ragueneau?

CYRANO [*same business*]   ". . . *who loves you devotedly . . .*" [*In the act
of signing the letter, he stops, rises, and tucks it inside his doublet.*] No
need to sign it, I deliver it myself.

RAGUENEAU [*to SECOND POET*]   I have rhymed a recipe.

THIRD POET [*establishing himself beside a tray of cream puffs*]   Let us
hear this recipe!

FOURTH POET [*examining a brioche of which he has possessed himself*]
It should not wear its cap so saucily on one side . . . it scarcely
looks well! . . . [*Bites off the top.*]

FIRST POET   See, the spice-cake there, ogling a susceptible poet
with eyes of almond under citron brows! . . . [*He takes the spice-
cake.*]

SECOND POET   We are listening!

THIRD POET [*slightly squeezing a cream puff between his fingers*]   This
puff creams at the mouth. . . . I water!

SECOND POET [*taking a bite out of the large pastry lyre*]   For once the
Lyre will have filled my stomach!

RAGUENEAU [*who has made ready to recite, has coughed, adjusted his cap,
    struck an attitude*]   A recipe in rhyme!
SECOND POET [*to* FIRST POET, *nudging him*]   Is it breakfast,
    with you?
FIRST POET [*to* SECOND POET]   And with you, is it dinner?
RAGUENEAU   How Almond Cheese-Cakes should be made.

> Briskly beat to lightness due,
>   Eggs, a few;
> With the eggs so beaten, beat—
> Nicely strained for this same use,—
>   Lemon-juice,
> Adding milk of almonds, sweet.
>
> With fine pastry dough, rolled flat,
>   After that,
> Line each little scallopped mold;
> Round the sides, light-fingered, spread
>   Marmalade;
> Pour the liquid eggy gold,
>
> Into each delicious pit;
>   Prison it
> In the oven,—and, bye and bye,
> Almond cheesecakes will in gay
>   Blond array
> Bless your nostril and your eye!

THE POETS [*their mouths full*]   Exquisite! . . . Delicious!
ONE OF THE POETS [*choking*]   Humph!
    [*They go toward the back, eating.* CYRANO, *who has been watching them,
    approaches RAGUENEAU.*]
CYRANO   While you recite your works to them, have you a notion
    how they stuff?

RAGUENEAU [*low, with a smile*]   Yes, I see them . . . without looking, lest they should be abashed. I get a double pleasure thus from
saying my verses over: I satisfy a harmless weakness of which I
stand convicted, at the same time as giving those who have not fed
a needed chance to feed!

CYRANO [*slapping him on the shoulder*]   You, . . . I like you!
[RAGUENEAU *joins his friends.* CYRANO *looks after him; then,
somewhat sharply.*] Hey, Lise! [LISE, *absorbed in tender conversation
with the* MOUSQUETAIRE, *starts and comes forward toward*
CYRANO.] Is that captain . . . laying siege to you?

LISE [*offended*]   My eyes, sir, have ever held in respect those who
meant hurt to my character. . . .

CYRANO   For eyes so resolute . . . I thought yours looked a little
languishing!

LISE [*choking with anger*]   But . . .

CYRANO [*bluntly*]   I like your husband. Wherefore, Madame Lise, I
say he shall not be sc . . . horned!*

LISE   But . . .

CYRANO [*raising his voice so as to be heard by the* MOUSQUETAIRE]
A word to the wise! [*He bows to the* MOUSQUETAIRE, *and after
looking at the clock, goes to the door at the back and stands in watch.*]

LISE [*to the* MOUSQUETAIRE, *who has simply returned* CYRANO's
bow]   Really . . . I am astonished at you. . . . Defy him . . . to
his face!

THE MOUSQUETAIRE   To his face, indeed! . . . to his
face! . . . [*He quickly moves off.* LISE *follows him.*]

CYRANO [*from the door at the back, signalling to* RAGUENEAU *that he
should clear the room*]   Pst! . . .

RAGUENEAU [*urging the* POETS *toward the door at the right*]   We
shall be much more comfortable in there. . . .

CYRANO [*impatiently*]   Pst! . . . Pst! . . .

---

*That is, "scorned," but also literally "horned": traditionally, the cuckolded husband
grows horns.

RAGUENEAU [*driving along the* POETS]　I want to read you a little thing of mine. . . .

FIRST POET [*despairingly, his mouth full*]　But the provisions. . . .

SECOND POET　Shall not be parted from us!

[*They follow RAGUENEAU in procession, after making a raid on the eatables.*]

SCENE V

Cyrano, Roxane, the Duenna

CYRANO　If I feel that there is so much as a glimmer of hope . . . I will out with my letter! . . .

[*ROXANE, masked, appears behind the glass door, followed by the DUENNA.*]

CYRANO [*instantly opening the door*]　Welcome! [*Approaching the* DUENNA.] Madame, a word with you!

THE DUENNA　A dozen.

CYRANO　Are you fond of sweets?

THE DUENNA　To the point of indigestion!

CYRANO [*snatching some paper bags off the counter*]　Good. Here are two sonnets of Benserade's . . .*

THE DUENNA　Pooh!

CYRANO　Which I fill for you with grated almond drops.

THE DUENNA [*with a different expression*]　Ha!

CYRANO　Do you look with favor upon the cate they call a trifle?

THE DUENNA　I affect it out of measure, when it has whipped cream inside.

CYRANO　Six shall be yours, thrown in with a poem by Saint-Amant.† And in these verses of Chapelain‡ I place this wedge of

---

*Isaac de Benserade (1613–1691), a precious poet.

†Antoine Girard, sieur de Saint-Amant (1594–1661), a poet and satirist.

‡Jean Chapelain (1595–1674), literary critic and poet.

fruit-cake, light by the side of them. . . . Oh! And do you like tarts . . . little jam ones . . . fresh?

THE DUENNA   I dream of them at night!

CYRANO [*loading her arms with crammed paper bags*]   Do me the favor to go and eat these in the street.

THE DUENNA   But . . .

CYRANO [*pushing her out*]   And do not come back till you have finished! [*He closes the door upon her, comes forward toward* ROXANE, *and stands, bareheaded, at a respectful distance.*]

SCENE VI

Cyrano, Roxane, the Duenna for a moment

CYRANO   Blessed forevermore among all hours the hour in which, remembering that so lowly a being still draws breath, you were so gracious as to come to tell me . . . to tell me? . . .

ROXANE [*who has removed her mask*]   First of all, that I thank you. For that churl, that coxcomb yesterday, whom you taught manners with your sword, is the one whom a great nobleman, who fancies himself in love with me. . . .

CYRANO   De Guiche?

ROXANE [*dropping her eyes*]   Has tried to force upon me as a husband.

CYRANO   Honorary? [*Bowing.*] It appears, then, that I fought, and I am glad of it, not for my graceless nose, but your thrice-beautiful eyes.

ROXANE   Further than that . . . I wished . . . But, before I can make the confession I have in mind to make, I must find in you once more the . . . almost brother, with whom as a child I used to play, in the park—do you remember?—by the lake!

CYRANO   I have not forgotten. Yes . . . you came every summer to Bergerac.

ROXANE   You used to fashion lances out of reeds . . .

CYRANO   The silk of the tasselled corn furnished hair for your doll . . .

ROXANE   It was the time of long delightful games . . .

CYRANO   And somewhat sour berries . . .

ROXANE   The time when you did everything I bade you!

CYRANO   Roxane, wearing short frocks, was known as Magdeleine.

ROXANE   Was I pretty in those days?

CYRANO   You were not ill-looking.

ROXANE   Sometimes, in your venturesome climbings you used to hurt yourself. You would come running to me, your hand bleeding. And, playing at being your mamma, I would harden my voice and say . . . [*She takes his hand.*] "Will you never keep out of mischief?" [*She stops short, amazed.*] Oh, it is too much! Here you have done it again! [CYRANO *tries to draw back his hand.*] No! Let me look at it! . . . Aren't you ashamed? A great boy like you! . . . How did this happen, and where?

CYRANO   Oh, fun . . . near the Porte de Nesle.

ROXANE [*sitting down at a table and dipping her handkerchief into a glass of water*]   Let me have it.

CYRANO [*sitting down too*]   So prettily, so cheeringly maternal!

ROXANE   And tell me, while I wash this naughty blood away . . . with how many were you fighting?

CYRANO   Oh, not quite a hundred.

ROXANE   Tell me about it.

CYRANO   No. What does it matter? You tell me, you . . . what you were going to tell me before, and did not dare . . .

ROXANE [*without releasing his hand*]   I do dare, now. I have breathed in courage with the perfume of the past. Oh, yes, now I dare. Here it is. There is someone whom I love.

CYRANO   Ah! . . .

ROXANE   Oh, he does not know it.

CYRANO   Ah! . . .

ROXANE   As yet . . .

CYRANO   Ah! . . .

ROXANE   But if he does not know it, he soon will.

CYRANO   Ah! . . .

ROXANE   A poor boy who until now has loved me timidly, from a distance, without daring to speak. . . .

CYRANO   Ah! . . .

ROXANE   No, leave me your hand. It is hot, this will cool it . . . But I have read his heart in his face.

CYRANO   Ah! . . .

ROXANE [*completing the bandaging of his hand with her small pocket-handkerchief*]   And, cousin, is it not a strange coincidence—that he should serve exactly in your regiment!

CYRANO   Ah! . . .

ROXANE [*laughing*]   Yes. He is a cadet, in the same company!

CYRANO   Ah! . . .

ROXANE   He bears plain on his forehead the stamp of wit, of genius! He is proud, noble, young, brave, handsome. . . .

CYRANO [*rising, pale*]   Handsome! . . .

ROXANE   What . . . what is the matter?

CYRANO   With me? . . . Nothing! . . . It is . . . it is . . . [*Showing his hand, smiling.*] You know! . . . It smarts a little . . .

ROXANE   In short, I love him. I must tell you, however, that I have never seen him save at the play.

CYRANO   Then you have never spoken to each other?

ROXANE   Only with our eyes.

CYRANO   But, then . . . how can you know? . . .

ROXANE   Oh, under the lindens of Place Royale, people will talk. A trustworthy gossip told me many things!

CYRANO   A cadet, did you say?

ROXANE   A cadet, in your company.

CYRANO   His name?

ROXANE   Baron Christian de Neuvillette.

CYRANO   What? He is not in the cadets.

ROXANE   He is! He certainly is, since morning. Captain Carbon de Castel-Jaloux.

CYRANO   And quickly, quickly, she throws away her heart! . . . But my poor little girl . . .

THE DUENNA [*opening the door at the back*]   Monsieur de Bergerac, I have eaten them, every one!

CYRANO   Now read the poetry printed upon the bags! [*The* DUENNA *disappears*] My poor child, you who can endure none but the choicest language, who savor eloquence and wit, . . . if he should be a barbarian!

ROXANE   No! no! . . . He has hair like one of D'Urfé's heroes!*

CYRANO   If he had on proof as homely a wit as he has pretty hair!

ROXANE   No! No! . . . I can see at a single glance, his utterances are fine, pointed . . .

CYRANO   Ah, yes! A man's utterances are invariably like his moustache! . . . Still, if he *were* a ninny? . . .

ROXANE [*stamping with her foot*]   I should die, there!

CYRANO [*after a time*]   You bade me come here that you might tell me this? I scarcely see the appropriateness, Madame.

ROXANE   Ah, it was because someone yesterday let death into my soul by telling me that in your company you are all Gascons, . . . all!

CYRANO   And that we pick a quarrel with every impudent fledgling, not Gascon, admitted by favor to our thoroughbred Gascon ranks? That is what you heard?

ROXANE   Yes, and you can imagine how distracted I am for him!

CYRANO [*in his teeth*]   You well may be!

ROXANE   But I thought, yesterday, when you towered up, great and

---

*Honoré d'Urfé (1567–1625) was author of the pastoral novel *L'Astrée*, in which the heroes are handsome and noble shepherds; he was the object of an early essay by Rostand.

invincible, giving his due to that miscreant, standing your ground against those caitiffs, I thought "Were he but willing, he of whom all are in awe . . ."

CYRANO   Very well, I will protect your little baron.

ROXANE   Ah, you will . . . you will protect him for me? . . . I have always felt for you the tenderest regard!

CYRANO   Yes, yes.

ROXANE   You will be his friend?

CYRANO   I will!

ROXANE   And never shall he have to fight a duel?

CYRANO   I swear it.

ROXANE   Oh, I quite love you! . . . Now I must go. [*She hurriedly resumes her mask, throws a veil over her head; says absentmindedly*] But you have not yet told me about last night's encounter. It must have been amazing! . . . Tell him to write to me. [*She kisses her hand to him.*] I love you dearly!

CYRANO   Yes, yes.

ROXANE   A hundred men against you? . . . Well, adieu. We are fast friends.

CYRANO   Yes, yes.

ROXANE   Tell him to write me! . . . A hundred men! You shall tell me another time. I must not linger now . . . A hundred men! What a heroic thing to do!

CYRANO [*bowing*]   Oh, I have done better since!

[*Exit ROXANE. CYRANO stands motionless, staring at the ground. Silence. The door at the right opens. RAGUENEAU thrusts in his head.*]

SCENE VII

Cyrano, Ragueneau, the Poets, Carbon de Castel-Jaloux, the Cadets, the Crowd, etc., then De Guiche

RAGNENEAU   May we come back?

CYRANO [*without moving*]   Yes . . .

[RAGUENEAU beckons, his friends come in again. At the same time, in the doorway at the back, appears CARBON DE CASTEL-JALOUX, costume of a Captain of the Guards. On seeing CYRANO, he gesticulates exaggeratedly by way of signal to someone out of sight.]

CARBON DE CASTEL-JALOUX   He is here!

CYRANO [*looking up*]   Captain!

CARBON DE CASTEL-JALOUX [*exultant*]   Hero! We know all! . . . About thirty of my cadets are out there! . . .

CYRANO [*drawing back*]   But . . .

CARBON DE CASTEL-JALOUX [*trying to lead him off*] Come! . . . You are in request!

CYRANO   No!

CARBON DE CASTEL-JALOUX   They are drinking across the way, at the Cross of the Hilt.

CYRANO   I . . .

CARBON DE CASTEL-JALOUX [*going to the door and shouting toward the street corner, in a voice of thunder*]   The hero refuses. He is not in the humor!

A VOICE [*outside*]   Ah, sandious! . . .*

[Tumult outside, noise of clanking swords and of boots drawing nearer.]

CARBON DE CASTEL-JALOUX [*rubbing his hands*]   Here they come, across the street. . . .

THE CADETS [*entering the cookshop*]   Mille dious! . . . Capdedious! . . . Mordious! . . . Pocapdedious! . . .

RAGUENEAU [*backing in alarm*]   Messieurs, are you all natives of Gascony?

THE CADETS   All!

ONE OF THE CADETS [*to CYRANO*]   Bravo!

CYRANO   Baron!

OTHER CADET [*shaking both CYRANO's hands*]   Vivat!

---

*"Sandious," along with such terms as "Mille dious!" and "Capdedious!" and "Pocapdedious!," just below, are attempts to render the colorfully emotive language of the Gascons.

CYRANO   Baron!

THIRD CADET   Let me hug you to my heart!

CYRANO   Baron!

SEVERAL GASCONS   Bravo! Let us hug him!

CYRANO [not knowing which one to answer]   Baron! . . . baron! . . .
your pardon!

RAGUENEAU   Messieurs, are you all barons?

THE CADETS   All!

RAGUENEAU   Are they truly?

FIRST CADET   Our coats of arms piled up would dwindle in the
clouds!

LE BRET [entering, running to CYRANO]   They are looking for you!
A crowd, gone mad as March, led by those who were with you
last night.

CYRANO [alarmed]   You never told them where to find me?

LE BRET [rubbing his hands]   I did.

A BURGHER [entering, followed by a number of others]   Monsieur, the
Marais* is coming in a body!
[The street outside has filled with people. Sedan-chairs, coaches stop be-
fore the door.]

LE BRET [smiling, low to CYRANO]   And Roxane?

CYRANO [quickly]   Be quiet!

THE CROWD [outside.]   Cyrano!
[A rabble bursts into the cookshop. Confusion. Shouting.]

RAGUENEAU [standing upon a table]   My shop is invaded! They are
breaking everything! It is glorious!

PEOPLE [pressing round CYRANO]   My friend . . . my friend. . . .

CYRANO   I had not so many friends . . . yesterday!

LE BRET   This is success!

A YOUNG MARQUIS [running toward CYRANO, with outstretched
hands]   If you knew, my dear fellow . . .

---

*District of central Paris.

CYRANO   Dear? . . . Fellow? . . . Where was it we stood sentinel
  together?

OTHER MARQUIS   I wish to present you, sir, to several ladies, who
  are outside in my coach. . . .

CYRANO [*coldly*]   But you, to me, by whom will you first be presented?

LE BRET [*astonished*]   But what is the matter with you?

CYRANO   Be still!

A MAN OF LETTERS [*with an inkhorn*]   Will you kindly favor me
  with the details of . . .

CYRANO   No.

LE BRET [*nudging him*]   That is Theophrastus Renaudot, the inventor
  of the gazctte.*

CYRANO   Enough!

LE BRET   A sheet close packed with various information! It is an
  idea, they say, likely to take firm root and flourish!

A POET [*coming forward*]   Monsieur . . .

CYRANO   Another!

THE POET   I am anxious to make a pentacrostic on your name.

SOMEBODY ELSE [*likewise approaching* CYRANO]   Monsieur . . .

CYRANO   Enough, I say!

  [*At the gesture of impatience which* CYRANO *cannot repress, the crowd
  draws away. DE GUICHE appears, escorted by officers; among them
  CUIGY, BRISSAILLE, those who followed CYRANO at the end of the first
  act. CUIGY hurries toward CYRANO.*]

CUIGY [*to* CYRANO]   Monsieur de Guiche! [*Murmurs. Every one
  draws back*] He comes at the request of the Marshal de Gaussion.

DE GUICHE [*bowing to* CYRANO]   Who wishes to express his admiration for your latest exploit, the fame of which has reached
  him.

THE CROWD   Bravo!

---

*In addition to being physician to the king, Théophraste Renaudot (1586–1653)
founded the *Gazette*, one of the first newspapers.

CYRANO [*bowing*]   The Marshal is qualified to judge of courage.

DE GUICHE   He would scarcely have believed the report, had these gentlemen not been able to swear they had seen the deed performed.

CUIGY   With our own eyes!

LE BRET [*low to* CYRANO, *who wears an abstracted air*]   But . . .

CYRANO   Be silent!

LE BRET   You appear to be suffering . . .

CYRANO [*starting, and straightening himself*]   Before these people? . . . [*His moustache bristles; he expands his chest.*] I . . . suffering? . . . You shall see!

DE GUICHE [*in whose ear* CUIGY *has been whispering*]   But this is by no means the first gallant achievement marking your career. You serve in the madcap Gascon company, do you not?

CYRANO   In the cadets, yes.

ONE OF THE CADETS [*in a great voice*]   Among his countrymen!

DE GUICHE [*considering the* GASCONS, *in line behind* CYRANO] Ah, ha!—All these gentlemen then of the formidable aspect, are the famous . . .

CARBON DE CASTEL-JALOUX   Cyrano!

CYRANO   Captain? . . .

CARBON DE CASTEL-JALOUX   My company, I believe, is here in total. Be so obliging as to present it to the Count.

CYRANO [*taking a step toward* DE GUICHE, *and pointing at the* CADETS].

> They are the Gascony Cadets
> Of Carbon de Castel Jaloux;
> Famed fighters, liars, desperates,
> They are the Gascony Cadets!
> All, better-born than pickpockets,
> Talk couchant, rampant, . . . pendent, too!
> They are the Gascony Cadets
> Of Carbon de Castel-Jaloux!

Cat-whiskered, eyed like falconets,
Wolf-toothed and heron-legged, they hew
The rabble down that snarls and threats . . .
Cat-whiskered, eyed like falconets!
Great pomp of plume hides and offsets
Holes in those hats they wear askew . . .
Cat-whiskered, eyed like falconets,
They drive the snarling mob, and hew!

The mildest of their sobriquets
Are Crack-my-crown and Run-me-through,
Mad drunk on glory Gascon gets!
These boasters of soft sobriquets
Wherever rapier rapier whets
Are met in punctual rendezvous . . .
The mildest of their sobriquets
Are Crack-my-crown and Run-me-through!

They are the Gascony Cadets
That give the jealous spouse his due!
Lean forth, adorable coquettes,
They are the Gascony Cadets,
With plumes and scarfs and aigulets!
The husband gray may well look blue . . .
They are the Gascony Cadets
That give the jealous spouse his due!

DE GUICHE [*nonchalantly seated in an armchair which* RAGUENEAU
  has hurriedly brought for him]   A gentleman provides himself to-
  day, by way of luxury, with a poet. May I look upon you as mine?
CYRANO   No, your lordship, as nobody's.
DE GUICHE   My uncle Richelieu yesterday found your spontaneity
  diverting. I shall be pleased to be of use to you with him.
LE BRET [*dazzled*]   Great God!

DE GUICHE   I cannot think I am wrong in supposing that you have rhymed a tragedy?*

LE BRET [*whispering to* CYRANO]   My boy, your Agrippina will be played!

DE GUICHE   Take it to him. . . .

CYRANO [*tempted and pleased*] Really . . .

DE GUICHE   He has taste in such matters. He will no more than, here and there, alter a word, recast a passage. . . .

CYRANO [*whose face has instantly darkened*]   Not to be considered, monsieur! My blood runs cold at the thought of a single comma added or suppressed.

DE GUICHE   On the other hand, my dear sir, when a verse finds favor with him, he pays for it handsomely.

CYRANO   He scarcely can pay me as I pay myself, when I have achieved a verse to my liking, by singing it over to myself!

DE GUICHE   You are proud.

CYRANO   You have observed it?

ONE OF THE CADETS [*coming in with a number of disreputable, draggled tattered hats threaded on his sword*]   Look, Cyrano! at the remarkable feathered game we secured this morning near the Porte de Nesle! The hats of the fugitives!

CARBON DE CASTEL-JALOUX   *Spoliæ opimæ!*†

ALL [*laughing*]   Ha! Ha! Ha! . . .

CUIGY   The one who planned that military action, my word! must be proud of it to-day!

BRISSAILLE   Is it known who did it?

DE GUICHE   I!—[*The laughter stops short*] They had instructions to chastise—a matter one does not attend to in person,—a drunken scribbler. [*Constrained silence.*]

---

*Cyrano de Bergerac in fact wrote a tragedy, *La Mort d'Agrippine* (*The Death of Agrippine*), performed in 1654 at the Hôtel de Bourgogne.

†Literally, the hide of an enemy general killed by the opposing general (Latin); figuratively, rich booty or spoils gained in battle.

THE CADET [*under breath, to* CYRANO, *indicating the hats*]   What can we do with them? They are oily. . . . Make them into a hotch pot?

CYRANO [*taking the sword with the hats, and bowing, as he shakes them off at* DE GUICHE'*s feet*]   Monsieur, if you should care to return them to your friends? . . .

DE GUICHE [*rises, and in a curt tone*]   My chair and bearers, at once. [*To* CYRANO, *violently*.] As for you, sir . . .

A VOICE [*in the street, shouting*]   The chairmen of Monseigneur the Comte de Guiche!

DE GUICHE [*who has recovered control over himself, with, a smile*]   Have you read *Don Quixote?**

CYRANO   I have. And at the name of that divine madman, I uncover . . .

DE GUICHE   My advice to you is to ponder. . . .

A CHAIRMAN [*appearing at the back*]   The chair is at the door!

DE GUICHE   The chapter of the windmills.

CYRANO [*bowing*]   Chapter thirteen.

DE GUICHE   For when a man attacks them, it often happens. . . .

CYRANO   I have attacked, am I to infer, a thing that veers with every wind?

DE GUICHE   That one of their far-reaching canvas arms pitches him down into the mud!

CYRANO   Or up among the stars!

[*Exit DE GUICHE. He is seen getting into his chair. The gentlemen withdraw whispering. LE BRET goes to the door with them. The crowd leaves.*]

---

*Hero of the novel of the same name by Miguel de Cervantes (1547–1616). Don Quixote is an idealist who, among other exploits, fights windmills, believing them to be his enemies.

SCENE VIII

Cyrano, Le Bret, the Cadets

[*The CADETS remain seated at the right and left at tables where food and drink is brought to them*].

CYRANO [*bowing with a derisive air to those who leave without daring to take leave of him*]   Gentlemen . . . gentlemen . . . gentlemen. . . .

LE BRET [*coming forward, greatly distressed, lifting his hands to Heaven*] Oh, in what a pretty pair of shoes. . . .

CYRANO   Oh, you! . . . I expect you to grumble!

LE BRET   But yourself, you will agree with me that invariably to cut the throat of opportunity becomes an exaggeration! . . .

CYRANO   Yes. I agree. I do exaggerate.

LE BRET [*triumphant*]   You see, you admit it! . . .

CYRANO   But for the sake of principle, and of example, as well, I think it a good thing to exaggerate as I do!

LE BRET   Could you but leave apart, once in a while, your mousquetaire of a soul, fortune, undoubtedly, fame. . . .

CYRANO   And what should a man do? Seek some grandee, take him for patron, and like the obscure creeper clasping a tree-trunk, and licking the bark of that which props it up, attain to height by craft instead of strength? No, I thank you. Dedicate, as they all do, poems to financiers? Wear motley in the humble hope of seeing the lips of a minister distend for once in a smile not ominous of ill? No, I thank you. Eat every day a toad? Be threadbare at the belly with groveling? Have his skin dirty soonest at the knees? Practice feats of dorsal elasticity? No, I thank you. With one hand stroke the goat while with the other he waters the cabbage? Make gifts of senna* that counter-gifts of rhubarb may accrue, and indefatigably swing his censer in some beard? No, I thank you. Push himself from lap to lap, become a little great man in a great little circle, propel his

---

*Leguminous herb, used medicinally.

ship with madrigals for oars and in his sails the sighs of the elderly
ladies? No, I thank you. Get the good editor Sercy to print his
verses at proper expense?* No, I thank you. Contrive to be nominated Pope in conclaves held by imbeciles in wineshops? No, I
thank you. Work to construct a name upon the basis of a sonnet,
instead of constructing other sonnets? No, I thank you. Discover
talent in tyros, and in them alone? Stand in terror of what gazettes
may please to say, and say to himself "At whatever cost, may I figure in the Paris Mercury!"† No, I thank you. Calculate, cringe,
peak, prefer making a call to a poem,—petition, solicit, apply?
No, I thank you! No, I thank you! No, I thank you! But . . .
sing, dream, laugh, loaf, be single, be free, have eyes that look
squarely, a voice with a ring; wear, if he chooses, his hat hindside
afore; for a yes, for a no, fight a duel or turn a ditty! . . . Work,
without concern of fortune or of glory, to accomplish the heart's-
desired journey to the moon! Put forth nothing that has not its
spring in the very heart, yet, modest, say to himself, "Old man, be
satisfied with blossoms, fruits, yea, leaves alone, so they be gath-
ered in your garden and not another man's!" Then, if it happens
that to some small extent he triumph, be obliged to render of the
glory, to Cæsar, not one jot, but honestly appropriate it all. In
short, scorning to be the parasite, the creeper, if even failing to be
the oak, rise, not perchance to a great height, . . . but rise alone!

LE BRET   Alone? Good! but not one against all! How the devil did
you contract the mania that possesses you for making enemies, always, everywhere?

CYRANO   By seeing you make friends, and smile to those same
flocks of friends with a mouth that takes for model an old purse!
I wish not to be troubled to return bows in the street, and I ex-
claim with glee "An enemy the more!"

---

*A humorous reference, since Sercy was Cyrano de Bergerac's editor.
†The reference is to the *Mercure français*, a literary review founded in 1611 that
molded French aesthetic taste.

LE BRET   This is mental aberration!

CYRANO   I do not dispute it. I am so framed. To displease is my pleasure. I love that one should hate me. Dear friend, if you but knew how much better a man walks under the exciting fire of hostile eyes, and how amused he may become over the spots on his doublet, spattered by Envy and Cowardice! . . . You, the facile friendship wherewith you surround yourself, resembles those wide Italian collars, loose and easy, with a perforated pattern, in which the neck looks like a woman's. They are more comfortable, but of less high effect; for the brow not held in proud position by any constraint from them, falls to nodding this way and that. . . . But for me every day Hatred starches and flutes the ruff whose stiffness holds the head well in place. Every new enemy is another plait in it, adding compulsion, but adding, as well, a ray: for, similar in every point to the Spanish ruff, Hatred is a bondage, . . . but is a halo, too!

LE BRET [*after a pause, slipping his arm through* CYRANO's]   To the hearing of all be proud and bitter, . . . but to me, below breath, say simply that she does not love you!

CYRANO [*sharply*]   Not a word!

[*CHRISTIAN has come in and mingled with the cadets; they ignore him; he has finally gone to a little table by himself, where LISE waits on him.*]

SCENE IX

Cyrano, Le Bret, the Cadets, Christian de Neuvillette

ONE OF THE CADETS [*seated at a table at the back, glass in hand*] Hey, Cyrano! [CYRANO *turns toward him*] Your story!

CYRANO   Presently! [*He goes toward the back on* LE BRET's *arm. They talk low.*]

THE CADET [*rising and coming toward the front*]   The account of your fight! It will be the best lesson [*stopping in front of the table at which* CHRISTIAN *is sitting*] for this timorous novice!

CHRISTIAN [*looking up*]   . . . Novice?

OTHER CADET   Yes, sickly product of the North!

CHRISTIAN   Sickly?

FIRST CADET [*impressively*]   Monsieur de Neuvillette, it is a good deed to warn you that there is a thing no more to be mentioned in our company than rope in the house of the hanged!

CHRISTIAN   And what is it?

OTHER CADET [*in a terrifying voice*]   Look at me! [*Three times, darkly, he places his finger upon his nose.*] You have understood?

CHRISTIAN   Ah, it is the . . .

OTHER CADET   Silence! . . . Never must you so much as breathe that word, or . . . [*He points toward* CYRANO *at the back talking with* LE BRET.] You will have him, over there, to deal with!

OTHER CADET [*who while* CHRISTIAN *was turned toward the first, has noiselessly seated himself on the table behind him*]   Two persons were lately cut off in their pride by him for talking through their noses. He thought it personal.

OTHER CADET [*in a cavernous voice, as he rises from under the table where he had slipped on all fours*]   Not the remotest allusion, ever, to the fatal cartilage, . . . unless you fancy an early grave!

OTHER CADET   A word will do the business! What did I say? . . . A word? . . . A simple gesture! Make use of your pocket handkerchief, you will shortly have use for your shroud!
[*Silence. All around* CHRISTIAN *watch him, with folded arms. He rises and goes to* CARBON DE CASTEL-JALOUX, *who, in conversation with an officer, affects to notice nothing.*]

CHRISTIAN   Captain!

CARBON [*turning and looking him rather contemptuously up and down*]   Monsieur?

CHRISTIAN   What is the proper course for a man when he finds gentlemen of the South too boastful?

CARBON DE CASTEL-JALOUX   He must prove to them that one can be of the North, yet brave. [*He turns his back upon him.*]

CHRISTIAN   I am much obliged.

FIRST CADET [*to* CYRANO]   And now, the tale of your adventure!

ALL   Yes, yes, now let us hear!

CYRANO [*coming forward among them*]   My adventure? [*All draw their stools nearer, and sit around him, with craned necks.* CHRISTIAN *sits astride a chair.*] Well, then, I was marching to meet them. The moon up in the skies was shining like a silver watch, when suddenly I know not what careful watch-maker having wrapped it in a cottony cloud, there occurred the blackest imaginable night; and, the streets being nowise lighted,—*mordious!*—you could see no further than . . .

CHRISTIAN   Your nose.

[*Silence. Everyone slowly gets up; all look with terror at* CYRANO. *He has stopped short, amazed. Pause.*]

CYRANO   Who is that man?

ONE OF THE CADETS [*low*]   He joined this morning.

CYRANO [*taking a step toward* CHRISTIAN]   This morning?

CARBON DE CASTEL-JALOUX [*low*]   His name is Baron de Neuvill . . .

CYRANO [*stopping short*]   Ah, very well. . . . [*He turns pale, then red, gives evidence of another impulse to throw himself upon* CHRISTIAN.] I. . . . [*He conquers it, and says in a stifled voice.*] Very well. [*He takes up his tale.*] As I was saying . . . [*with a burst of rage.*] *Mordious!* . . . [*He continues in a natural tone*] one could not see in the very least. [*Consternation. All resume their seats, staring at one another.*] And I was walking along, reflecting that for a very insignificant rogue I was probably about to offend some great prince who would bear me a lasting grudge, that, in brief, I was about to thrust my . . .

CHRISTIAN   Nose . . .

[*All get up.* CHRISTIAN *has tilted his chair and is rocking on the hind legs.*]

CYRANO [*choking*]   Finger . . . between the tree and the bark; for the aforesaid prince might be of sufficient power to trip me and throw me . . .

CHRISTIAN   On my nose . . .

CYRANO [*wipes the sweat from his brow.*]   But, said I, "Gascony forward! Never falter when duty prompts! Forward, Cyrano!" and, saying this, I advance—when suddenly, in the darkness, I barely avoid a blow . . .

CHRISTIAN   Upon the nose . . .

CYRANO   I ward it. . . . and thereupon find myself . . .

CHRISTIAN   Nose to nose . . .

CYRANO [*springing toward him*]   *Ventre-Saint-Gris!* . . . [*All the GAS-CONS rush forward, to see;* CYRANO, *on reaching* CHRISTIAN, *controls himself and proceeds*] . . . with a hundred drunken brawlers, smelling . . .

CHRISTIAN   To the nose's limit . . .

CYRANO [*deathly pale, and smiling*]   . . . of garlic and of grease. I leap forward, head lowered . . .

CHRISTIAN   Nose to the wind! . . .

CYRANO   And I charge them. I knock two breathless and run a third through the body. One lets off at me: Paf! and I retort . . .

CHRISTIAN   Pif!

CRYANO [*exploding*]   Death and damnation! Go,—all of you!
[*All the CADETS make for the door.*]

FIRST CADET   The tiger is roused at last!

CYRANO   All! and leave me with this man.

SECOND CADET   *Bigre!* When we see him again, it will be in the shape of mince-meat!

RAGUENEAU   Mince-meat? . . .

OTHER CADET   In one of your pies.

RAGUENEAU   I feel myself grow white and flabby as a table-napkin!

CARBON DE CASTEL-JALOUX   Let us go!

OTHER CADET   Not a smudge of him will be left!

OTHER CADET   What these walls are about to behold gives me gooseflesh to think upon!

OTHER CADET [*closing the door at the right*]   Ghastly! . . . Ghastly!

[All have left, by the back or the sides, a few up the stairway. CYRANO and CHRISTIAN remain face to face, and look at each other a moment.]

SCENE X

Cyrano, Christian

CYRANO   Embrace me!

CHRISTIAN   Monsieur . . .

CYRANO   Brave fellow.

CHRISTIAN   But what does this . . .

CYRANO   Very brave fellow. I wish you to.

CHRISTIAN   Will you tell me? . . .

CYRANO   Embrace me, I am her brother.

CHRISTIAN   Whose?

CYRANO   Hers!

CHRISTIAN   What do you mean?

CYRANO   Roxane's!

CHRISTIAN *[running to him]*   Heavens! You, her brother?

CYRANO   Or the same thing: her first cousin.

CHRISTIAN   And she has . . .

CYRANO   Told me everything!

CHRISTIAN   Does she love me?

CYRANO   Perhaps!

CHRISTIAN *[seizing his hands]*   How happy I am, Monsieur, to make your acquaintance! . . .

CYRANO   That is what I call a sudden sentiment!

CHRISTIAN   Forgive me! . . .

CYRANO *[looking at him, laying his hand upon his shoulder]*   It is true that he is handsome, the rascal!

CHRISTIAN   If you but knew, Monsieur, how greatly I admire you! . . .

CYRANO   But all those noses which you . . .

CHRISTIAN   I take them back!

CYRANO   Roxane expects a letter to-night . . .

CHRISTIAN   Alas!

CYRANO   What is the matter?

CHRISTIAN   I am lost if I cease to be dumb!

CYRANO   How is that?

CHRISTIAN   Alas! I am such a dunce that I could kill myself for shame!

CYRANO   But, no . . . no. . . . You are surely not a dunce, if you believe you are! Besides, you scarcely attacked me like a dunce.

CHRISTIAN   Oh, it is easy to find words in mounting to the assault! Indeed, I own to a certain cheap military readiness, but when I am before women, I have not a word to say. . . . Yet their eyes, when I pass by, express a kindness toward me . . .

CYRANO   And do their hearts not express the same when you stop beside them?

CHRISTIAN   No! . . . for I am of those—I recognize it, and am dismayed!—who do not know how to talk of love.

CYRANO   *Tiens!* . . . It seems to me that if Nature had taken more pains with my shape, I should have been of those who do know how to talk of it.

CHRISTIAN   Oh, to be able to express things gracefully!

CYRANO   Oh, to be a graceful little figure of a passing mousquetaire!

CHRISTIAN   Roxane is a précieuse, . . . * there is no chance but that I shall be a disillusion to Roxane!

CYRANO [*looking at* CHRISTIAN]   If I had, to express my soul, such an interpreter! . . .

CHRISTIAN [*desperately*]   I ought to have eloquence! . . .

CYRANO [*abruptly*]   Eloquence I will lend you! . . . And you, to me, shall lend all-conquering physical charm . . . and between us we will compose a hero of romance!

CHRISTIAN   What?

---

*A précieuse, someone who is extremely refined and follows the behavior known as preciosity; see note on p. 12 and discussion in the Introduction.

CYRANO   Should you be able to say, as your own, things which I day
by day would teach you?

CHRISTIAN   You are suggesting? . . .

CYRANO   Roxane shall not have disillusions! Tell me, shall we win
her heart, we two as one? will you submit to feel, transmitted
from my leather doublet into your doublet stitched with silk, the
soul I wish to share?

CHRISTIAN   But Cyrano! . . .

CYRANO   Christian, will you?

CHRISTIAN   You frighten me!

CYRANO   Since you fear, left to yourself, to chill her heart, will you
consent,—and soon it will take fire, I vouch for it!—to con-
tribute your lips to my phrases?

CHRISTIAN   Your eyes shine! . . .

CYRANO   Will you?

CHRISTIAN   What, would it please you so much?

CYRANO [with rapture]   It would . . . [Remembering, and confining
himself to expressing an artistic pleasure] . . . amuse me! It is an ex-
periment fit surely to tempt a poet. Will you complete me, and
let me in exchange complete you? We will walk side by side: you
in full light, I in your shadow. . . . I will be wit to you . . . you,
to me, shall be good looks!

CHRISTIAN   But the letter, which should be sent to her without
delay? . . . Never shall I be able . . .

CYRANO [taking from his doublet the letter written in the first part of the
act]   The letter? Here it is!

CHRISTIAN   How? . . .

CYRANO   It only wants the address.

CHRISTIAN   I . . .

CYRANO   You can send it without uneasiness. It is a good letter.

CHRISTIAN   You had? . . .

CYRANO   You shall never find us—poets!—without epistles in our
pockets to the Chlorises . . . of our imagining! For we are those
same that have for mistress a dream blown into the bubble of a

name! Take,—you shall convert this feigning into earnest; I was sending forth at random these confessions and laments: you shall make the wandering birds to settle . . . Take it! You shall see . . . I was as eloquent as if I had been sincere! Take, and have done!

CHRISTIAN   But will it not need to be altered in any part? . . . Written without object, will it fit Roxane?

CYRANO   Like a glove!

CHRISTIAN   But . . .

CYRANO   Trust to the blindness of love . . . and vanity! Roxane will never question that it was written for her.

CHRISTIAN   Ah, my friend! [*He throws himself into* CYRANO's *arms. They stand embraced.*]

SCENE XI

Cyrano, Christian, the Cadets, the Mousquetaire, Lise

ONE OF THE CADETS [*opening the door a very little*]   Nothing more. . . . The stillness of death. . . . I dare not look . . . [*He thrusts in his head.*] What is this?

ALL THE CADETS [*entering and seeing* CYRANO *and* CHRISTIAN *locked in each others arms*]   Ah! . . . Oh! . . .

ONE OF THE CADETS   This passes bounds! [*Consternation*].

THE MOUSQUETAIRE [*impudent*]   Ouais?

CARBON DE CASTEL-JALOUX   Our demon is waxen mild as an apostle; smitten upon one nostril, he turns the other also!

THE MOUSQUETAIRE   It is in order now to speak of his nose, is it? [*Calling* LISE, *with a swaggering air*] Hey, Lise! now listen and look. [*Pointedly sniffing the air.*] Oh, . . . oh, . . . it is surprising! . . . what an odor! [*Going to* CYRANO.] But Monsieur must have smelled it, too? Can you tell me what it is, so plain in the air?

CYRANO [*beating him*]   Why, sundry blows!

[*Joyful antics of the* CADETS *in beholding* CYRANO *himself again. Curtain.*]

ACT THREE

Roxane's Kiss

> *A small square in the old Marais. Old-fashioned houses. Narrow streets seen in perspective. At the right, ROXANE'S house and the wall of her garden, above which spreading tree-tops. Over the house-door, a balcony and window. A bench beside the doorstep.*
>
> *The wall is overclambered by ivy, the balcony wreathed with jasmine.*
>
> *By means of the bench and projecting stones in the wall, the balcony can easily be scaled.*
>
> *On the opposite side, old house in the same style of architecture, brick and stone, with entrance-door. The door-knocker is swaddled in linen.*
>
> *At the rise of the curtain, the DUENNA is seated on the bench. The window on ROXANE'S balcony is wide open.*
>
> *RAGUENEAU, in a sort of livery, stands near the DUENNA; he is finishing the tale of his misfortunes, drying his eyes.*

SCENE I

Ragueneau, the Duenna, then Roxane, Cyrano, and two Pages

RAGUENEAU   And then, she eloped with a mousquetaire! Ruined, forsaken, I was hanging myself. I had already taken leave of earth, when Monsieur de Bergerac happening along, unhanged me, and proposed me to his cousin as her steward . . .

THE DUENNA   But how did you fall into such disaster?

RAGUENEAU   Lise was fond of soldiers, I, of poets! Mars ate up all left over by Apollo. Under those circumstances, you conceive, the pantry soon was bare.

THE DUENNA [*rising and calling toward the open window*]   Roxane, are you ready? . . . They are waiting for us! . . .

ROXANE'S VOICE [*through the window*]   I am putting on my mantle!

THE DUENNA [*to* RAGUENEAU, *pointing at the door opposite*]   It is over there, opposite, we are expected. At Clomire's. She holds a meeting in her little place. A disquisition upon the Softer Sentiments is to be read.*

RAGUENEAU   Upon the Softer Sentiments?

THE DUENNA [*coyly*]   Yes! . . . [*Calling toward the window.*] Roxane, you must make haste, or we shall miss the disquisition upon the Softer Sentiments!

ROXANE'S VOICE   I am coming!

[*A sound of string-instruments is heard, drawing nearer.*]

CYRANO'S VOICE [*singing in the wings*] La! la! la! la! la! . . .

THE DUENNA [*surprised*]   We are to have music?

CYRANO [*enters followed by two* PAGES *with theorbos*]†   I tell you it is a demi-semi-quaver! . . . you demi-semi-noddle!

FIRST PAGE [*ironically*]   Monsieur knows then about quavers, semi and demi?

CYRANO   I know music, as do all Gassendi's disciples!‡

THE PAGE [*playing and singing*]   La! la!

CYRANO [*snatching the theorbo from him and continuing the musical phrase*]   I can carry on the melody. . . . La, la, la, la, . . .

ROXANE [*appearing on the balcony*]   It is you?

CYRANO [*singing upon the tune he is continuing*]   I, indeed, who salute your lilies and present my respects to your ro-o-oses! . . .

ROXANE   I am coming down! [*She leaves the balcony.*]

---

*The reference is to the *Carte du Tendre* (*Map of Tenderness*), a map that plotted in allegorical fashion the stations of love and the torturous path leading to it.

†Large, double-necked lutes.

‡Pierre Gassendi (1592–1655) was a philosopher and libertine, under whom Cyrano de Bergerac studied.

THE DUENNA   [*pointing at the* PAGES]   What is the meaning of these two virtuosi?

CYRANO   A wager I won, from D'Assoucy. We were disputing upon a question of grammar. Yes! No! Yes! No! Suddenly pointing at these two tall knaves, expert at clawing strings, by whom he constantly goes attended, he said, "I wager a day long of music!" He lost. Until therefore the next rise of the sun, I shall have dangling after me these arch-lute players, harmonious witnesses of all I do! . . . At first I liked it very well, but now it palls a little. [*To the musicians*] Hey! . . . Go, from me, to Montfleury, and play him a pavane! . . . [*The* PAGES *go toward the back. To the* DUENNA.] I have come to inquire of Roxane, as I do every evening. . . . [*To the* PAGES *who are leaving.*] Play a long time . . . and out of tune! [*To the* DUENNA] . . . whether in the friend of her soul she can still detect no fault?

ROXANE [*coming out of the house*]   Ah, how beautiful he is, what wit he has, how deeply I love him!

CYRANO [*smiling*]   Christian has so much wit? . . .

ROXANE   Cousin, more than yourself!

CYRANO   I grant you.

ROXANE   There is not one alive, I truly believe, more apt at turning those pretty nothings which yet are everything. . . . Sometimes he is of an absent mood, his muse is wool-gathering, then, suddenly, he will say the most enchanting things!

CYRANO [*incredulous*]   Come! . . .

ROXANE   Oh, it is too bad! Men are all alike, narrow, narrow: because he is handsome, he cannot possibly be witty!

CYRANO   So he talks of the heart in acceptable fashion?

ROXANE   Talks, cousin, is feeble. . . . He dissertates!

CYRANO   And writes? . . .

ROXANE   Still better! Listen now to this . . . [*Declaiming.*] *"The more of my heart you steal from me, the more heart I have!"* [*Triumphantly to* CYRANO]. Well? . . .

CYRANO   Pooh!

ROXANE   And to this: *"Since you have stolen my heart, and since I must suffer, to suffer with send me your own!"*

CYRANO   Now he has too much heart, now he has not enough, . . . just what does he want, in the matter of quantity?

ROXANE   You vex me! You are eaten up with jealousy. . . .

CYRANO [*starting*]   Hein?

ROXANE   Author's jealousy! And this, could anything be more exquisitely tender? *"Unanimously, believe it, my heart cries out to you, and if kisses could be sent in writing, Love, you should read my letter with your lips. . . ."*

CYRANO [*in spite of himself smiling with satisfaction*]   Ha! Ha! Those particular lines seem to me . . . ho! . . . ho! . . . [*Remembering himself, disdainfully*] . . . puny, pretty . . .

ROXANE   This, then . . .

CYRANO [*delighted*]   You know his letters by heart?

ROXANE   All!

CYRANO   It is flattering, one cannot deny.

ROXANE   In this art of expressing love he is a master!

CYRANO [*modest*]   Oh, . . . a master!

ROXANE [*peremptory*]   A master!

CYRANO   As you please, then . . . a master!

THE DUENNA [*who had gone toward the back, coming quickly forward*]   Monsieur de Guiche! [*To* CYRANO, *pushing him toward the house*] Go in! It is perhaps better that he should not see you here! it might put him on the scent . . .

ROXANNE [*to* CYRANO]   Yes, of my dear secret! He loves me, he is powerful, . . . he must not find out! He might cut in sunder our loves . . . with an axe!

CYRANO [*going into the house*]   Very well, very well.
     [*DE GUICHE appears.*]

SCENE II

Roxane, De Guiche, the Duenna in the background

ROXANE [*to* DE GUICHE, *with a curtsey*]   I was leaving the house.

DE GUICHE   I have come to bid you farewell.

ROXANE   You are going away?

DE GUICHE   To war.

ROXANE   Ah!

DE GUICHE   I have my orders. Arras is besieged.

ROXANE   Ah! . . . it is besieged?

DE GUICHE   Yes. . . . I see that my departure does not greatly affect you.

ROXANE   Oh! . . .

DE GUICHE   As for me, I own it wrings my heart. Shall I see you again? . . . When? . . . You know that I am made commander-in-general?

ROXANE [*uninterested*]   I congratulate you.

DE GUICHE   Of the Guards.

ROXANE [*starting*]   Ah, . . . of the Guards?

DE GUICHE   Among whom your cousin serves, . . . the man of the boasts and tirades. I shall have opportunity in plenty to retaliate upon him down there.

ROXANE [*suffocating*]   What? The Guards are going down there?

DE GUICHE   Surely. It is my regiment.

ROXANE [*falls sitting upon the bench; aside*]   Christian!

DE GUICHE   What is it troubles you?

ROXANE [*greatly moved*]   This departure . . . grieves me mortally. When one cares for a person . . . to know him away at the war!

DE GUICHE [*surprised and charmed*]   For the first time you utter a kind and feeling word, when I am leaving!

ROXANE [*in a different tone, fanning herself*]   So . . . you are thinking of revenge upon my cousin?

DE GUICHE [*smiling*]   You side with him?

ROXANE   No . . . against him.

DE GUICHE   Do you see much of him?

ROXANE   Very little.

DE GUICHE   He is everywhere to be met with one of the
cadets . . . [*trying to remember*] that Neu . . . villen . . . viller . . .

ROXANE   A tall man?

DE GUICHE   Light haired.

ROXANE   Red haired.

DE GUICHE   Good looking.

ROXANE   Pooh!

DE GUICHE   But a fool!

ROXANE   He looks like one. [*In a different tone.*] Your vengeance
upon Cyrano is then to place him within reach of shot, which is
the thing of all he loves! . . . A miserable vengeance! . . . I know,
I do, what would more seriously concern him!

DE GUICHE   And that is?

ROXANE   Why . . . that the regiment should march, and leave him
behind, with his beloved cadets, arms folded, the whole war
through, in Paris! That is the only way to cast down a man like
him. You wish to punish him? Deprive him of danger.

DE GUICHE   A woman! A woman! None but a woman could devise
a vengeance of the sort!

ROXANE   His friends will gnaw their fists, and he his very soul, with
chagrin at not being under fire; and you will be abundantly avenged!

DE GUICHE [*coming nearer*]   Then you do love me a little? [ROX-
ANE *smiles.*] I wish to see in this fact of your espousing my grudge
a proof of affection, Roxane . . .

ROXANE   . . . You may!

DE GUICHE [*showing several folded papers*]   I have here upon me the
orders to be transmitted at once to each of the companies . . .
except . . . [*he takes one from among the others.*] This one! . . . the
company of the cadets . . . [*He puts it in his pocket.*] This, I will keep.
[*Laughing*]   Ah, ah, ah! Cyrano! his belligerent humor! . . . So
you sometimes play tricks upon people, you? . . .

ROXANE   Sometimes.

DE GUICHE [*very near her*]   I love you to distraction! This evening . . . listen, . . . it is true that I must be gone. But to go when I feel that it is a matter for your caring! Listen! . . . There is, not far from here, in Rue Orléans, a convent founded by the Capuchins. Father Athanasius. A layman may not enter. But the good fathers . . . I fear no difficulty with them! They will hide me up their sleeve . . . their sleeve is wide. They are the Capuchins that serve Richelieu at home. Fearing the uncle, they proportionately fear the nephew. I shall be thought to have left. I will come to you masked. Let me delay by a single day, wayward enchantress!

ROXANE   But if it should transpire . . . your fame . . .

DE GUICHE   Bah!

ROXANE   But . . . the siege . . . Arras! . . .

DE GUICHE   Must wait! Allow me, I beg . . .

ROXANE   No!

DE GUICHE   I beseech!

ROXANE [*tenderly*]   No! Love itself bids me forbid you!

DE GUICHE   Ah!

ROXANE   You must go! [*Aside.*] Christian will stay! [*Aloud.*] For my sake, be heroic . . . Antony!*

DE GUICHE   Ah, heavenly word upon your lips! . . . Then you love the one who . . .

ROXANE   Who shall have made me tremble for his sake . . .

DE GUICHE [*in a transport of joy*]   Ah, I will go! [*He kisses her hand.*] Are you satisfied with me?

ROXANE   My friend, I am.

[*Exit DE GUICHE*]

THE DUENNA [*dropping a mocking curtsey toward his back*]   My friend, we are!

---

*Informal, endearing name for de Guiche, whose full name was Antoine de Gramont, duc de Guiche.

SCENE III

Roxane, the Duenna, Cyrano

ROXANE [*to the* DUENNA]   Not a word of what I have done:
Cyrano would never forgive me for defrauding him of his war!
[*She calls toward the house.*] Cousin! [CYRANO *comes out.*] We are
going to Clomire's. [*She indicates the house opposite.*] Alcandre has
engaged to speak, and so has Lysimon.

THE DUENNA [*putting her little finger to her ear*]   Yes, but my little
finger tells me that we shall be too late to hear them!

CYRANO [*to* ROXANE]   Of all things do not miss the trained
monkeys!

[*They have reached Clomire's door*]

THE DUENNA   See! . . . See! they have muffled the doorknocker!
[*To the door-knocker.*] You have been gagged, that your voice should
not disturb the beautiful lecture, . . . little brutal disturber! [*She
lifts it with infinite care and knocks softly*]

ROXANE [*seeing the door open*]   Come! [*From the threshold to*
CYRANO.] If Christian should come, as probably he will, say he
must wait!

CYRANO [*hurriedly, as she is about to disappear*]   Ah! [*She turns.*] Upon
what shall you, according to your custom, question him to-day?

ROXANE   Upon . . .

CYRANO [*eagerly*]   Upon? . . .

ROXANE   But you will be silent . . .

CYRANO   As that wall!

ROXANE   Upon nothing! I will say: Forward! Free rein! No curb!
Improvise! Talk of love! Be magnificent!

CYRANO [*smiling*]   Good.

ROXANE   Hush!

CYRANO   Hush!

ROXANE   Not a word! [*She goes in and closes the door.*]

CYRANO [*bowing, when the door is closed*]   A thousand thanks!

[The door opens again and ROXANE looks out]

ROXANE   He might prepare his speeches . . .

CYRANO   Ah no! . . . the devil, no!

BOTH *[together]*   Hush! . . .

[The door closes]

SCENE IV

Cyrano, Christian

CYRANO *[calling]*   Christian! *[Enter CHRISTIAN.]* I know all that
we need to. Now make ready your memory. This is your chance
to cover yourself with glory. Let us lose no time. Do not look
sullen, like that. Quick! Let us go to your lodgings and I will rehearse you . . .

CHRISTIAN   No!

CYRANO   What?

CHRISTIAN   No, I will await Roxane here.

CYRANO   What insanity possesses you? Come quickly and
learn . . .

CHRISTIAN   No, I tell you! I am weary of borrowing my letters,
my words . . . of playing a part, and living in constant fear. . . . It
was very well at first, but now I feel that she loves me. I thank you
heartily. I am no longer afraid. I will speak for myself . . .

CYRANO   *Ouais?* . . .

CHRISTIAN   And what tells you that I shall not know how? I am
not such an utter blockhead, after all! You shall see! Your lessons
have not been altogether wasted. I can shift to speak without
your aid! And, that failing, by Heaven! I shall still know enough
to take her in my arms! *[Catching sight of* ROXANE *who is coming
out from Clomire's.]* She is coming! Cyrano, no, do not leave
me! . . .

CYRANO *[bowing to him]*   I will not meddle, Monsieur.

[He disappears behind the garden wall]

SCENE V

Christian, Roxane, briefly the Duenna, several Prieux and Précieuses

ROXANE [*coming from CLOMIRE's house with a number of people from whom she is taking leave. Curtseys and farewells.*] Barthénoide! . . . Alcandre! . . . Grémione! . . .

THE DUENNA [*comically desperate*] We missed the disquisition upon the Softer Sentiments! [*She goes into ROXANE's house.*]

ROXANE [*still taking leave of this one and that*] Urimédonte! . . . Good-bye!

[*All bow to ROXANE, to one another, separate and go off by the various streets. ROXANE sees CHRISTIAN.*]

ROXANE You are here! [*She goes to him.*] Evening is closing round. . . . Wait! . . . They have all gone. . . . The air is so mild. . . . Not a passer in sight. . . . Let us sit here. . . . Talk! . . . I will listen.

CHRISTIAN [*sits beside her, on the bench. Silence.*] I love you.

ROXANE [*closing her eyes*] Yes. Talk to me of love.

CHRISTIAN I love you.

ROXANE Yes. That is the theme. Play variations upon it.

CHRISTIAN I love . . .

ROXANE Variations!

CHRISTIAN I love you so much . . .

ROXANE I do not doubt it. What further? . . .

CHRISTIAN And further. I should be so happy if you loved me! Tell me, Roxane, that you love me . . .

ROXANE [*pouting*] You proffer cider to me when I was hoping for champagne! . . . Now tell me a little *how* you love me?

CHRISTIAN Why . . . very, very much.

ROXANE Oh! . . . unravel, disentangle your sentiments!

CHRISTIAN Your throat! . . . I want to kiss it! . . .

ROXANE Christian!

CHRISTIAN I love you! . . .

ROXANE [*attempting to rise*]   Again! . . .

CHRISTIAN [*hastily, holding her back*]. No, I do not love you! . . .

ROXANE [*sitting down again*]   That is fortunate!

CHRISTIAN   I adore you!

ROXANE [*rising and moving away*]   Oh! . . .

CHRISTIAN   Yes, . . . love makes me into a fool!

ROXANE [*drily*]   And I am displeased at it! as I should be displeased
at your no longer being handsome.

CHRISTIAN   But . . .

ROXANE   Go, and rally your routed eloquence!

CHRISTIAN   I . . .

ROXANE   You love me. I have heard it. Good-evening. [*She goes toward the house.*]

CHRISTIAN   No, no, not yet! . . . I wish to tell you . . .

ROXANE [*pushing open the door to go in*]   That you adore me. Yes, I
know. No! No! Go away! . . . Go! . . . Go! . . .

CHRISTIAN   But I . . .

[*She closes the door in his face.*]

CYRANO [*who has been on the scene a moment, unnoticed*]   Unmistak-
ably a success.

SCENE VI

Christian, Cyrano, briefly the Pages

CHRISTIAN   Help me!

CYRANO   No, sir, no.

CHRISTIAN   I will go kill myself if I am not taken back into favor
at once . . . at once!

CYRANO   And how can I . . . how, the devil? . . . make you learn
on the spot . . .

CHRISTIAN [*seizing him by the arm*]   Oh, there! . . . Look! . . . See!
[*Light has appeared in the balcony window.*]

CYRANO [*with emotion*]   Her window!

CHRISTIAN   Oh, I shall die!

CYRANO   Not so loud!

CHRISTIAN [*in a whisper*]   I shall die!

CYRANO   It is a dark night. . . .

CHRISTIAN   Well?

CYRANO   All may be mended. But you do not deserve. . . . There! stand there, miserable boy! . . . in front of the balcony! I will stand under it and prompt you.

CHRISTIAN   But . . .

CYRANO   Do as I bid you!

THE PAGES [*reappearing at the back, to* CYRANO]   Hey!

CYRANO   Hush! [*He signs to them to lower their voices.*]

FIRST PAGE [*in a lower voice*]   We have finished serenading Montfleury!

CYRANO [*low, quickly*]   Go and stand out of sight. One at this street corner, the other at that; and if any one comes near, play! . . .

SECOND PAGE   What sort of tune, Monsieur the Gassendist?

CYRANO   Merry if it be a woman, mournful if it be a man. [*The pages disappear, one at each street corner. To* CHRISTIAN.] Call her!

CHRISTIAN   Roxane!

CYRANO [*picking up pebbles and throwing them at the window-pane*]   Wait! A few pebbles . . .

SCENE VII

Roxane, Christian, Cyrano, at first hidden under the balcony

ROXANE [*opening the window*]   Who is calling me?

CHRISTIAN   It is I . . .

ROXANE   Who is . . . I?

CHRISTIAN   Christian!

ROXANE [*disdainfully*]   Oh, you!

CHRISTIAN   I wish to speak with you.

CYRANO [*under the balcony, to* CHRISTIAN]   Speak low! . . .

ROXANE   No, your conversation is too common. You may go home!

CHRISTIAN   In mercy! . . .

ROXANE   No . . . you do not love me any more!

CHRISTIAN [*whom* CYRANO *is prompting*]   You accuse me . . . just Heaven! of loving you no more. . . . when I can love you no more!

ROXANE [*who was about to close her window, stopping*]   Ah, that is a little better!

CHRISTIAN [*same business*]   To what a . . . size has Love grown in my . . . sigh-rocked soul which the . . . cruel cherub has chosen for his cradle!

ROXANE [*stepping nearer to the edge of the balcony*]   That is distinctly better! . . . But, since he is so cruel, this Cupid, you were unwise not to smother him in his cradle!

CHRISTIAN [*same business*]   I tried to, but, Madame, the . . . attempt was futile. This . . . new-born Love is . . . a little Hercules . . .

ROXANE   Much, much better!

CHRISTIAN [*same business*]   . . . Who found it merest baby-play to . . . strangle the serpents . . . twain, Pride and . . . Mistrust.

ROXANE [*leaning her elbows on the balcony-rail*]   Ah, that is very good indeed! . . . But why do you speak so slowly and stintedly? Has your imagination gout in its wings?

CYRANO [*drawing* CHRISTIAN *under the balcony, and taking his place*]   Hush! It is becoming too difficult!

ROXANE   To-night your words come falteringly. . . . Why is it?

CYRANO [*talking low like* CHRISTIAN]   Because of the dark. They have to grope to find your ear.

ROXANE   My words do not find the same difficulty.

CYRANO   They reach their point at once? Of course they do! That is because I catch them with my heart. My heart, you see, is very large, your ear particularly small. . . . Besides, your words drop . . . that goes quickly; mine have to climb . . . and that takes longer!

ROXANE   They have been climbing more nimbly, however, in the last few minutes.

CYRANO   They are becoming used to this gymnastic feat!

ROXANE   It is true that I am talking with you from a very mountain top!

CYRANO   It is sure that a hard word dropped from such a height upon my heart would shatter it!

ROXANE [*with the motion of leaving*]   I will come down.

CYRANO [*quickly*]   Do not!

ROXANE [*pointing at the bench at the foot of the balcony*]   Then do you get up on the seat! . . .

CYRANO [*drawing away in terror*]   No!

ROXANE   How do you mean . . . no?

CYRANO [*with ever-increasing emotion*]   Let us profit a little by this chance of talking softly together without seeing each other . . .

ROXANE   Without seeing each other? . . .

CYRANO   Yes, to my mind, delectable! Each guesses at the other, and no more. You discern but the trailing blackness of a mantle, and I a dawn-grey glimmer which is a summer gown. I am a shadow merely, a pearly phantom are you! You can never know what these moments are to me! If ever I was eloquent . . .

ROXANE   You were!

CYRANO   My words never till now surged from my very heart . . .

ROXANE   And why?

CYRANO   Because, till now, they must strain to reach you through . . .

ROXANE   What?

CYRANO   Why, the bewildering emotion a man feels who sees you, and whom you look upon! . . . But this evening, it seems to me that I am speaking to you for the first time!

ROXANE   It is true that your voice is altogether different.

CYRANO [*coming nearer, feverishly*]   Yes, altogether different, because, protected by the dark, I dare at last to be myself. I dare . . . [*He stops, and distractedly.*] What was I saying? . . . I do

not know. . . . All this . . . forgive my incoherence! . . . is so delicious . . . is so new to me!

ROXANE   So new? . . .

CYRANO [*in extreme confusion, still trying to mend his expressions*]   So
new . . . yes, new, to be sincere; the fear of being mocked always
constrains my heart . . .

ROXANE   Mocked . . . for what?

CYRANO   Why, . . . for its impulses, its flights! . . . Yes, my heart
always cowers behind the defence of my wit. I set forth to capture
a star . . . and then, for dread of laughter, I stop and pick a
flower . . . of rhetoric!

ROXANE   That sort of flower has its pleasing points . . .

CYRANO   But yet, to-night, let us scorn it!

ROXANE   Never before had you spoken as you are speaking! . . .

CYRANO   Ah, if far from Cupid-darts and quivers, we might seek a
place of somewhat fresher things! If instead of drinking, flat sip by
sip, from a chiselled golden thimble, drops distilled and dulcified,
we might try the sensation of quenching the thirst of our souls by
stooping to the level of the great river, and setting our lips to the
stream!

ROXANE   But yet, wit . . . fancy . . . delicate conceits. . . .

CYRANO   I gave my fancy leave to frame conceits, before, to make
you linger, . . . but now it would be an affront to this balm-
breathing night, to Nature and the hour, to talk like characters in
a pastoral performed at Court! . . . Let us give Heaven leave,
looking at us with all its earnest stars, to strip us of disguise and
artifice: I fear, . . . oh, fear! . . . lest in our mistaken alchemy
sentiment should be subtilized to evaporation; lest the life of the
heart should waste in these empty pastimes, and the final refinement of the fine be the undoing of the refined!

ROXANE   But yet, wit, . . . aptness, . . . ingenuity . . .

CYRANO   I hate them in love! Criminal, when one loves, to pro-
long over-much that paltry thrust and parry! The moment, however, comes inevitably,—and I pity those for whom it never

comes!—in which, we apprehending the noble depth of the love
we harbor, a shallow word hurts us to utter!

ROXANE   If . . . if, then, that moment has come for us two, what
words will you say to me?

CYRANO   All those, all those, all those that come to me! Not in formal nosegay order, . . . I will throw them to you in a wild sheaf!
I love you, choke with love, I love you, dear. . . . My brain reels,
I can bear no more, it is too much. . . . Your name is in my heart
the golden clapper in a bell; and as I know no rest, Roxane, always
the heart is shaken, and ever rings your name! . . . Of you, I remember all, all have I loved! Last year, one day, the twelfth of May,
in going out at morning you changed the fashion of your hair. . . .
I have taken the light of your hair for my light, and as having stared
too long at the sun, on everything one sees a scarlet wheel, on
everything when I come from my chosen light, my dazzled eye
sets swimming golden blots! . . .

ROXANE [in a voice unsteady with emotion]   Yes . . . this is love . . .

CYRANO   Ah, verily! The feeling which invades me, terrible and
jealous, is love . . . with all its mournful frenzy! It is love, yet
self-forgetting more than the wont of love! Ah, for your happiness now readily would I give mine, though you should never
know it, might I but, from a distance, sometimes, hear the happy
laughter bought by my sacrifice! Every glance of yours breeds in
me new strength, new valor! Are you beginning to understand?
Tell me, do you grasp my love's measure? Does some little part
of my soul make itself felt of you there in the darkness? . . . Oh,
what is happening to me this evening is too sweet, too deeply
dear! I tell you all these things, and you listen to me, you! Not in
my least modest hoping did I ever hope so much! I have now only
to die! It is because of words of mine that she is trembling among
the dusky branches! For you are trembling, like a flower among
leaves! Yes, you tremble, . . . for whether you will or no, I have
felt the worshipped trembling of your hand all along this thrilled

and blissful jasmin-bough! [*He madly kisses the end of a pendant bough.*]

ROXANE   Yes, I tremble . . . and weep . . . and love you . . . and am yours! . . . For you have carried me away . . . away! . . .

CYRANO   Then, let death come! I have moved you, I! . . . There is but one thing more I ask . . .

CHRISTIAN [*under the balcony*]   A kiss!

ROXANE [*drawing hastily back*]   What?

CYRANO   Oh!

ROXANE   You ask? . . .

CYRANO   Yes . . . I . . . [*To* CHRISTIAN.] You are in too great haste!

CHRISTIAN   Since she is so moved, I must take advantage of it!

CYRANO [*to* ROXANE]   I . . . Yes, it is true I asked . . . but, merciful heavens! . . . I knew at once that I had been too bold.

ROXANE [*a shade disappointed*]   You insist no more than so?

CYRANO   Indeed, I insist . . . without insisting! Yes! yes! but your modesty shrinks! . . . I insist, but yet . . . the kiss I begged . . . refuse it me!

CHRISTIAN [*to* CYRANO, *pulling at his mantle*]   Why?

CYRANO   Hush, Christian!

ROXANE [*bending over the balcony-rail*]   What are you whispering?

CYRANO   Reproaches to myself for having gone too far; I was saying "Hush, Christian!" [*The theorbos are heard playing*] Your pardon! . . . a second! . . . Someone is coming!

[*ROXANE closes the window. CYRANO listens to the theorbos, one of which plays a lively, and the other a lugubrious tune*]

CYRANO   A dance? . . . A dirge? . . . What do they mean? Is it a man or a woman? . . . Ah, it is a monk!

[*Enter a CAPUCHIN MONK, who goes from house to house, with a lantern, examining the doors.*]

SCENE VIII

Cyrano, Christian, a Capuchin

CYRANO [*to* THE CAPUCHIN]   What are you looking for, Diogenes?*

THE CAPUCHIN   I am looking for the house of Madame . . .

CHRISTIAN   He is in the way!

THE CAPUCHIN   Magdeleine Robin . . .

CYRANO [*pointing up one of the streets*]   This way! . . . Straight ahead . . . go straight ahead . . .

THE CAPUCHIN   I thank you. I will say ten Aves for your peace. [*Exit.*]

CYRANO   My good wishes speed your cowl! [*He comes forward toward* CHRISTIAN.]

SCENE IX

Cyrano, Christian

CHRISTIAN   Insist upon the kiss! . . .

CYRANO   No, I will not!

CHRISTIAN   Sooner or later . . .

CYRANO   It is true! It must come, the moment of inebriation when your lips shall imperiously be impelled toward each other, because the one is fledged with youthful gold and the other is so soft a pink! . . . [*To himself.*] I had rather it should be because . . . [*Sound of the window reopening;* CHRISTIAN *hides under the balcony.*]

---

*Diogenes the Cynic (413–323 B.C.), a Greek philosopher, was seen in broad daylight in the marketplace in Athens, carrying a lantern; "I am looking for an honest man," he said, when questioned.

SCENE X

Cyrano, Christian, Roxane

ROXANE [*stepping forward on the balcony*]   Are you there? We were speaking of . . . of . . . of a . . .

CYRANO   Kiss. The word is sweet. Why does your fair lip stop at it? If the mere word burns it, what will be of the thing itself? Do not make it into a fearful matter, and then fear! Did you not a moment ago insensibly leave playfulness behind and slip without trepidation from a smile to a sigh, from a sigh to a tear? Slip but a little further in the same blessed direction: from a tear to a kiss there is scarcely a dividing shiver!

ROXANE   Say no more!

CYRANO   A kiss! When all is said, what is a kiss? An oath of allegiance taken in closer proximity, a promise more precise, a seal on a confession, a rose-red dot upon the letter i in loving; a secret which elects the mouth for ear; an instant of eternity murmuring like a bee; balmy communion with a flavor of flowers; a fashion of inhaling each other's heart, and of tasting, on the brink of the lips, each other's soul!

ROXANE   Say no more . . . no more!

CYRANO   A kiss, Madame, is a thing so noble that the Queen of France, on the most fortunate of lords, bestowed one, did the queen herself!

ROXANE   If that be so . . .

CYRANO [*with increasing fervor*]   Like Buckingham* I have suffered in long silence, like him I worship a queen, like him I am sorrowful and unchanging . . .

ROXANE   Like him you enthrall through the eyes the heart that follows you!

---

*Allusion to the clandestine love between the Duke of Buckingham and Anne of Austria (wife of French King Louis XIII), related in Dumas's *The Three Musketeers*.

CYRANO [*to himself, sobered*]   True, I am handsome . . . I had forgotten!

ROXANE   Come then and gather it, the supreme flower . . .

CYRANO [*pushing* CHRISTIAN *toward the balcony*]   Go!

ROXANE   . . . tasting of the heart.

CYRANO   Go! . . .

ROXANE   . . . murmuring like a bee . . .

CYRANO   Go!

CHRISTIAN [*hesitating*]   But now I feel as if I ought not!

ROXANE   . . . making Eternity an instant . . .

CYRANO [*pushing* CHRISTIAN]   Scale the balcony, you donkey!

[*CHRISTIAN springs toward the balcony, and climbs by means of the bench, the vine, the posts and balusters*]

CHRISTIAN   Ah, Roxane! [*He clasps her to him, and bends over her lips*]

CYRANO   Ha! . . . What a turn of the screw to my heart! . . . Kiss, banquet of Love at which I am Lazarus, a crumb drops from your table even to me,* here in the shade. . . . Yes, in my outstretched heart a little falls, as I feel that upon the lip pressing her lip Roxane kisses the words spoken by me! . . . [*The theorbos are heard.*] A merry tune . . . a mournful one . . . The monk! [*He goes through the pretence of arriving on the spot at a run, as if from a distance; calling.*] Ho, there!

ROXANE   What is it?

CYRANO   It is I. I was passing this way. Is Christian there?

CHRISTIAN [*astonished*]   Cyrano!

ROXANE   Good-evening, cousin!

CYRANO   Cousin, good-evening!

ROXANE   I will come down.

[*ROXANE disappears in the house. THE CAPUCHIN re-enters at the back.*]

CHRISTIAN [*seeing him*]   Oh, again! [*He follows* ROXANE.]

---

*In the Bible, Luke 16:21, Lazarus has only the crumbs from the table of the rich to feed on.

SCENE XI

Cyrano, Christian, Roxane, the Capuchin, Ragueneau

THE CAPUCHIN   It is here she lives, I am certain . . .
Magdeleine Robin.

CYRANO   You said Ro-lin.

THE CAPUCHIN   No, bin, . . . b, i, n, bin!

ROXANE [*appearing upon the threshold, followed by* RAGUENEAU *carrying a lantern, and* CHRISTIAN]   What is it?

THE CAPUCHIN   A letter.

CHRISTIAN   What?

THE CAPUCHIN [*to* ROXANE]   Oh, the contents can be only of a
sacred character! It is from a worthy nobleman who . . .

ROXANE [*to* CHRISTIAN]   It is from De Guiche!

CHRISTIAN   He dares to . . . ?

ROXANE   Oh, he will not trouble me much longer! [*Opening the letter.*] I love you, and if . . . [*By the light of* RAGUENEAU's *lantern she reads, aside, low.*] Mademoiselle: The drums are beating. My regiment is buckling on its corselet. It is about to leave. I am thought to have left already, but lag behind. I am disobeying you. I am in the convent here. I am coming to you, and send you word by a friar, silly as a sheep, who has no suspicion of the import of this letter. You smiled too sweetly upon me an hour ago: I must see you smile again. Provide to be alone, and deign graciously to receive the audacious worshipper, forgiven already, I can but hope, who signs himself your—etc. . . . [*To* THE CAPUCHIN.] Father, this is what the letter tells me . . . Listen: [*All draw nearer; she reads aloud.*] Mademoiselle: The wishes of the cardinal may not be disregarded, however hard compliance with them prove. I have therefore chosen as bearer of this letter a most reverend, holy, and sagacious Capuchin; it is our wish that he should at once, in your own dwelling, pronounce the nuptial blessing over you. Christian must secretly become your husband. I send him to you. You dislike him. Bow to Heaven's will in resignation, and be sure that it will bless your zeal, and sure, likewise, Mademoiselle, of the respect of him who is and will be ever your most humble and . . . etc.

THE CAPUCHIN [*beaming*]   The worthy gentleman! . . . I knew it! You remember that I said so: The contents of that letter can be only of a sacred character!

ROXANE [*low, to* CHRISTIAN]   I am a fluent reader, am I not?

CHRISTIAN   Hm!

ROXANE [*with feigned despair*]   Ah . . . it is horrible!

THE CAPUCHIN [*who has turned the light of his lantern upon* CYRANO]   You are the one?

CHRISTIAN   No, I am.

THE CAPUCHIN [*turning the light upon him, and as if his good looks aroused suspicion*]   But . . .

ROXANE [*quickly*] Postscript: You will bestow upon the convent two hundred and fifty crowns.

THE CAPUCHIN   The worthy, worthy gentleman! [*To* ROXANE.] Be reconciled!

ROXANE [*with the expression of a martyr*]   I will endeavor! [*While* RAGUENEAU *opens the door for* THE CAPUCHIN, *whom* CHRISTIAN *is showing into the house,* ROXANE *says low to* CYRANO.] De Guiche is coming! . . . Keep him here! Do not let him enter until . . .

CYRANO   I understand! [*To* THE CAPUCHIN.] How long will it take to marry them?

THE CAPUCHIN   A quarter of an hour.

CYRANO [*pushing all toward the house*]   Go in! I shall be here!

ROXANE [*to* CHRISTIAN]   Come!

[*They go in.*]

SCENE XII

Cyrano, alone

CYRANO   How can I detain De Guiche for a quarter of an hour? [*He jumps upon the bench, climbs the wall toward the balcony rail.*] So! . . . I climb up here! . . . I know what I will do! . . . [*The theorbos play a melancholy tune.*] Ho, it is a man! [*The tune quavers lugubriously.*] Ho, ho, this time there is no mistake! [*He is on the balcony; he pulls the brim of his hat over his eyes, takes off his sword, wraps his cloak about him, and bends over the balcony-rail.*] No, it is not too far! [*He climbs over the balcony-rail, and reaching for a long bough that projects beyond the garden wall, holds on to it with both hands, ready to let himself drop.*] I shall make a slight commotion in the atmosphere!

SCENE XIII

Cyrano, De Guiche

DE GUICHE [*enters masked, groping in the dark*]   What can that thrice-damned Capuchin be about?

CYRANO   The devil! if he should recognize my voice? [*Letting go with one hand, he makes show of turning a key.*] Cric! crac! [*Solemnly.*] Cyrano, resume the accent of Bergerac!

DE GUICHE [*looking at* ROXANE's *house*]   Yes, that is it. I can scarcely see. This mask bothers my eyes! [*He is about to enter* ROXANE's *house;* CYRANO *swings from the balcony, holding on to the bough, which bends and lets him down between the door and* DE GUICHE. *He intentionally drops very heavily, to give the effect of dropping from a great height, and lies flattened upon the ground, motionless, as if stunned.*]

DE GUICHE   What is it? [*When he looks up, the bough has swung into place; sees nothing but the sky*]   Where did this man drop from?

CYRANO [*rising to a sitting posture*]   From the moon!

DE GUICHE   From the . . . ?

CYRANO [*in a dreamy voice*]   What time is it?

DE GUICHE   Is he mad?

CYRANO   What time? What country? What day? What season?

DE GUICHE   But . . .

CYRANO   I am dazed!

DE GUICHE   Monsieur . . .

CYRANO   I have dropped from the moon like a bomb!

DE GUICHE [*impatiently*]   What are you babbling about?

CYRANO [*rising, in a terrible voice*]   I tell you I have dropped from the moon!

DE GUICHE [*backing a step*]   Very well. You have dropped from the moon! . . . He is perhaps a lunatic!

CYRANO [*walking up close to him*]   Not metaphorically, mind that!

DE GUICHE   But . . .

CYRANO   A hundred years ago, or else a minute,—for I have no conception how long I have been falling,—I was up there, in that saffron-colored ball!

DE GUICHE [*shrugging his shoulders*]   You were. Now, let me pass!

CYRANO [*standing in his way*]   Where am I? Be frank with me! Keep nothing from me! In what region, among what people, have I been shot like an aerolite?

DE GUICHE   I wish to pass!

CYRANO   While falling I could not choose my way, and have no notion where I have fallen! Is it upon a moon, or is it upon an earth, I have been dragged by my posterior weight?

DE GUICHE   I tell you, sir . . .

CYRANO [*with a scream of terror at which* DE GUICHE *starts backward a step*]   Great God! . . . In this country men's faces are soot-black!

DE GUICHE [*lifting his hand to his face*]   What does he mean?

CYRANO [*still terrified*]   Am I in Algeria? Are you a native? . . .

DE GUICHE [*who has felt his mask*]   Ah, my mask!

CYRANO [*pretending to be easier*]   So I am in Venice! . . . Or am I in Genoa?

DE GUICHE [*attempting to pass*]   A lady is expecting me!

CYRANO [*completely reassured*]   Ah, then I am in Paris.

DE GUICHE [*smiling in spite of himself*]   The rogue is not far from amusing!

CYRANO   Ah, you are laughing!

DE GUICHE   I laugh . . . but intend to pass!

CYRANO [*beaming*]   To think I should strike Paris! [*Quite at his ease, laughing, brushing himself, bowing.*] I arrived—pray, pardon my appearance!—by the last whirlwind. I am rather unpresentable— Travel, you know! My eyes are still full of star-dust. My spurs are clogged with bristles off a planet. [*Appearing to pick something off his sleeve.*] See, on my sleeve, a comet's hair! [*He makes a feint of blowing it away.*]

DE GUICHE [*beside himself*]   Sir . . .

CYRANO [*as DE GUICHE is about to pass, stretching out his leg as if to show something on it, thereby stopping him.*]   Embedded in my calf, I have brought back one of the Great Bear's teeth . . . and as, falling too near the Trident, I strained aside to clear one of its prongs, I landed sitting in Libra, . . . yes, one of the scales! . . . and now my weight is registered up there! [*Quickly preventing DE GUICHE from passing, and taking hold of a button on his doublet.*] And if, Monsieur, you should take my nose between your fingers and compress it . . . milk would result!

DE GUICHE   What are you saying? Milk? . . .

CYRANO   Of the Milky Way.

DE GUICHE   Go to the devil!

CYRANO   No! I am sent from Heaven, literally. [*Folding his arms.*] Will you believe—I discovered it in passing—that Sirius at night puts on a night-cap? [*Confidentially.*] The lesser Bear is too little yet to bite. . . . [*Laughing.*] I tumbled plump through Lyra, and snapped a string! . . . [*Magnificent.*] But I intend setting all this down in a book, and the golden stars I have brought back caught in my shaggy mantle, when the book is printed, will be seen serving as asterisks!

DE GUICHE   I have stood this long enough! I want . . .

CYRANO   I know perfectly what you want!

DE GUICHE   Man . . .

CYRANO   You want to know, from me, at first hand, what the moon is made of, and whether that monumental pumpkin is inhabited?

DE GUICHE [*shouting*]   Not in the very least! I want . . .

CYRANO   To know how I got there? I got there by a method of my own invention.

DE GUICHE [*discouraged*]   He is mad! . . . stark!

CYRANO [*disdainfully*]   Do not imagine that I resorted to anything so absurd as Regiomontanus's eagle, or anything so lacking in enterprise as Archytas's pigeon! . . .*

DE GUICHE   The madman is erudite.

CYRANO   I drew up nothing that had ever been thought of before! [DE GUICHE *has succeeded in getting past* CYRANO, *and is nearing* ROXANE's *door;* CYRANO *follows him, ready to buttonhole him.*] I invented no less than six ways of storming the blue fort of Heaven!

DE GUICHE [*turning around*]   Six, did you say?

CYRANO [*volubly*]   One way was to stand naked in the sunshine, in a harness thickly studded with glass phials, each filled with morning dew. The sun in drawing up the dew, you see, could not have helped drawing me up too!

DE GUICHE [*surprised, taking a step toward* CYRANO]   True. That is one!

CYRANO [*taking a step backward, with a view to drawing* DE GUICHE *away from the door*]   Or else, I could have let the wind into a cedar coffer, then rarified the imprisoned element by means of cunningly adjusted burning-glasses, and soared up with it!

DE GUICHE [*taking another step toward* CYRANO]   Two!

---

*References are to Johann Müller Regiomontanus (1436–1476), a German astronomer, and Archytas (428–347 B.C.), a Greek philosopher.

CYRANO [*backing*]   Or else, mechanic as well as artificer, I could have fashioned a giant grasshopper, with steel joints, which, impelled by successive explosions of salt-peter, would have hopped with me to the azure meadows where graze the starry flocks!

DE GUICHE [*unconsciously following* CYRANO, *and counting on his fingers*]   That makes three!

CYRANO   Since smoke by its nature ascends, I could have blown into an appropriate globe a sufficient quantity to ascend with me!

DE GUICHE [*as above, more and more astonished*]   Four!

CYRANO   Since Phœbe, the moon-goddess, when she is at wane, is greedy, O beeves! of your marrow, . . . with that marrow have besmeared myself!

DE GUICHE [*amazed*]   Five!

CYRANO [*who while talking has backed, followed by* DE GUICHE, *to the further side of the square, near a bench*]   Or else, I could have placed myself upon an iron plate, have taken a magnet of suitable size, and thrown it in the air! That way is a very good one! The magnet flies upward, the iron instantly after; the magnet no sooner overtaken than you fling it up again. . . . The rest is clear! You can go upward indefinitely.

DE GUICHE   Six! . . . But here are six excellent methods! Which of the six, my dear sir, did you select?

CYRANO   A seventh!

DE GUICHE   Did you, indeed? And what was that?

CYRANO   I give you a hundred guesses!

DE GUICHE   I must confess that I should like to know!

CYRANO [*imitating the noise of the surf, and making great, mysterious gestures*]   Hoo-ish! hoo-ish!

DE GUICHE   Well! What is that?

CYRANO   Cannot you guess?

DE GUICHE   No!

CYRANO   The tide! . . . At the hour in which the moon attracts the deep, I lay down upon the sands, after a sea-bath . . . and, my head being drawn up first,—the reason of this, you see, that the hair will hold a quantity of water in its mop!——I rose in the air, straight, beautifully straight, like an angel. I rose . . . I rose softly . . . without an effort . . . when, suddenly, I felt a shock. Then . . .

DE GUICHE [*lured on by curiosity, taking a seat on the bench*]   Well, then? . . .

CYRANO   Then . . . [*resuming his natural voice.*]   The time is up, Monsieur, and I release you. They are married.

DE GUICHE [*getting to his feet with a leap*]   I am dreaming or drunk! That voice? [*The door of* ROXANE's *house opens; lackeys appear carrying lighted candelabra.* CYRANO *removes his hat.*] And that nose! . . . Cyrano!

CYRANO [*bowing*]   Cyrano. They have exchanged rings within the quarter of the hour.

DE GUICHE   Who have? [*He turns round. Tableau. Behind the lackey stand* ROXANE *and* CHRISTIAN *holding hands.* THE CAPUCHIN *follows them smiling.* RAGUENEAU *holds high a flambeau.* THE DUENNA *closes the procession, bewildered, in her bedgown.*]

SCENE XIV

The Same, Roxane, Christian, the Capuchin, Ragueneau, Lackeys, the Duenna

DE GUICHE   Heavens! [*to* ROXANE.] You! [*Recognizing* CHRISTIAN *with amazement.*] He? [*Bowing to* ROXANE.] Your astuteness compels my admiration! [*To* CYRANO.] My compliments to you, ingenious inventor of flying machines. Your experiences would have beguiled a saint on the threshold of Paradise! Make a note of them. . . . They can be used again, with profit, in a book!

CYRANO [*bowing*]   I will confidently follow your advice.

THE CAPUCHIN [*to* DE GUICHE, *pointing at the lovers, and wagging his great white beard with satisfaction*] A beautiful couple, my son, brought together by you!

DE GUICHE [*eyeing him frigidly*] As you say! [*To* ROXANE.] And now proceed, Madame, to take leave of your husband.

ROXANE What?

DE GUICHE [*to* CHRISTIAN] The regiment is on the point of starting. You are to join it!

ROXANE To go to war?

DE GUICHE Of course!

ROXANE But the cadets are not going!

DE GUICHE They are! [*Taking out the paper which he had put in his pocket.*] Here is the order. [*To* CHRISTIAN.] I beg you will take it to the Captain, baron, yourself.

ROXANE [*throwing herself in* CHRISTIAN'*s arms*] Christian!

DE GUICHE [*to* CYRANO, *with a malignant laugh*] The wedding night is somewhat far as yet!

CYRANO [*aside*] He thinks that he is giving me great pain!

CHRISTIAN [*to* ROXANE] Oh, once more, dear! . . . Once more!

CYRANO Be reasonable . . . Come! . . . Enough!

CHRISTIAN [*still clasping* ROXANE] Oh, it is hard to leave her. . . . You cannot know . . .

CYRANO [*trying to draw him away*] I know.

[*Drums are heard in the distance sounding a march.*]

DE GUICHE [*at the back*] The regiment is on its way!

ROXANE [*to* CYRANO, *while she clings to* CHRISTIAN *whom he is trying to draw away*] Oh! . . . I entrust him to your care! Promise that under no circumstance shall his life be placed in danger!

CYRANO I will endeavor . . . but obviously cannot promise . . .

ROXANE [*same business*] Promise that he will be careful of himself!

CYRANO I will do my best, but . . .

ROXANE [*as above*] That during this terrible siege he shall not take harm from the cold!

CYRANO I will try, but . . .

ROXANE [*as above*]   That he will be true to me!

CYRANO   Of course, but yet, you see . . .

ROXANE [*as above*]   That he will write to me often!

CYRANO [*stopping*]   Ah, that . . . I promise freely!

   [*Curtain.*]

ACT FOUR

The Gascony Cadets

The post occupied at the siege of Arras* by the company of CARBON DE CASTEL-JALOUX. At the back, across the whole stage, sloping earthwork. Beyond this is seen a plain stretching to the horizon; the country is covered with constructions relating to the siege. In the distance, against the sky, the outlines of the walls and roofs of Arras. Tents; scattered arms; drums, etc. It is shortly before sunrise. The East is yellow. Sentinels at even intervals. Camp-fires. The GASCONY CADETS lie asleep, rolled in their cloaks. CARBON DE CASTEL-JALOUX and LE BRET are watching. All are very pale and gaunt. CHRISTIAN lies sleeping among the others, in his military cape, in the foreground, his face lighted by one of the camp-fires. Silence.

SCENE I

Christian, Carbon de Castel-Jaloux, Le Bret, the Cadets, then Cyrano

LE BRET   It is dreadful!

CARBON   Yes. Nothing left.

LE BRET   *Mordious!*

CARBON [*warning him by a gesture to speak lower*]   Curse in a whisper! You will wake them! . . . [*To the* CADETS.] Hush! Go to sleep! [*To* LE BRET.] Who sleeps dines.

---

*In 1640, during the Thirty Years War, the town of Arras in northeastern France was occupied by the Spanish. The historical Cyrano fought and was wounded in this siege.

LE BRET   Who lies awake misses two good things . . . What a situation!

[A few shots are heard in the distance.]

CARBON   The devil take their popping! They will wake my young ones! . . . [*To the* CADETS *who lift their heads.*] Go to sleep!

[The CADETS lie down again. Other shots are heard, nearer.]

ONE OF THE CADETS [*stirring*]   The devil! Again?

CARBON   It is nothing. It is Cyrano getting home. [*The heads which had started up, go down again.*]

A SENTINEL [*outside*]   *Ventrebleu!* Who goes there?

CYRANO'S VOICE   Bergerac!

THE SENTINEL [*upon the embankment*]   *Ventrebieu!* Who goes there?

CYRANO [*appearing at the top of the embankment*]   Bergerac, blockhead!

[He comes down. LE BRET goes to him, uneasy]

LE BRET   Ah, thank God!

CYRANO [*warning him by a sign to wake no one*]   Hush!

LE BRET   Wounded?

CYRANO   Do you not know that it has become a habit with them to miss me?

LE BRET   To me, it seems a little excessive that you should, every morning, for the sake of taking a letter, risk . . .

CYRANO [*stopping in front of* CHRISTIAN]   I promised that he would write often. [*He looks at* CHRISTIAN] He sleeps. He has grown pale. If the poor little girl could know that he is starving. . . . But handsome as ever!

LE BRET   Go at once and sleep.

CYRANO   Le Bret, do not grumble! Learn this: I nightly cross the Spanish lines at a point where I know beforehand every one will be drunk.

LE BRET   You ought some time to bring us back some victuals!

CYRANO   I must be lightly burdened to flit through! . . . But I know that there will be events before the evening. The French, unless I am much mistaken, will eat or die.

LE BRET   Oh, tell us!

CYRANO   No, I am not certain . . . You will see!

CARBON   What a shameful reversal of the order of things, that the besieger should be starved!

LE BRET   Alas! never was more complicated siege than this of Arras: We besiege Arras, and, caught in a trap, are ourselves besieged by the Cardinal-prince of Spain . . .

CYRANO   Someone now ought to come and besiege him.

LE BRET   I am not joking!

CYRANO   Oh, oh!

LE BRET   To think, ungrateful boy, that every day you risk a life precious as yours, solely to carry . . . [CYRANO *goes toward one of the tents.*] Where are you going?

CYRANO   I am going to write another. [*He lifts the canvas flap, and disappears in the tent.*]

SCENE II

The Same, without Cyrano

[*Daybreak has brightened. Rosy flush. The city of Arras at the horizon catches a golden light. The report of a cannon is heard, followed at once by a drum-call, very far away, at the left. Other drums beat, nearer. The drum-calls answer one another, come nearer, come very near, and go off, decreasing, dying in the distance, toward the right, having made the circuit of the camp. Noise of general awakening. Voices of officers in the distance*]

CARBON [*with a sigh*]   The reveille Ah, me! . . . [*The* CADETS *stir in their cloaks, stretch.*] An end to the succulent slumbers! I know but too well what their first word will be!

ONE OF THE CADETS [*sitting up*]   I am famished!

OTHER CADET   I believe I am dying!

ALL   Oh! . . .

CARBON   Get up!

THIRD CADET   I cannot go a step!

FOURTH CADET   I have not strength to stir!

FIRST CADET [*looking at himself in a bit of armor.*] My tongue is coated: it must be the weather that is indigestible!

OTHER CADET   Any one who wants them, can have all my titles of nobility for a Chester cheese . . . or part of one!

OTHER CADET   If my stomach does not have something put into it to take up the attention of my gastric juice, I shall retire into my tent before long . . . like Achilles!

OTHER CADET   Yes, they ought to provide us with bread!

CARBON [*going to the tent into which* CYRANO *has retired; low.*] Cyrano!

OTHER CADETS   We cannot stand this much longer!

CARBON [*as above, at the door of the tent*]   To the rescue, Cyrano! You who succeed so well always in cheering them, come and make them pluck up spirits!

SECOND CADET [*falling upon* FIRST CADET *who is chewing something*]   What are you chewing, man?

FIRST CADET   A bit of gun-tow fried in axle-grease. . . . using a burganet as frying pan. The suburbs of Arras are not precisely rich in game. . . .

OTHER CADET [*entering*]   I have been hunting!

OTHER CADET [*the same*]   I have been fishing!

ALL [*rising and falling upon the newcomers*]   What?—what did you catch?—A pheasant?—A carp?—Quick! quick! . . . Let us see!

THE HUNTSMAN   A sparrow!

THE ANGLER   A gudgeon!

ALL [*exasperated*]   Enough of this! Let us revolt!

CARBON   To the rescue, Cyrano!

[*It is now broad daylight.*]

SCENE III

The Same, Cyrano

CYRANO [*coming out of the tent, tranquil, a pen behind his ear, a book in his hand*]   What is the matter? [*Silence. To* FIRST CADET.] Why do you go off like that, with that slouching gait?

THE CADET   I have something away down in my heels which inconveniences me.

CYRANO   And what is that?

THE CADET   My stomach.

CYRANO   That is where mine is, too.

THE CADET   Then you too must be inconvenienced.

CYRANO   No. The size of the hollow within me merely increases my sense of my size.

SECOND CADET   I happen to have teeth, long ones!

CYRANO   The better will you bite . . . in good time!

THIRD CADET   I reverberate like a drum!

CYRANO   You will be of use . . . to sound the charge!

OTHER CADET   I have a buzzing in my ears!

CYRANO   A mistake. Empty belly, no ears. You hear no buzzing.

OTHER CADET   Ah, a trifling article to eat . . . and a little oil upon it!

CYRANO [*taking off the* CADET's *morion* and placing it in his hand*]   That is seasoned.

OTHER CADET   What is there we could devour?

CYRANO [*tossing him the book he has been holding*]   Try the Iliad!

OTHER CADET   The minister, in Paris, makes his four meals a day!

CYRANO   You feel it remiss in him not to send you a bit of partridge?

THE SAME   Why should he not? And some wine!

CYRANO   Richelieu, some Burgundy, if you please?

---

*Type of visorless helmet, worn in the sixteenth and seventeenth centuries.

THE SAME   He might, by one of his capuchins!

CYRANO   By his Eminence, perhaps, in sober gray?

OTHER CADET   No ogre was ever so hungry!

CYRANO   You may have your fill yet of humble-pie!

FIRST CADET [*shrugging his shoulders*]   Forever jests! . . .
    puns! . . . *mots!*

CYRANO   *Le mot** forever, indeed! And I would wish to die, on a
    fine evening, under a rose-flushed sky, delivering myself of a good
    mot in a good cause! . . . Ah, yes, the best were indeed, far from
    fever bed and potion, pierced with the only noble weapon, by an
    adversary worthy of oneself, to fall upon a glorious field, the
    point of a sword through his heart, the point of a jest on his
    lips! . . .

ALL [*in a wail*]   I am hungry!

CYRANO [*folding his arms*]   God ha' mercy! can you think of noth-
    ing but eating? . . . Come here, Bertrandou the fifer, once the
    shepherd! Take from the double case one of your fifes: breathe
    into it, play to this pack of guzzlers and of gluttons our homely
    melodies, of haunting rhythm, every note of which appeals like a
    little sister, through whose every strain are heard strains of
    beloved voices . . . mild melodies whose slowness brings to mind
    the slowness of the smoke upcurling from our native hamlet
    hearths . . . melodies that seem to speak to a man in his native di-
    alect! . . . [*The old fifer sits down and makes ready his fife.*] To-day let
    the fife, martial unwillingly, be reminded, while your fingers
    upon its slender stem flutter like birds in a delicate minuet, that
    before being ebony it was reed; surprise itself by what you make
    it sing, . . . let it feel restored to it the soul of its youth, rustic and
    peaceable! [*The old man begins playing Languedoc tunes*] Listen, Gas-
    cons! It is no more, beneath his fingers, the shrill fife of the camp,
    but the soft flute of the woodland! It is no more, between his lips,

---

*Literally, "word" (French), but also a sentence, particularly one combining elegance,
wit, and incisiveness.

the whistling note of battle, but the lowly lay of goatherds leading their flocks to feed! . . . Hark! . . . It sings of the valley, the heath, the forest! . . . of the little shepherd, sunburned under his crimson cap! . . . the green delight of evening on the river! . . . Hark, Gascons all! It sings of Gascony!

[*Every head has drooped; all eyes have grown dreamy; tears are furtively brushed away with a sleeve, the hem of a cloak*]

CARBON [*to* CYRANO, *low*]   You are making them weep!

CYRANO   With homesickness! . . . a nobler pain than hunger . . . not physical: mental! I am glad the seat of their suffering should have removed . . . that the gripe should now afflict their hearts!

CARBON   But you weaken them, making them weep!

CYRANO [*beckoning to a drummer*]   Never fear! The hero in their veins is quickly roused. It is enough to . . . [*He signs to the drummer who begins drumming.*]

ALL [*starting to their feet and snatching up their arms*]   Hein? . . . What? . . . What is it?

CYRANO [*smiling*]   You see? . . . The sound of the drum was enough! Farewell dreams, regrets, old homestead, love . . . What comes with the fife with the drum may go . . .

ONE OF THE CADETS [*looking off at the back*]   Ah! ah! . . . Here comes Monsieur de Guiche!

ALL THE CADETS [*grumbling*]   Hoo . . .

CYRANO [*smiling*]   Flattering murmur . . .

ONE OF THE CADETS   He bores us! . . .

OTHER CADET   Showing himself off, with his broad point collar on top of his armor! . . .

OTHER CADET   As if lace were worn with steel!

FIRST CADET   Convenient, if you have a boil on your neck to cover . . .

SECOND CADET   There is another courier for you!

OTHER CADET   His uncle's own nephew!

CARBON   He is a Gascon, nevertheless!

FIRST CADET   Not genuine! . . . Never trust him. For a Gascon,

look you, must be something of a madman: nothing is so deadly
to deal with as a Gascon who is completely rational!

LE BRET   He is pale!

OTHER CADET   He is hungry, as hungry as any poor devil of us!
But his corslet being freely embellished with gilt studs, his
stomach-ache is radiant in the sun!

CYRANO [*eagerly*]   Let us not appear to suffer, either! You, your
cards, your pipes, your dice . . . [*All briskly set themselves to playing
with cards and dice, on the heads of drums, on stools, on cloaks spread over
the ground. They light long tobacco pipes.*] And I will be reading
Descartes . . .

[*He walks to and fro, forward and backward, reading a small book which
he has taken from his pocket. Tableau. Enter DE GUICHE. Every one appears absorbed and satisfied. DE GUICHE is very pale. He goes toward
CARBON.*]

SCENE IV

The Same, De Guiche

DE GUICHE [*to CARBON*]   Ah, good-morning. [*They look at each
other attentively. Aside, with satisfaction*] He is pale as plaster.

CARBON [*same business*]   His eyes are all that is left of him.

DE GUICHE [*looking at the CADETS*]   So here are the wrong-
headed rascals? . . . Yes, gentlemen, it is reported to me on
every side that I am your scoff and derision; that the cadets,
highland nobility, Béarn clodhoppers, Périgord baronets, cannot
express sufficient contempt for their colonel; call me intriguer,
courtier, find it irksome to their taste that I should wear, with
my cuirass, a collar of Genoese point, and never cease to air
their wondering indignation that a man should be a Gascon
without being a vagabond! [*Silence. The CADETS continue smoking and playing*] Shall I have you punished by your captain? . . . I
do not like to.

CARBON   Did you otherwise, however, . . . I am free, and punish only . . .

DE GUICHE   Ah? . . .

CARBON   My company is paid by myself, belongs to me. I obey no orders but such as relate to war.

DE GUICHE   Ah, is it so? Enough, then. I will treat your taunts with simple scorn. My fashion of deporting myself under fire is well known. You are not unaware of the manner in which yesterday, at Bapaume, I forced back the columns of the Comte de Bucquoi; gathering my men together to plunge forward like an avalanche, three times I charged him. . . .

CYRANO [*without lifting his nose from his book*]   And your white scarf?

DE GUICHE [*surprised and self-satisfied*]   You heard of that circumstance? . . . In fact, it happened that as I was wheeling about to collect my men for the third charge, I was caught in a stream of fugitives which bore me onward to the edge of the enemy. I was in danger of being captured and cut off with an arquebuse, when I had the presence of mind to untie and let slip to the ground the white scarf which proclaimed my military grade. Thus was I enabled, undistinguished, to withdraw from among the Spaniards, and thereupon returning with my reinspirited men, to defeat them. Well? . . . What do you say to the incident?

[*The CADETS have appeared not to be listening; at this point, however, hands with cards and dice-boxes remain suspended in the air; no pipe-smoke is ejected; all expresses expectation.*]

CYRANO   That never would Henry the Fourth, however great the number of his opponents, have consented to diminish his presence by the size of his white plume.*

[*Silent joy. Cards fall, dice rattle, smoke upwreathes.*]

DE GUICHE   The trick was successful, however!

[*As before, expectation suspends gambling and smoking.*]

----

*In French, the word for "white plume" is *panache*; see the Introduction for a discussion of this word.

CYRANO   Very likely. But one should not resign the honor of being a target. [*Cards, dice, smoke, fall, rattle, and upwreathe, as before, in expression of increasing glee.*] Had I been at hand when you allowed your scarf to drop—the quality of our courage, monsieur, shows different in this,—I would have picked it up and worn it. . . .

DE GUICHE   Ah, yes,—more of your Gascon bragging! . . .

CYRANO   Bragging? . . . Lend me the scarf. I engage to mount, ahead of all, to the assault, wearing it crosswise upon my breast!

DE GUICHE   A Gascon's offer, that too! You know that the scarf was left in the enemy's camp, by the banks of the Scarpe, where bullets since then have hailed . . . whence no one can bring it back!

CYRANO [*taking a white scarf from his pocket and handing it to* DE GUICHE]   Here it is.
[*Silence. The CADETS smother their laughter behind cards and in dice-boxes. DE GUICHE turns around, looks at them; instantly they become grave; one of them, with an air of unconcern, whistles the tune played earlier by the fifer*]

DE GUICHE [*taking the scarf*]   I thank you. I shall be able with this shred of white to make a signal . . . which I was hesitating to make . . . [*He goes to the top of the bank and waves the scarf.*]

ALL   What now? . . . What is this?

THE SENTINEL [*at the top of the bank*]   A man . . . over there . . . running off . . .

DE GUICHE [*coming forward again*]   It is a supposed Spanish spy. He is very useful to us. The information he carries to the enemy is that which I give him,—so that their decisions are influenced by us.

CYRANO   He is a scoundrel!

DE GUICHE [*coolly tying on his scarf*]   He is a convenience. We were saying? . . . Ah, I was about to tell you. Last night, having resolved upon a desperate stroke to obtain supplies, the Marshal secretly set out for Dourlens. The royal sutlers* are encamped there. He expects to join them by way of the tilled fields; but, to

---

*Those who follow an army and sell provisions to the officers and soldiers.

provide against interference, he took with him troops in such number that, certainly, if we were now attacked, the enemy would find easy work. Half of the army is absent from the camp.

CARBON   If the Spaniards knew that, it might be serious. But they do not know.

DE GUICHE   They do. And are going to attack us.

CARBON   Ah!

DE GUICHE   My pretended spy came to warn me of their intention. He said, moreover: I can direct the attack. At what point shall it be? I will lead them to suppose it the least strong, and they will centre their efforts against it. I answered: Very well. Go from the camp. Look down the line. Let them attack at the point I signal from.

CARBON [*to the* CADETS]   Gentlemen, get ready! [*All get up. Noise of swords and belts being buckled on.*]

DE GUICHE   They will be here in an hour.

FIRST CADET   Oh! . . . if there is a whole hour! . . .
[*All sit down again, and go on with their games.*]

DE GUICHE [*to CARBON*]   The main object is to gain time. The Marshal is on his way back.

CARBON   And to gain time?

DE GUICHE   You will be so obliging as to keep them busy killing you.

CYRANO   Ah, this is your revenge!

DE GUICHE   I will not pretend that if I had been fond of you, I would have thus singled out you and yours; but, as your bravery is unquestionably beyond that of others, I am serving my King at the same time as my inclination.

CYRANO   Suffer me, monsieur, to express my gratitude.

DE GUICHE   I know that you affect fighting one against a hundred. You will not complain of lacking opportunity. [*He goes toward the back with CARBON.*]

CYRANO [*to the* CADETS]   We shall now be able, gentlemen, to add to the Gascon escutcheon, which bears, as it is, six chevrons,

or* and azure, the chevron that was wanting to complete it,—
blood-red!

[DE GUICHE at the back speaks low with CARBON. Orders are given. All
is made ready to repel an attack. CYRANO goes toward CHRISTIAN, who
stands motionless, with folded arms.]

CYRANO [laying his hand on CHRISTIAN's shoulder]   Christian?

CHRISTIAN [shaking his head]   Roxane!

CYRANO   Ah me!

CHRISTIAN   I wish I might at least put my whole heart's last blessing in a beautiful letter!

CYRANO   I mistrusted that it would come to-day . . . [he takes a letter from his doublet] and I have written your farewells.

CHRISTIAN   Let me see!

CYRANO   You wish to see it? . . .

CHRISTIAN [taking the letter]   Yes! [He opens the letter, begins to read,
stops short.] Ah? . . .

CYRANO   What?

CHRISTIAN   That little round blister?

CYRANO [hurriedly taking back the letter, and looking at it with an artless
air]   A blister?

CHRISTIAN   It is a tear!

CYRANO   It looks like one, does it not? . . . A poet, you see, is
sometimes caught in his own snare,—that is what constitutes the
interest, the charm! . . . This letter, you must know, is very
touching. In writing it I apparently made myself shed tears.

CHRISTIAN   Shed tears? . . .

CYRANO   Yes, because . . . well, to die is not terrible at all . . . but
never to see her again, . . . never! . . . that, you know, is horrible
beyond all thinking. . . . And, things having taken the turn they
have, I shall not see her . . . [CHRISTIAN looks at him] we shall
not see her . . . [Hastily] you will not see her. . . .

---

*Gold (French).

CHRISTIAN [*snatching the letter from him*]   Give me the letter!
   [*Noise in the distance.*]
VOICE OF A SENTINEL   *Ventrebieu*, who goes there?
   [*Shots. Noise of voices, tinkling of bells.*]
CARBON   What is it?
THE SENTINEL [*on the top of the bank*]   A coach!
   [*All run to see.*]
   [*Noisy exclamations.*] What?—In the camp?—It is driving into the
   camp!—It comes from the direction of the enemy! The devil! Fire upon
   it!—No! the coachman is shouting something!—What does he say?—
   He shouts: Service of the King!
DE GUICHE   What? Service of the King?
   [*All come down from the bank and fall into order.*]
CARBON   Hats off, all!
DE GUICHE [*at the corner*]   Service of the King! Stand back, low rab-
   ble, and give it room to turn around with a handsome sweep!
   [*The coach comes in at a trot. It is covered with mud and dust. The curtains
   are drawn. Two lackeys behind. It comes to a standstill.*]
CARBON [*shouting*]   Salute!
   [*Drums roll. All the CADETS uncover.*]
DE GUICHE   Let down the steps!
   [*Two men hurry forward. The coach door opens.*]
ROXANE [*stepping from the carriage*]   Good-morning!
   [*At the sound of a feminine voice, all the men, in the act of bowing low,
   straighten themselves. Consternation.*]

SCENE V

The Same, Roxane

DE GUICHE   Service of the King! You?
ROXANE   Of the only King! . . . of Love!
CYRANO   Ah, great God!
CHRISTIAN [*rushing to her*]   You! Why are you here?

ROXANE   This siege lasted too long!

CHRISTIAN   Why have you come?

ROXANE   I will tell you!

CYRANO [*who at the sound of her voice has started, then stood motionless without venturing to look her way*]   God! . . . can I trust myself to look at her?

DE GUICHE   You cannot remain here.

ROXANE   But I can,—I can, indeed! Will you favor me with a drum? [*She seats herself upon a drum brought forward for her.*] There! I thank you! [*She laughs.*] They fired upon my carriage. [*Proudly.*] A patrol! It does look rather as if it were made out of a pumpkin, does it not? like Cinderella's coach! and the footmen made out of rats! [*Blowing a kiss to* CHRISTIAN.] How do you do? [*Looking at them all.*] You do not look overjoyed! . . . Arras is a long way from Paris, do you know it? [*Catching sight of* CYRANO.] Cousin, delighted!

CYRANO [*coming toward her*]   But how did you . . . ?

ROXANE   How did I find the army? Dear me, cousin, that was simple: I followed straight along the line of devastation. . . . Ah, I should never have believed in such horrors had I not seen them! Gentlemen, if that is the service of your King, I like mine better!

CYRANO   But this is mad! . . . By what way did you come?

ROXANE   Way? . . . I drove through the Spaniards' camp.

FIRST CADET   Ah, what will keep lovely woman from her way!

DE GUICHE   But how did you contrive to get through their lines?

LE BRET   That must have been difficult . . .

ROXANE   No, not very. I simply drove through them, in my coach, at a trot. If a hidalgo,* with arrogant front, showed likely to stop us, I put my face at the window, wearing my sweetest smile, and, those gentlemen being,—let the French not grudge my saying so!—the most gallant in the world, . . . I passed!

---

*Spanish nobleman or gentleman by birth.

CARBON   Such a smile is a passport, certainly! . . . But you must have been not unfrequently bidden to stand and deliver where you were going?

ROXANE   Not unfrequently, you are right. Whereupon I would say, "I am going to see my lover!" At once, the fiercest looking Spaniard of them all would gravely close my carriage door; and, with a gesture the King might emulate, motion aside the musket-barrels levelled at me; and, superb at once for grace and haughtiness, bringing his spurs together, and lifting his plumed hat, bow low and say, "Pass, senorita, pass!"

CHRISTIAN   But, Roxane . . .

ROXANE   I said, "My lover!" yes, forgive me!—You see, if I had said, "My husband!" they would never have let me by!

CHRISTIAN   But . . .

ROXANE   What troubles you?

DE GUICHE   You must leave at once.

ROXANE   I?

CYRANO   At once!

LE BRET   As fast as you can.

CHRISTIAN   Yes, you must.

ROXANE   But why?

CHRISTIAN [*embarrassed*]   Because . . .

CYRANO [*embarrassed too*]   In three quarters of an hour . . .

DE GUICHE [*the same*]   Or an hour . . .

CARBON [*the same*]   You had much better . . .

LE BRET [*the same*]   You might . . .

ROXANE   I shall remain. You are going to fight.

ALL   Oh, no! . . . No!

ROXANE   He is my husband! [*She throws herself in* CHRISTIAN's *arms.*] Let me be killed with you!

CHRISTIAN   How your eyes shine!

ROXANE   I will tell you why they shine!

DE GUICHE [*desperately*]   It is a post of horrible probabilities!

ROXANE [*turning toward him*]   What—of horrible? . . .

CYRANO   In proof of which he appointed us to it! . . .

ROXANE   Ah, you wish me made a widow?

DE GUICHE   I swear to you . . .

ROXANE   No! Now I have lost all regard. . . . Now I will surely not
go. . . . Besides, I think it fun!

CYRANO   What? The précieuse contained a heroine?

ROXANE   Monsieur de Bergerac, I am a cousin of yours!

ONE OF THE CADETS   Never think but that we will take good care
of you!

ROXANE [*more and more excited*]   I am sure you will, my friends!

OTHER CADET   The whole camp smells of iris!

ROXANE   By good fortune I put on a hat that will look well in battle! [*Glancing toward* DE GUICHE.] But perhaps it is time the
Count should go.—The battle might begin.

DE GUICHE   Ah, it is intolerable!—I am going to inspect my guns,
and coming back.—You still have time: think better of it!

ROXANE   Never!

[*Exit DE GUICHE*]

SCENE VI

The Same, without De Guiche

CHRISTIAN [*imploring*]   Roxane!

ROXANE   No!

FIRST CADET   She is going to stay!

ALL [*hurrying about, pushing one another, snatching things from one
another*]   A comb!—Soap!—My jacket is torn, a needle!—
A ribbon!—Lend me your pocket-mirror!—My cuffs!—
Curling-irons!—A razor!

ROXANE [*to* CYRANO, *who is still pleading with her*]   No! Nothing
shall prevail upon me to stir from this spot!

CARBON [*after having, like the others, tightened his belt, dusted himself,
brushed his hat, straightened his feather, pulled down his cuffs, approaches*

ROXANE, *and ceremoniously*]   It is, perhaps, proper, since you are going to stay, that I should present to you a few of the gentlemen about to have the honor of dying in your presence . . . [ROXANE *bows, and stands waiting, with her arm through* CHRISTIAN's.] Baron Peyrescous de Colignac!

THE CADET [*bowing*]   Madame!

CARBON [*continuing to present the* CADETS] Baron de Casterac de Cahuzac,—Vidame do Malgouyre Estressac Lesbas d'Escara-biot,—Chevalier d'Antignac-Juzet,—Baron Hillot de Blagnac-Saléchan de Castel Crabioules . . .

ROXANE   But how many names have you apiece?

BARON HILLOT   Innumerable!

CARBON [*to* ROXANE]   Open your hand with the handkerchief!

ROXANE [*opens her hand; the handkerchief drops*]   Why?
[*The whole company starts forward to pick it up*]

CARBON [*instantly catching it*]   My company had no flag! Now, my word, it will have the prettiest one in the army!

ROXANE [*smiling*]   It is rather small!

CARBON [*fastening the handkerchief on the staff of his captain's spear*] But it is lace!

ONE OF THE CADETS [*to the others*]   I could die without a murmur, having looked upon that beautiful face, if I had so much as a walnut inside me! . . .

CARBON [*who has overheard, indignant*]   Shame! . . . to talk of food when an exquisite woman . . .

ROXANE   But the air of the camp is searching, and I myself am hungry: Patties, jellied meat, light wine . . . are what I should like best! Will you kindly bring me some?
[*Consternation*]

ONE OF THE CADETS   Bring you some?

OTHER CADET   And where, great God, shall we get them?

ROXANE [*quietly*]   In my coach.

ALL   What?

ROXANE   But there is much to be done, carving and boning and

serving. Look more closely at my coachman, gentlemen, and you
will recognize a precious individual: the sauces, if we wish, can be
warmed over . . .

THE CADETS [*springing toward the coach*]   It is Ragueneau! [*Cheers.*]
Oh! Oh!

ROXANE [*watching them*]   Poor fellows!

CYRANO [*kissing her hand*]   Kind fairy!

RAGUENEAU [*standing upon the box-seat like a vendor at a public fair*]
Gentlemen!
[*Enthusiasm*]

THE CADETS   Bravo! Bravo!

RAGUENEAU   How should the Spaniards, when so much beauty
passed, suspect the repast?
[*Applause.*]

CYRANO [*low to* CHRISTIAN]   Hm! Hm! Christian!

RAGUENEAU   Absorbed in gallantry, no heed took they . . . [*he
takes a dish from the box-seat*] . . . of galantine!*
[*Applause. The galantine is passed from hand to hand.*]

CYRANO [*low to* CHRISTIAN]   A word with you . . .

RAGUENEAU   Venus kept their eyes fixed upon herself, while
Diana slipped past with the . . . [*he brandishes a joint*] game!
[*Enthusiasm. The joint is seized by twenty hands at once.*]

CYRANO [*low to* CHRISTIAN]   I must speak with you.

ROXANE [*to the* CADETS *who come forward, their arms full of provisions*]
Spread it all upon the ground!
[*Assisted by the two imperturbable footmen who were on the back of the
coach, she arranges everything on the grass.*]

ROXANE [*to* CHRISTIAN *whom* CYRANO *is trying to draw aside*]
Make yourself useful, sir!
[*CHRISTIAN comes and helps her. CYRANO gives evidence of uneasiness.*]

RAGUENEAU   A truffled peacock!

---

*Sauce for fish or fowl; also a dish of various meats, boiled and served cold.

FIRST CADET [*radiant, comes forward cutting off a large slice of ham*] Praise the pigs, we shall not go to our last fight with nothing in our b . . . [*correcting himself at sight of* ROXANE] hm . . . stomachs!

RAGUENEAU [*flinging the carriage cushions*]   The cushions are stuffed with snipe!

[*Tumult. The cushions are ripped open. Laughter. Joy.*]

RAGUENEAU [*flinging bottles of red wine*]   Molten ruby! [*Bottles of white wine.*] Fluid topaz!

ROXANE [*throwing a folded tablecloth to* CYRANO]   Unfold the cloth: Hey! . . . be nimble!

RAGUENEAU [*waving one of the coach lanterns*]   Each lantern is a little larder!

CYRANO [*low to* CHRISTIAN, *while together they spread the cloth*]   I must speak with you before you speak with her . . .

RAGUENEAU   The handle of my whip, behold, is a sausage!

ROXANE [*pouring wine, dispensing it*]   Since we are the ones to be killed, *morbleu*, we will not fret ourselves about the rest of the army! Everything for the Gascons! . . . And if De Guiche comes, nobody must invite him! [*Going from one to the other.*] Gently! You have time . . . You must not eat so fast! There, drink. What are you crying about?

FIRST CADET   It is too good!

ROXANE   Hush! White wine or red?—Bread for Monsieur de Carbon!—A knife!—Pass your plate!—You prefer crust?—A little more?—Let me help you.—Champagne?—A wing?—

CYRANO [*following* ROXANE, *his hands full of dishes, helping her*]   I adore her!

ROXANE [*going to* CHRISTIAN]   What will you take?

CHRISTIAN   Nothing!

ROXANE   Oh, but you must take something! This biscuit—in a little Muscatel,—just a little?

CHRISTIAN [*trying to keep her from going*]   Tell me what made you come?

ROXANE   I   owe   myself   to   those   poor   fellows. . . . Be
patient, . . . By and by . . .

LE BRET [*who had gone toward the back to pass a loaf of bread on the end
of a pike to the SENTINEL upon the earthwork*]   De Guiche!

CYRANO   Presto! Vanish basket, flagon, platter and pan! Hurry! Let
us look as if nothing were! [*To* RAGUENEAU.] Take a flying leap
on to your box!—Is everything hidden?
[*In a wink, all the eatables have been pushed into the tents, or hidden
under clothes, cloaks, hats. Enter DE GUICHE, hurriedly; he stops short,
sniffing the air. Silence.*]

SCENE VII

The Same, De Guiche

DE GUICHE   What a good smell!

ONE OF THE CADETS [*singing, with effect of mental abstraction*]   To
lo lo lo. . . .

DE GUICHE [*stopping and looking at him closely*]   What is the matter
with you—you, there? You are red as a crab.

THE CADET   I? Nothing . . . It is just my blood. . . . We are going
to fight: it tells . . .

OTHER CADET   Poom . . . poom . . . poom . . .

DE GUICHE [*turning*]   What is this?

THE CADET [*slightly intoxicated*]   Nothing . . . A   song . . .
just a little song.

DE GUICHE   You look in good spirits, my boy!

THE CADET   Danger affects me that way!

DE GUICHE [*calling CARBON DE CASTEL-JALOUX to give an order*]
Captain, I . . . [*He stops at sight of his face.*] Peste! You look in good
spirits, too.

CARBON [*flushed, holding a bottle behind him; with an evasive gesture*]
Oh! . . .

DE GUICHE   I had a cannon left over, which I have ordered them to place [*he points in the wing*] there, in that corner, and which your men can use, if necessary . . .

ONE OF THE CADETS [*swaying from one foot to the other*]   Charming attention!

OTHER CADET [*smiling sugarily*]   Our thanks for your gracious thoughtfulness!

DE GUICHE   Have they gone mad? . . . [*Drily.*] As you are not accustomed to handling a cannon, look out for its kicking . . .

FIRST CADET   Ah, pfft! . . .

DE GUICHE [*going toward him, furious*]   But . . .

THE CADET   A cannon knows better than to kick a Gascon!

DE GUICHE [*seizing him by the arm and shaking him*]   You are all tipsy: on what?

THE CADET [*magnificently*]   The smell of powder!

DE GUICHE [*shrugs his shoulders, pushes aside the* CADET, *and goes rapidly toward* ROXANE]   Quick, Madame! what have you condescended to decide?

ROXANE   I remain.

DE GUICHE   Retire, I beseech you!

ROXANE   No.

DE GUICHE   If you are determined, then . . . Let me have a musket!

CARBON   What do you mean?

DE GUICHE   I, too, will remain.

CYRANO   At last, Monsieur, an instance of pure and simple bravery!

FIRST CADET   Might you be a Gascon, lace collar notwithstanding?

DE GUICHE   I do not leave a woman in danger.

SECOND CADET [*to* FIRST CADET]   Look here! I think he might be given something to eat!

[*All the food reappears, as if by magic.*]

DE GUICHE [*his eyes brightening*]   Provisions?

THIRD CADET   Under every waistcoat!

DE GUICHE [*mastering himself, haughtily*]   Do you imagine that I will eat your leavings?

CYRANO [*bowing*]   You are improving!

DE GUICHE [*proudly, falling at the last of the sentence into a slightly GAS-CON accent*]   I will fight before I eat!

FIRST CADET [*exultant*]   Fight! Eat! . . . He spoke with an accent!

DE GUICHE [*laughing*]   I did?

THE CADET   He is one of us!

[*All fall to dancing.*]

CARBON [*who a moment before disappeared behind the earth-works, reappearing at the top*]   I have placed my pikemen. They are a determined troop . . .

[*He points at a line of pikes projecting above the bank*]

DE GUICHE [*to* ROXANE, *bowing*]   Will you accept my hand and pass them in review?

[*She takes his hand; they go toward the bank. Every one uncovers and follows.*]

CHRISTIAN [*going to* CYRANO, *quickly*]   Speak! Be quick!

[*As* ROXANE *appears at the top of the bank, the pikes disappear, lowered in a salute, and a cheer goes up;* ROXANE *bows.*]

PIKEMEN [*outside*]   Vivat!

CHRISTIAN   What did you want to tell me?

CYRANO   In case Roxane . . .

CHRISTIAN   Well?

CYRANO   Should speak to you of the letters . . .

CHRISTIAN   Yes, the letters. I know!

CYRANO   Do not commit the blunder of appearing surprised . . .

CHRISTIAN   At what?

CYRANO   I must tell you! . . . It is quite simple, and merely comes into my mind to-day because I see her. You have . . .

CHRISTIAN   Hurry!

CYRANO   You . . . you have written to her oftener than you suppose . . .

CHRISTIAN   Oh, have I?

CYRANO   Yes. It was my business, you see. I had undertaken to interpret your passion, and sometimes I wrote without having told you I should write.

CHRISTIAN Ah?

CYRANO It is very simple.

CHRISTIAN But how did you succeed since we have been so closely surrounded, in . . . ?

CYRANO Oh, before daybreak I could cross the lines . . .

CHRISTIAN [*folding his arms*] Ah, that is very simple, too? . . . And how many times a week have I been writing? Twice? Three times? Four? . . .

CYRANO More.

CHRISTIAN Every day?

CYRANO Yes, every day . . . twice.

CHRISTIAN [*violently*] And you cared so much about it that you were willing to brave death. . . .

CYRANO [*seeing* ROXANE *who returns.*] Be still . . . Not before her! [*He goes quickly into his tent.*]
    [*CADETS come and go at the back. CARBON and DE GUICHE give orders.*]

SCENE VIII

Roxane, Christian, Cadets, Carbon de Castel-Jaloux,
De Guiche

ROXANE [*running to* CHRISTIAN] And now, Christian . . .

CHRISTIAN [*taking her hands*] And now, you shall tell me why, over these fearful roads, through these ranks of rough soldiery, you risked your dear self to join me?

ROXANE Because of the letters!

CHRISTIAN The . . . ? What did you say?

ROXANE It is through your fault that I have been exposed to such and so many dangers. It is your letters that have gone to my head! Ah, think how many you have written me in a month, each one more beautiful . . .

CHRISTIAN What? . . . Because of a few little love letters . . .

ROXANE   Say nothing! You cannot understand! Listen: The truth is
that I took to idolizing you one evening, when, below my window,
in a voice I did not know before, your soul began to reveal itself. . . . Think then what the effect should be of your letters,
which have been like your voice heard constantly for one month,
your voice of that evening, so tender, caressing . . . You must bear
it as you can, I have come to you! Prudent Penelope would not
have stayed at home with her eternal tapestry, if Ulysses, her lord,
had written as you write . . . but, impulsive as Helen, have tossed
aside her yarns, and flown to join him!*

CHRISTIAN   But . . .

ROXANE   I read them, I re-read them, in reading I grew faint . . . I
became your own indeed! Each fluttering leaf was like a petal of
your soul wafted to me . . . In every word of those letters, love
is felt as a flame would be felt,—love, compelling, sincere,
profound . . .

CHRISTIAN   Ah, sincere, profound? . . . You say that it can be felt,
Roxane?

ROXANE   He asks me!

CHRISTIAN   And so you came? . . .

ROXANE   I came—oh Christian, my own, my master! If I were to
kneel at your feet you would lift me, I know. It is my soul therefore which kneels, and never can you lift it from that posture!—
I came to implore your pardon—as it is fitting, for we are both
perhaps about to die!—your pardon for having done you the
wrong, at first, in my shallowness, of loving you . . . for mere
looking!

CHRISTIAN [*in alarm*]   Ah, Roxane! . . .

ROXANE   Later, dear one, grown less shallow—similar to a bird
which flutters before it can fly,—your gallant exterior appealing

---

*In Homer's *Odyssey*, Penelope is the virtuous wife of Ulysses who spends her days
weaving a tapestry and her nights undoing it.

to me still, but your soul appealing equally, I loved you for both! . . .

CHRISTIAN   And now?

ROXANE   Now at last yourself are vanquished by yourself: I love you for your soul alone . . .

CHRISTIAN [*drawing away*]   Ah, Roxane!

ROXANE   Rejoice! For to be loved for that wherewith we are clothed so fleetingly must put a noble heart to torture. . . . Your dear thought at last casts your dear face in shadow: the harmonious lineaments whereby at first you pleased me, I do not see them, now my eyes are open!

CHRISTIAN   Oh!

ROXANE   You question your own triumph?

CHRISTIAN [*sorrowfully*]   Roxane!

ROXANE   I understand, you cannot conceive of such a love in me?

CHRISTIAN   I do not wish to be loved like that! I wish to be loved quite simply . . .

ROXANE   For that which other women till now have loved in you? Ah, let yourself be loved in a better way.

CHRISTIAN   No . . . I was happier before! . . .

ROXANE   Ah, you do not understand! It is now that I love you most, that I truly love you. It is that which makes you, you—can you not grasp it?—that I worship . . . And did you no longer walk our earth like a young martial Apollo . . .

CHRISTIAN   Say no more!

ROXANE   Still would I love you! . . . Yes, though a blight should have fallen upon your face and form . . .

CHRISTIAN   Do not say it!

ROXANE   But I do say it, . . . I do!

CHRISTIAN   What? If I were ugly, distinctly, offensively?

ROXANE   If you were ugly, dear, I swear it!

CHRISTIAN   God!

ROXANE   And you are glad, profoundly glad?

CHRISTIAN [*in a smothered voice*]   Yes . . .

ROXANE   What is it?

CHRISTIAN [*pushing her gently away*]   Nothing. I have a word or two
to say to some one: your leave, for a second . . .

ROXANE   But . . .

CHRISTIAN [*pointing at a group of* CADETS *at the back*]   In my self-
ish love, I have kept you from those poor brothers. . . . Go, smile
on them a little, before they die, dear . . . go!

ROXANE [*moved*]   Dear Christian!

[*She goes toward the* GASCONS *at the back; they respectfully gather
around her.*]

SCENE IX

*Christian, Cyrano; in the background, Roxane, talking with
Carbon de Castel-Jaloux and some of the Cadets*

CHRISTIAN [*calling toward* CYRANO'*s tent*]   Cyrano!

CYRANO [*appears, armed for battle*]   What is it? . . . How pale you
are!

CHRISTIAN   She does not love me any more!

CYRANO   What do you mean?

CHRISTIAN   She loves you.

CYRANO   No!

CHRISTIAN   She only loves my soul!

CYRANO   No!

CHRISTIAN   Yes! Therefore it is you she loves . . . and you love
her . . .

CYRANO   I . . .

CHRISTIAN   I know it!

CYRANO   It is true.

CHRISTIAN   To madness!

CYRANO   More.

CHRISTIAN   Tell her then.

CYRANO   No!

CHRISTIAN   Why not?

CYRANO   Look at me!

CHRISTIAN   She would love me grown ugly.

CYRANO   She told you so?

CHRISTIAN   With the utmost frankness!

CYRANO   Ah! I am glad she should have told you that! But, believe me, believe me, place no faith in such a mad asseveration! Dear God, I am glad such a thought should have come to her, and that she should have spoken it, —but believe me, do not take her at her word: Never cease to be the handsome fellow you are. . . . She would not forgive me!

CHRISTIAN   That is what I wish to discover.

CYRANO   No! no!

CHRISTIAN   Let her choose between us! You shall tell her everything.

CYRANO   No . . . No . . . I refuse the ordeal!

CHRISTIAN   Shall I stand in the way of your happiness because my outside is not so much amiss?

CYRANO   And I? shall I destroy yours, because, thanks to the hazard that sets us upon earth, I have the gift of expressing . . . what you perhaps feel?

CHRISTIAN   You shall tell her everything!

CYRANO   He persists in tempting me . . . It is a mistake . . . and cruel!

CHRISTIAN   I am weary of carrying about, in my own self, a rival!

CYRANO   Christian!

CHRISTIAN   Our marriage . . . contracted without witnesses . . . can be annulled . . . if we survive!

CYRANO   He persists! . . .

CHRISTIAN   Yes. I will be loved for my sole self, or not at all!—I am going to see what they are about. Look! I will walk to the end of the line and back . . . Tell her, and let her pronounce between us.

CYRANO   She will pronounce for you.

CHRISTIAN   I can but hope she will! [*calling*] Roxane!

CYRANO   No! No!

ROXANE [*coming forward*]   What is it?

CHRISTIAN   Cyrano has something to tell you . . . something important!

[*ROXANE goes hurriedly to CYRANO. Exit CHRISTIAN.*]

SCENE X

Roxane, Cyrano, then Le Bret, Carbon de Castel-Jaloux, the Cadets, Ragueneau, De Guiche, etc.

ROXANE   Something important?

CYRANO [*distracted*]   He is gone! . . . [*To* ROXANE.] Nothing whatever! He attaches—but you must know him of old!—he attaches importance to trifles . . .

ROXANE [*quickly*]   He did not believe what I told him a moment ago? . . . I saw that he did not believe . . .

CYRANO [*taking her hand*]   But did you in very truth tell him the truth?

ROXANE   Yes. Yes. I should love him even . . . [*She hesitates a second.*]

CYRANO [*smiling sadly*]   You do not like to say it before me?

ROXANE   But . . .

CYRANO   I shall not mind! . . . Even if he were ugly?

ROXANE   Yes . . . Ugly. [*Musket shots outside.*] They are firing!

CYRANO [*ardently*]   Dreadfully ugly?

ROXANE   Dreadfully.

CYRANO   Disfigured?

ROXANE   Disfigured!

CYRANO   Grotesque?

ROXANE   Nothing could make him grotesque . . . to me.

CYRANO   You would love him still?

ROXANE   I believe that I should love him more . . . if that were possible!

CYRANO [*losing his head, aside*]   My God, perhaps she means it . . . perhaps it is true . . . and that way is happiness! [*To* ROX-ANE.] I . . . Roxane . . . listen!

LE BRET [*comes in hurriedly; calls softly*]   Cyrano!

CYRANO [*turning*]   Hein?

LE BRET   Hush! [*He whispers a few words to* CYRANO.]

CYRANO [*letting* ROXANE'*s hand drop, with a cry*]   Ah! . . .

ROXANE   What ails you?

CYRANO [*to himself, in consternation*]   It is finished!
   [*Musket reports.*]

ROXANE   What is it? What is happening? Who is firing? [*She goes to the back to look off.*]

CYRANO   It is finished. . . . My lips are sealed for evermore!
   [CADETS *come in, attempting to conceal something they carry among them; they surround it, preventing* ROXANE'S *seeing it.*]

ROXANE   What has happened?

CYRANO [*quickly stopping her as she starts toward them*]   Nothing!

ROXANE   These men? . . .

CYRANO [*drawing her away*]   Pay no attention to them!

ROXANE   But what were you about to say to me before?

CYRANO   What was I about to say? . . . Oh, nothing! . . . Nothing whatever, I assure you. [*Solemnly.*] I swear that Christian's spirit, that his soul, were . . . [*in terror, correcting himself*] are the greatest that . . .

ROXANE   Were? . . . [*With a great cry.*] Ah! . . . [*Runs to the group of* CADETS, *and thrusts them aside.*]

CYRANO   It is finished!

ROXANE [*seeing* CHRISTIAN *stretched out in his cloak*]   Christian!

LE BRET [*to* CYRANO]   At the enemy's first shot!

[ROXANE throws herself on CHRISTIAN'S body. Musket reports. Clashing of swords. Tramping. Drums.]

CARBON *[sword in hand]*   The attack! To your muskets! *[Followed by the* CADETS *he goes to the further side of the earthworks.]*

ROXANE   Christian!

CARBON'S VOICE *[beyond the earthworks]*   Make haste!

ROXANE   Christian!

CARBON   Fall into line!

ROXANE   Christian!

CARBON   Measure . . . match!

[RAGUENEAU has come running in with water in a steel cap.]

CHRISTIAN *[in a dying voice]*   Roxane!

CYRANO *[quick, low in CHRISTIAN's ear, while ROXANE, distracted, dips into the water a fragment of linen torn from her breast to bind his wound]* I have told her everything! . . . You are still the one she loves!

[CHRISTIAN closes his eyes.]

ROXANE   What, dear love?

CARBON   Muzzle . . . high!

ROXANE *[to CYRANO]*   He is not dead? . . .

CARBON   Open charge . . . with teeth!

ROXANE   I feel his cheek grow cold against my own!

CARBON   Take aim!

ROXANE   A letter on his breast. . . . *[She opens it.]* To me!

CYRANO *[aside]*   My letter!

CARBON   Fire!

[Musket shots. Cries. Roar of battle.]

CYRANO *[trying to free his hand which ROXANE clasps kneeling]*   But, Roxane, they are fighting.

ROXANE *[clinging]*   No! . . . Stay with me a little! . . . He is dead. You are the only one that truly knew him. . . . *[She cries subduedly.]* Was he not an exquisite being, . . . an exceptional, marvellous being? . . .

CYRANO *[standing bareheaded]*   Yes. Roxane.

ROXANE   A poet without his peer, . . . one verily to reverence?

CYRANO   Yes, Roxane.

ROXANE   A sublime spirit?

CYRANO   Yes, Roxane.

ROXANE   A profound heart, such as the profane could never have understood . . . a soul as noble as it was charming? . . .

CYRANO [*firmly*]   Yes, Roxane.

ROXANE [*throwing herself on* CHRISTIAN's *body*]   And he is dead!

CYRANO [*aside, drawing his sword*]   And I have now only to die, since, without knowing it, she mourns my death in his!
[*Trumpets in the distance.*]

DE GUICHE [*reappears on the top of the bank, bareheaded, his forehead bloody; in a thundering voice*]   The signal they promised! The flourish of trumpets! . . . The French are entering the camp with supplies! . . . Stand fast a little longer!

ROXANE   Upon his letter . . . blood, . . . tears!

A VOICE [*outside, shouting*]   Surrender!

VOICES OF THE CADETS   No!

RAGUENEAU [*who from the top of the coach is watching the battle beyond the bank*]   The conflict rages hotter! . . .

CYRANO [*to* DE GUICHE *pointing at* ROXANE]   Take her away! . . . I am going to charge.

ROXANE [*kissing the letter, in a dying voice*]   His blood! . . . his tears!

RAGUENEAU [*leaping from the coach and running to* ROXANE]   She is fainting!

DE GUICHE [*at the top of the bank, to the* CADETS, *madly*]   Stand fast!

VOICE [*outside*]   Surrender!

VOICES OF THE CADETS   No!

CYRANO [*to* DE GUICHE]   Your courage none will question . . . [*Pointing at* ROXANE.] Fly for the sake of saving her!

DE GUICHE [*Runs to* ROXANE *and lifts her in his arms*]   So be it! But we shall win the day if you can hold out a little longer . . .

CYRANO   We can. [*To* ROXANE, *whom* DE GUICHE, *helped by*
RAGUENEAU, *is carrying off insensible.*] Good-bye, Roxane!
[*Tumult. Cries.* CADETS *reappear, wounded, and fall upon the stage.*
CYRANO *dashing forward to join the combatants is stopped on the crest
of the bank by* CARBON *covered with blood.*]

CARBON   We are losing ground . . . I have got two halberd
wounds . . .

CYRANO [*yelling to the* GASCONS]   Steadfast! . . . Never give
them an inch! . . . Brave boys! [*To CARBON.*] Fear nothing! I have
various deaths to avenge: Christian's and all my hopes'! [*They
come down.* CYRANO *brandishes the spear at the head of which* ROX-
ANE'*s handkerchief is fastened.*] Float free, little cobweb flag, em-
broidered with her initials! [*He drives the spear-staff into the earth;
shouts to the* CADETS.] Fall on them, boys! . . . Crush them! [*To
the fifer.*] Fifer, play!
[*The fifer plays. Some of the wounded get to their feet again. Some of the
CADETS, coming down the bank, group themselves around* CYRANO *and
the little flag. The coach, filled and covered with men, bristles with muskets and becomes a redoubt.*]

ONE OF THE CADETS [*appears upon the top of the bank backing
while he fights; he cries*]   They are coming up the slope! [*Falls
dead.*]

CYRANO   We will welcome them!
[*Above the bank suddenly rises a formidable array of enemies. The great
banners of the Imperial Army appear.*]

CYRANO   Fire!
[*General discharge.*]

CRY [*among the hostile ranks.*] Fire!
[*Shots returned.* CADETS *drop on every side*]

A SPANISH OFFICER [*taking off his hat*]   What are these men, so determined all to be killed?

CYRANO [*declaiming, as he stands in the midst of flying bullets.*]
They are the Gascony Cadets
Of Carbon de Castel-Jaloux;

Famed fighters, liars, desperates . . .
[*He leaps forward, followed by a handful of survivors.*]
They are the Gascony Cadets! . . .
[*The rest is lost in the confusion of battle.*]
[*Curtain.*]

ACT FIVE

Cyrano's Gazette

Fifteen years later, 1655. The park belonging to the convent of the Sisters of the Cross, in Paris.

Superb shade-trees. At the left, the house; several doors opening on to broad terrace with steps. In the centre of the stage, huge trees standing alone in a clear oval space. At the right, first wing, a semicircular stone seat, surrounded by large box-trees.

All along the back of the stage, an avenue of chestnut-trees, which leads, at the right, fourth wing, to the door of a chapel seen through trees. Through the double row of trees overarching the avenue are seen lawns, other avenues, clumps of trees, the further recesses of the park, the sky.

The chapel opens by a small side-door into a colonnade, overrun by a scarlet creeper; the colonnade comes forward and is lost to sight behind the box-trees at the right.

It is Autumn. The leaves are turning, above the still fresh grass. Dark patches of evergreens, box and yew. Under each tree a mat of yellow leaves. Fallen leaves litter the whole stage, crackle underfoot, lie thick on the terrace and the seats.

Between the seat at the right and the tree in the centre, a large embroidery frame, in front of which a small chair. Baskets full of wools, in skeins and balls. On the frame, a piece of tapestry, partly done.

At the rise of the curtain, nuns come and go in the park; a few are seated on the stone seat around an older nun; leaves are falling.

SCENE I

Mother Margaret, Sister Martha, Sister Claire, other Nuns

SISTER MARTHA [*to* MOTHER MARGARET]   Sister Claire, after putting on her cap went back to the mirror, to see herself again.

MOTHER MARGARET [*to* SISTER CLAIRE]   It was unbecoming, my child.

SISTER CLAIRE   But Sister Martha, to-day, after finishing her portion, went back to the tart for a plum. I saw her!

MOTHER MARGARET [*to* SISTER MARTHA]   My child, it was ill done.

SISTER CLAIRE   I merely glanced! . . . .

SISTER MARTHA   The plum was about so big! . . .

MOTHER MARGARET   This evening, when Monsieur Cyrano comes, I will tell him.

SISTER CLAIRE [*alarmed*]   No! He will laugh at us!

SISTER MARTHA   He will say that nuns are very vain!

SISTER CLAIRE   And very greedy!

MOTHER MARGARET   And really very good.

SISTER CLAIRE   Mother Margaret, is it not true that he has come here every Saturday in the last ten years?

MOTHER MARGARET   Longer! Ever since his cousin brought among our linen coifs her coif of crape, the worldly symbol of her mourning, which settled like a sable bird amidst our flock of white some fourteen years ago.

SISTER MARTHA   He alone, since she took her abode in our cloister, has art to dispel her never-lessening sorrow.

ALL THE NUNS   He is so droll!—It is merry when he comes!—He teases us!—He is delightful!—We are greatly attached to him!—We are making Angelica paste* to offer him!

---

*Based on angelica, an aromatic root with alleged medicinal properties that is also often candied and served as a sweet.

SISTER MARTHA   He is not, however, a very good Catholic!

SISTER CLAIRE   We will convert him.

THE NUNS   We will! We will!

MOTHER MARGARET   I forbid your renewing that attempt, my children. Do not trouble him: he might not come so often!

SISTER MARTHA   But . . . God!

MOTHER MARGARET   Set your hearts at rest: God must know him of old!

SISTER MARTHA   But every Saturday, when he comes, he says to me as soon as he sees me, "Sister, I ate meat, yesterday!"

MOTHER MARGARET   Ah, that is what he says? . . . Well, when he last said it, he had eaten nothing for two days.

SISTER MARTHA   Mother!

MOTHER MARGARET   He is poor.

SISTER MARTHA   Who told you?

MOTHER MARGARET   Monsieur Le Bret.

SISTER MARTHA   Does no one offer him assistance?

MOTHER MARGARET   No, he would take offence.

[*In one of the avenues at the back, appears ROXANE, in black, wearing a widow's coif and long mourning veil; DE GUICHE, markedly older, magnificently dressed, walks beside her. They go very slowly. MOTHER MARGARET gets up.*]

MOTHER MARGARET   Come, we must go within. Madame Magdeleine is walking in the park with a visitor.

SISTER MARTHA [*low to* SISTER CLAIRE.]   Is not that the Marshalduke de Grammont?

SISTER CLAIRE [*looking*]   I think it is!

SISTER MARTHA   He has not been to see her in many months!

THE NUNS   He is much engaged!—The Court!—The Camp!—

SISTER CLAIRE   Cares of this world!

[*Exeunt. DE GUICHE and ROXANE come forward silently, and stop near the embroidery frame. A pause.*]

SCENE II

Roxane, De Guiche (now the Duke of Grammont), then Le Bret and Ragueneau

DE GUICHE   And so you live here, uselessly fair, always in mourning?

ROXANE   Always.

DE GUICHE   As faithful as of old?

ROXANE   As faithful.

DE GUICHE [*after a time*]   Have you forgiven me?

ROXANE   Since I am here.

   [*Other silence.*]

DE GUICHE   And he was really such a rare being?

ROXANE   To understand, one must have known him!

DE GUICHE   Ah, one must have known him! . . . Perhaps I did not know him well enough. And his last letter, still and always, against your heart?

ROXANE   I wear it on this velvet, as a more holy scapular.*

DE GUICHE   Even dead, you love him?

ROXANE   It seems to me sometimes he is but half dead, that our hearts have not been severed, that his love still wraps me round, no less than ever living!

DE GUICHE [*after another silence*]   Does Cyrano come here to see you?

ROXANE   Yes, often. That faithful friend fulfils by me the office of gazette. His visits are regular. He comes: when the weather is fine, his armchair is brought out under the trees. I wait for him here with my work; the hour strikes; on the last stroke, I hear—I do not even turn to see who comes!—his cane upon the steps; he takes his seat; he rallies me upon my never-ending tapestry†; he

---

*Object of devotion, often made of cloth, worn around the neck.

†Allusion to the tapestry that Penelope, wife of Ulysses, wove day in and day out.

tells off the events of the week, and . . . [LE BRET *appears on the steps*] Ah, Le Bret! [LE BRET *comes down the steps*] How does your friend?

LE BRET   Ill.

THE DUKE   Oh!

ROXANE   He exaggerates! . . .

LE BRET   All is come to pass as I foretold: neglect! poverty! his writings ever breeding him new enemies! Fraud he attacks in every embodiment: usurpers, pious pretenders, plagiarists, asses in lions' skins . . . all! He attacks all!

ROXANE   No one, however, but stands in profound respect of his sword. They will never succeed in silencing him.

DE GUICHE [*shaking his head*]   Who knows?

LE BRET   What I fear is not the aggression of man; what I fear is loneliness and want and winter creeping upon him like stealthy wolves in his miserable attic; they are the insidious foes that will have him by the throat at last! . . . Every day he tightens his belt by an eyelet; his poor great nose is pinched, and turned the sallow of old ivory; the worn black serge you see him in is the only coat he has!

DE GUICHE   Ah, there is one who did not succeed! . . . Nevertheless, do not pity him too much.

LE BRET [*with a bitter smile*]   Marshal! . . .

DE GUICHE   Do not pity him too much: he signed no bonds with the world; he has lived free in his thought as in his actions.

LE BRET [*as above*]   Duke . . .

DE GUICHE [*haughtily*]   I know, yes: I have everything, he has nothing. . . . But I should like to shake hands with him. [*Bowing to* ROXANE.] Good-bye.

ROXANE   I will go with you to the door.

[*DE GUICHE bows to LE BRET and goes with ROXANE toward the terrace steps.*]

DE GUICHE [*stopping, while she goes up the steps*]   Yes, sometimes I envy him. You see, when a man has succeeded too well in life, he is not unlikely to feel—dear me! without having committed any very serious wrong!—a multitudinous disgust of himself, the sum of which does not constitute a real remorse, but an obscure uneasiness; and a ducal mantle, while it sweeps up the stairs of greatness, may trail in its furry lining a rustling of sere illusions and regrets, as, when you slowly climb toward those doors, your black gown trails the withered leaves.

ROXANE [*ironical*]   Are you not unusually pensive? . . .

DE GUICHE   Ah, yes! [*As he is about to leave, abruptly.*]   Monsieur Le Bret! [*To* ROXANE] Will you allow me? A word. [*He goes to* LE BRET, *and lowering his voice.*] It is true that no one will dare overtly to attack your friend, but many have him in particular disrelish; and some one was saying to me yesterday, at the Queen's, "It seems not unlikely that this Cyrano will meet with an accident."

LE BRET   Ah? . . .

DE GUICHE   Yes. Let him keep indoors. Let him be cautious.

LE BRET [*lifting his arms toward Heaven*]   Cautious! . . . He is coming here. I will warn him. Warn him! . . . Yes, but . . .

ROXANE [*who has been standing at the head of the steps, to a nun who comes toward her*]   What is it?

THE NUN   Ragueneau begs to see you, Madame.

ROXANE   Let him come in. [*To* DE GUICHE *and* LE BRET.] He comes to plead distress. Having determined one day to be an author, he became in turn precentor . . .*

LE BRET   Bath-house keeper . . .

ROXANE   Actor . . .

LE BRET   Beadle . . .

ROXANE   Barber . . .

LE BRET   Arch-lute teacher . . .

ROXANE   I wonder what he is now!

---

*Choirmaster.

RAGUENEAU [*entering precipitately*]   Ah, Madame! [*He sees* LE
BRET.] Monsieur!

ROXANE [*smiling*]   Begin telling your misfortunes to Le Bret. I am
coming back.

RAGUENEAU   But, Madame . . .

[*ROXANE leaves without listening, with the* DUKE. *RAGUENEAU goes
to* LE BRET]

SCENE III

Le Bret, Ragueneau

RAGUENEAU   It is better so. Since you are here, I had liefer not tell
her! Less than half an hour ago, I was going to see your friend. I
was not thirty feet from his door, when I saw him come out. I hurried to catch up with him. He was about to turn the corner. I
started to run, when from a window below which he was passing—was it pure mischance? It may have been!—a lackey drops a
block of wood . . .

LE BRET   Ah, the cowards! . . . Cyrano!

RAGUENEAU   I reach the spot, and find him . . .

LE BRET   Horrible!

RAGUENEAU   Our friend, Monsieur, our poet, stretched upon the
ground, with a great hole in his head!

LE BRET   He is dead?

RAGUENEAU   No, but . . . God have mercy! I carried him to his
lodging . . . Ah, his lodging! You should see that lodging of his!

LE BRET   Is he in pain?

RAGUENEAU   No, Monsieur, he is unconscious.

LE BRET   Has a doctor seen him?

RAGUENEAU   One came . . . out of good nature.

LE BRET   My poor, poor Cyrano! . . . We must not tell Roxane
outright. And the doctor?

RAGUENEAU He talked . . . I hardly grasped . . . of fever . . . cerebral inflammation! Ah, if you should see him, with his head done up in cloths! . . . Let us hurry . . . No one is there to tend him . . . And he might die if he attempted to get up!

LE BRET [*dragging* RAGUENEAU *off at the right*] This way. Come, it is shorter through the chapel.

ROXANE [*appearing at the head of the steps, catching sight of* LE BRET *hurrying off through the colonnade which leads to the chapel side-door*] Monsieur Le Bret! [LE BRET *and* RAGUENEAU *make their escape without answering.*] Le Bret not turning back when he is called? . . . Poor Ragueneau must be in some new trouble! [*She comes down the steps.*]

SCENE IV

Roxane, alone, then briefly two Sisters

ROXANE How beautiful . . . how beautiful, this golden-hazy waning day of September at its wane! My sorrowful mood, which the exuberant gladness of April offends, Autumn, the dreamy and subdued, lures on to smile . . . [*She sits down at her embroidery frame. Two NUNS come from the house bringing a large armchair which they place under the tree.*] Ah, here comes the classic armchair in which my old friend always sits!

SISTER MARTHA The best in the convent parlor!

ROXANE I thank you, sister. [*The nuns withdraw.*] He will be here in a moment. [*She adjusts the embroidery frame before her.*] There! The clock is striking . . . My wools! . . . The clock has struck? . . . I wonder at this! . . . Is it possible that for the first time he is late? . . . It must be that the sister who keeps the door . . . my thimble? ah, here it is! . . . is detaining him to exhort him to repentance . . . [*A pause.*] She exhorts him at some length! . . . He cannot be much longer . . . A withered leaf! [*She brushes away the dead leaf which has dropped on the embroidery.*] Surely nothing could keep . . . My scissors? . . . in my workbag! . . . could keep him from coming!

A NUN [*appearing at the head of the steps*]   Monsieur de Bergerac!

SCENE V

Roxane, Cyrano, briefly Sister Martha

ROXANE [*without turning round*]   What was I saying? . . . [*She begins to embroider. CYRANO appears, exceedingly pale, his hat drawn down over his eyes. The NUN who has shown him into the garden, withdraws. He comes down the steps very slowly, with evident difficulty to keep on his feet, leaning heavily on his cane. ROXANE proceeds with her sewing.*] Ah, these dull soft shades! . . . How shall I match them? [*To CYRANO, in a tone of friendly chiding.*] After fourteen years, for the first time you are late!

CYRANO [*who has reached the armchair and seated himself, in a jolly voice which contrasts with his face.*]   Yes, it seems incredible! I am savage at it. I was detained, spite of all I could do! . . .

ROXANE   By? . . .

CYRANO   A somewhat inopportune call.

ROXANE [*absent-minded, sewing*]   Ah, yes . . . some troublesome fellow!

CYRANO   Cousin, it was a troublesome Madam.

ROXANE   You excused yourself?

CYRANO   Yes. I said, "Your pardon, but this is Saturday, on which day I am due in certain dwelling. On no account do I ever fail. Come back in an hour!"

ROXANE [*lightly*]   Well, she will have to wait some time to see you. I shall not let you go before evening.

CYRANO   Perhaps . . . I shall have to go a little earlier. [*He closes his eyes and is silent a moment.*]

[*SISTER MARTHA is seen crossing the park from the chapel to the terrace. ROXANE sees her and beckons to her by a slight motion of her head.*]

ROXANE [*to* CYRANO]   Are you not going to tease Sister Martha
to-day?

CYRANO [*quickly, opening his eyes*]   I am indeed! [*In a comically
gruff voice.*] Sister Martha, come nearer! [*The* NUN *demurely
comes toward him.*] Ha! ha! ha! Beautiful eyes, ever studying the
ground!

SISTER MARTHA [*lifting her eyes and smiling*]   But . . . [*She sees his
face and makes a gesture of surprise*] Oh!

CYRANO [*low, pointing at* ROXANE]   Hush! . . . It is nothing! [*In a
swaggering voice, aloud.*] Yesterday, I ate meat!

SISTER MARTHA   I am sure you did! [*Aside.*] That is why he is so
pale! [*Quickly, low.*] Come to the refectory presently. I shall have
ready for you there a good bowl of broth . . . You will come!

CYRANO   Yes, yes, yes.

SISTER MARTHA   Ah, you are more reasonable to-day!

ROXANE [*hearing them whisper*]   She is trying to convert you?

SISTER MARTHA   Indeed I am not!

CYRANO   It is true, you, usually almost discursive in the holy cause,
are reading me no sermon! You amaze me! [*With comical fury.*] I
will amaze you, too! Listen, you are authorized . . . [*With the air
of casting about in his mind, and finding the jest he wants.*] Ah, now I
shall amaze you! to . . . pray for me, this evening . . . in the
chapel.

ROXANE   Oh! oh!

CYRANO [*laughing*]   Sister Martha . . . lost in amazement!

SISTER MARTHA [*gently*]   I did not wait for your authorization. [*She
goes in.*]

CYRANO [*turning to* ROXANE, *who is bending over her embroidery*]
The devil, tapestry . . . the devil, if I hope to live to see the end
of you!

ROXANE   I was waiting for that jest.
[*A slight gust of wind makes the leaves fall.*]

CYRANO   The leaves!

ROXANE [*looking up from her work and gazing off toward the avenues*]

They are the russet gold of a Venetian beauty's hair . . . Watch them fall!

CYRANO   How consummately they do it! In that brief fluttering from bough to ground, how they contrive still to put beauty! And though foredoomed to moulder upon the earth that draws them, they wish their fall invested with the grace of a free bird's flight!

ROXANE   Serious, you?

CYRANO [*remembering himself*]   Not at all, Roxane!

ROXANE   Come, never mind the falling leaves! Tell me the news, instead . . . Where is my budget?*

CYRANO   Here it is!

ROXANE   Ah!

CYRANO [*growing paler and paler, and struggling with pain*]   Saturday, the nineteenth: The king having filled his dish eight times with Cette† preserves, and emptied it, was taken with a fever; his distemper, for high treason, was condemned to be let blood, and now the royal pulse is rid of febriculosity! On Sunday: at the Queen's great ball, were burned seven hundred and sixty-three wax candles; our troops, it is said, defeated Austrian John;‡ four sorcerers were hanged; Madame Athis's little dog had a distressing turn, the case called for a . . .

ROXANE   Monsieur de Bergerac, leave out the little dog!

CYRANO   Monday, . . . nothing, or next to it: Lygdamire took a fresh lover.

ROXANE   Oh!

CYRANO [*over whose face is coming a change more and more marked*]   Tuesday: the whole Court assembled at Fontainebleau. Wednesday, the fair Monglat said to Count Fiesco "No!" Thursday, Mancini, Queen of France, . . . or little less. Twenty-fifth, the

---

*Common title for a newspaper or gazette; for example, the *Pall Mall Budget*.
†Old spelling for Sète, a town in southern France on the Mediterranean.
‡Reference to Don Juan of Austria, viceroy of the Netherlands, defeated during the Thirty Years War in 1658 by the great French commander the vicomte de Turenne.

fair Monglat said to Count Fiesco "Yes!" And Saturday, the twenty-sixth . . . [*He closes his eyes. His head drops on his breast. Silence.*]

ROXANE [*surprised at hearing nothing further, turns, looks at him and starts to her feet in alarm*]   Has he fainted? [*She runs to him, calling.*] Cyrano!

CYRANO [*opening his eyes, in a faint voice*]   What is it? . . . What is the matter! [*He sees* ROXANE *bending over him, hurriedly readjusts his hat, pulling it more closely over his head, and shrinks back in his armchair in terror*] No! no! I assure you, it is nothing! . . . Do not mind me!

ROXANE   But surely . . .

CYRANO   It is merely the wound I received at Arras . . . Sometimes . . . you know . . . even now . . .

ROXANE   Poor friend!

CYRANO   But it is nothing . . . It will pass . . . [*He smiles with effort*] It has passed.

ROXANE   Each one of us has his wound: I too have mine. It is here, never to heal, that ancient wound . . . [*She places her hand on her breast.*] It is here, beneath the yellowing letter on which are still faintly visible tear-drops and drops of blood!

[*The light is beginning to grow less*]

CYRANO   His letter? . . . Did you not once say that some day . . . you might show it to me?

ROXANE   Ah! . . . Do you wish? . . . His letter?

CYRANO   Yes . . . to-day . . . I wish to . . .

ROXANE [*handing him the little bag from her neck*]   Here!

CYRANO   I may open it?

ROXANE   Open it . . . read! [*She goes back to her embroidery frame, folds it up, orders her wools.*]

CYRANO   "Good-bye, Roxane! I am going to die!"

ROXANE [*stopping in astonishment*]   You are reading it aloud?

CYRANO [*reading*]   "It is fated to come this evening, beloved, I believe! My soul is heavy, oppressed with love it had not time to utter . . . and now Time is at end! Never again, never again shall my worshipping eyes . . ."

ROXANE   How strangely you read his letter!

CYRANO [*continuing*]   ". . . whose passionate revel it was, kiss in its fleeting grace your every gesture. One, usual to you, of tucking back a little curl, comes to my mind . . . and I cannot refrain from crying out . . .

ROXANE   How strangely you read his letter! . . .

[*The darkness gradually increases*]

CYRANO   "and I cry out: Good-bye!"

ROXANE   You read it . . .

CYRANO   "my dearest, my darling, . . . my treasure . . ."

ROXANE   . . . in a voice . . .

CYRANO   ". . . my love! . . ."

ROXANE   . . . in a voice . . . a voice which I am not hearing for the first time!

[*ROXANE comes quietly nearer to him, without his seeing it; she steps behind his armchair, bends noiselessly over his shoulder, looks at the letter. The darkness deepens.*]

CYRANO   ". . . My heart never desisted for a second from your side . . . and I am and shall be in the world that has no end, the one who loved you without measure, the one . . ."

ROXANE [*laying her hand on his shoulder*]   How can you go on reading? It is dark. [CYRANO *starts, and turns round; sees her close to him, makes a gesture of dismay and hangs his head. Then, in the darkness which has completely closed round them, she says slowly, clasping her hands.*] And he, for fourteen years, has played the part of the comical old friend who came to cheer me!

CYRANO   Roxane!

ROXANE   So it was you.

CYRANO   No, no, Roxane!

ROXANE   I ought to have divined it, if only by the way in which he speaks my name!

CYRANO   No, it was not I!

ROXANE   So it was you!

CYRANO   I swear to you . . .

ROXANE   Ah, I detect at last the whole generous imposture: The
     letters . . . were yours!

CYRANO   No!

ROXANE   The tender fancy, the dear folly. . . . yours!

CYRANO   No!

ROXANE   The voice in the night, was yours!

CYRANO   I swear to you that it was not!

ROXANE   The soul . . . was yours!

CYRANO   I did not love you, no!

ROXANE   And you loved me!

CYRANO   Not I . . . it was the other!

ROXANE   You loved me!

CYRANO   No!

ROXANE   Already your denial comes more faintly!

CYRANO   No, no, my darling love, I did not love you!

ROXANE   Ah, how many things within the hour have died . . . how
     many have been born! Why, why have you been silent these long
     years, when on this letter, in which he had no part, the tears were
     yours?

CYRANO [*handing her the letter*]   Because . . . the blood was his.

ROXANE   Then why let the sublime bond of this silence be loosed
     to-day?

CYRANO   Why?

     [*LE BRET and RAGUENEAU enter running.*]

SCENE VI

The Same, Le Bret and Ragueneau

LE BRET   Madness! Monstrous madness! . . . Ah, I was sure of it!
     There he is!

CYRANO [*smiling and straightening himself*]   *Tiens!* Where else?

LE BRET   Madame, he is likely to have got his death by getting out of bed!

ROXANE   Merciful God! A moment ago, then . . . that faintness . . . that . . . ?

CYRANO   It is true. I had not finished telling you the news. And on Saturday, the twenty-sixth, an hour after sundown, Monsieur de Bergerac died of murder done upon him. [*He takes off his hat; his head is seen wrapped in bandages.*]

ROXANE   What is he saying? . . . Cyrano? . . . Those bandages about his head? . . . Ah, what have they done to you? . . . Why? . . .

CYRANO   "Happy who falls, cut off by a hero, with an honest sword through his heart!" I am quoting from myself! . . . Fate will have his laugh at us! . . . Here am I killed, in a trap, from behind, by a lackey, with a log! Nothing could be completer! In my whole life I shall have not had anything I wanted . . . not even a decent death!

RAGUENEAU   Ah, monsieur! . . .

CYRANO   Ragueneau, do not sob like that! [*Holding out his hand to him.*] And what is the news with you, these latter days, fellow-poet?

RAGUENEAU [*through his tears*]   I am candle-snuffer at Molière's theatre.

CYRANO   Molière!

RAGUENEAU   But I intend to leave no later than to-morrow. Yes, I am indignant! Yesterday, they were giving Scapin, and I saw that he has appropriated a scene of yours.*

LE BRET   A whole scene?

RAGUENEAU   Yes, monsieur. The one in which occurs the famous "What the devil was he doing in . . ."

---

*Les Fourberies de Scapin (The Cheats of Scapin, 1677), by the great French playwright Molière (1622–1673), contains a line that seems borrowed from Cyrano de Bergerac's play Le Pédant joué (The Pedant Imitated).

LE BRET   Molière has taken that from you!

CYRANO   Hush! hush! He did well to take it! [*To* RAGUENEAU.] The scene was very effective, was it not?

RAGUENEAU   Ah, monsieur, the public laughed . . . laughed!

CYRANO   Yes, to the end, I shall have been the one who prompted . . . and was forgotten! [*To* ROXANE.] Do you remember that evening on which Christian spoke to you from below the balcony? There was the epitome of my life: while I have stood below in darkness, others have climbed to gather the kiss and glory! It is well done, and on the brink of my grave I approve it: Molière has genius . . . Christian was a fine fellow! [*At this moment, the chapel bell having rung, the NUNS are seen passing at the back, along the avenue, on their way to service.*] Let them hasten to their prayers . . . the bell is summoning them . . .

ROXANE [*rising and calling*]   Sister! Sister!

CYRANO [*holding her back*]   No! No! do not leave me to fetch anybody! When you come back I might not be here to rejoice . . . [*The NUNS have gone into the chapel; the organ is heard.*] I longed for a little music . . . it comes in time!

ROXANE   I love you . . . you shall live!

CYRANO   No! for it is only in the fairy-tale that the shy and awkward prince when he hears the beloved say "I love you!" feels his ungainliness melt and drop from him in the sunshine of those words! . . . But you would always know full well, dear Heart, that there had taken place in your poor slave no beautifying change!

ROXANE   I have hurt you . . . I have wrecked your life, I! . . . I!

CYRANO   You? . . . The reverse! Woman's sweetness I had never known. My mother . . . thought me unflattering. I had no sister. Later, I shunned Love's cross-road in fear of mocking eyes. To you I owe having had, at least, among the gentle and fair, a friend. Thanks to you there has passed across my life the rustle of a woman's gown.

LE BRET [*calling his attention to the moonlight peering through the*

branches]   Your other friend, among the gentle and fair, is
there . . . she comes to see you!

CYRANO [*smiling to the moon*]   I see her!

ROXANE   I never loved but one . . . and twice I lose him!

CYRANO   Le Bret, I shall ascend into the opalescent moon, without
need this time of a flying-machine!

ROXANE   What are you saying?

CYRANO   Yes, it is there, you may be sure, I shall be sent for my
Paradise. More than one soul of those I have loved must be ap-
portioned there . . . There I shall find Socrates and Galileo!

LE BRET [*in revolt*]   No! No! It is too senseless, too cruel, too unfair!
So true a poet! So great a heart! To die . . . like this! To die! . . .

CYRANO   As ever . . . Le Bret is grumbling!

LE BRET [*bursting into tears*]   My friend! My friend!

CYRANO [*lifting himself, his eyes wild*]   They are the Gascony
Cadets! . . . Man in the gross . . . Eh, yes! . . . the weakness of
the weakest point . . .

LE BRET   Learned . . . even in his delirium! . . .

CYRANO   Copernicus said . . .

ROXANE   Oh!

CYRANO   But what the devil was he doing . . . and what the devil
was he doing in that galley?

> Philosopher and physicist,
> Musician, rhymester, duellist,
> Explorer of the upper blue,
> Retorter apt with point and point,
> Lover as well,—not for his peace!
> Here lies Hercule Savinien
> De Cyrano de Bergerac,
> Who was everything . . . but of account!*

---

*In French, *Qui fut tout, et qui ne fut rien*, which translates literally as "Who was everything, and who was nothing"; that is, he was of no account.

But, your pardons, I must go . . . I wish to keep no one waiting . . . See, a moon-beam, come to take me home! [*He has dropped in his chair; ROXANE's weeping calls him back to reality; he looks at her and gently stroking her mourning veil.*] I do not wish . . . indeed, I do not wish . . . that you should sorrow less for Christian, the comely and the kind! Only I wish that when the everlasting cold shall have seized upon my fibres, this funereal veil should have a twofold meaning, and the mourning you wear for him be worn for me too . . . a little!

ROXANE   I promise . . .

CYRANO [*seized with a great shivering, starts to his feet*]   Not there! No! Not in an elbow-chair! [*All draw nearer to help him.*] Let no one stay me! No one! [*He goes and stands against the tree.*] Nothing but this tree! [*Silence.*] She comes, Mors, the indiscriminate Madam! . . . Already I am booted with marble . . . gauntleted with lead! [*He stiffens himself.*] Ah, since she is on her way, I will await her standing . . . [*He draws his sword.*] Sword in hand!

LE BRET   Cyrano!

ROXANE [*swooning*]   Cyrano!

[*All start back, terrified.*]

CYRANO   I believe she is looking at me . . . that she dares to look at my nose, the bony baggage who has none! [*He raises his sword.*] What are you saying? That it is no use? . . . I know it! But one does not fight because there is hope of winning! No! . . . no! . . . it is much finer to fight when it is no use! . . . What are all those? You are a thousand strong? . . . Ah, I know you now . . . all my ancient enemies! . . . Hypocrisy? . . . [*He beats with his sword, in the vacancy.*] Take this! And this! Ha! Ha! Compromises? . . . and Prejudices? and dastardly Expedients? [*He strikes.*] That I should come to terms, I? . . . Never! Never! . . . Ah, you are there too, you, bloated and pompous Silliness! I know full well that you will lay me low at last . . . No matter: whilst I have breath, I will fight you, I will fight you, I will fight you! [*He waves his sword in great sweeping circles, and stops, panting.*] Yes, you have wrested from me everything, laurel as well as rose . . . Work your wills! . . . Spite of your worst, something will still be left me to take whither I go . . . and to-night when I enter God's house, in saluting, broadly will I sweep the azure threshold with what despite of all I carry forth unblemished and unbent . . . [*He starts forward, with lifted sword.*] . . . and that is . . . [*The sword falls from his hands, he staggers, drops in the arms of* LE BRET *and* RAGUENEAU.]

ROXANE [*bending over him and kissing his forehead*]   That is? . . .

CYRANO [*opens his eyes again, recognizes her and says with a smile*]   . . .
My plume!

[*Curtain.*]

Inspired by
CYRANO DE BERGERAC

Edmond Rostand's beloved tragicomic character has inspired other works almost from the moment he appeared on the Paris stage for the first time in 1897.

MUSIC

Cyrano de Bergerac has been transliterated into many musical forms— from Dutch composer Johan Wagenaar's fourteen-minute Overture to *Cyrano de Bergerac*, Opus 23 (1905), to Estonian composer Eino Tamberg's opera (1974) called, not surprisingly, *Cyrano de Bergerac*. In fact, in 1899, just two years after Rostand's play opened in France, Victor Herbert's comic operetta *Cyrano de Bergerac* premiered on Broadway. The three-act work, with a book by Stuart Reed, portrays the nasally endowed hero as particularly boastful, playing up Cyrano's roosterly theatricality.

American composer Walter Damrosch wrote an opera, *Cyrano*, in 1913, and Italian composer Franco Alfano also brought the story into the opera house, with his 1936 *Cyrano de Bergerac*, in which the soft, spare, intricate music is reminiscent of Maurice Ravel and Claude Debussy, and in which Cyrano, a tenor, proffers a memorable, whispered serenade to his cousin Roxane in a balcony scene.

In 1971 Anthony Burgess, author of the novel *A Clockwork Orange* (1962), translated *Cyrano* into book and lyrics, composed incidental music, and created a wholly original musical. This acclaimed production led to a Broadway version starring Christopher Plummer, with new music composed by Michael J. Lewis. *Cyrano de Bergerac*, in two acts, opened on Broadway on May 13, 1973, and lasted for forty-nine performances.

FILM

Cyrano has been filmed a number of times. The screen versions include a silent production in 1925 starring Pierre Magnier and Michael Gordon's 1950 version starring José Ferrer, for which the latter received an Oscar. (Orson Wells was apparently interested in making a version of it but abandoned the project in 1947.) But it was 1987's *Roxanne*, starring Steve Martin, that brought *Cyrano* to life for contemporary audiences. Directed by Fred Schepisi (*Six Degrees of Separation*) and adapted by Martin, *Roxanne* is a latter-day retelling of *Cyrano* that sparkles with all of Rostand's rapier wit and florid romance while remaining faithful to the core of Rostand's play.

Hot on the heels of audiences' love for *Roxanne*, the French reclaimed a national treasure with *Cyrano de Bergerac* (1990), starring Gérard Depardieu. Directed by Jean-Paul Rappeneau, *Cyrano de Bergerac* is a lavish seventeenth-century costume epic and one of the most expensive productions in the history of French cinema. The script as adapted by Rappeneau and Jean-Claude Carriére strives to maintain Rostand's original verse, and the international version is subtitled with Anthony Burgess's droll rhymes.

COMMENTS & QUESTIONS

In this section, we aim to provide the reader with an array of perspectives on the text, as well as questions that challenge those perspectives. The commentary has been culled from sources as diverse as reviews contemporaneous with the work, letters written by the author, literary criticism of later generations, and appreciations written throughout the work's history. Following the commentary, a series of questions seeks to filter Edmond Rostand's Cyrano de Bergerac *through a variety of points of view and bring about a richer understanding of this enduring work.*

COMMENTS

Gertrude Hall

Cyrano is so comprehensible! To Cyrano the world he lives in must be filled with striking generous deeds and sounding generous phrases. The world is slow in performing the first, so he performs them himself. Then, the care of exalting them cannot be left with the world, afflicted with dullness as with slowness, so he talks about them. I am sure Cyrano cares very little that himself should be in question. He merely wishes fine deeds and fine sentiments to be, and to make surest and shortest work, furnishes them himself. It is very innocent.

On the other hand, I fancy it impossible to follow the whole play and not get the contagion of Cyrano's generosity. . . . When that night he entered God's house, and, in saluting, broadly swept the azure threshold with his very clean plume, what eloquent and touching tirade must he have made to Gascony Cadets in bliss, at the sure vision of his fighting not having been in vain, of his having inspired others—(remote audiences in America, among them)—to detest and fight the ancient enemies that were his: Lies, Compromises,

Prejudices, base Expedients,—the whole multitude of things ugly
and petty!

—from her Introduction to *Cyrano de Bergerac* (1910)

T. S. Eliot

In plays of realism we often find parts which are never allowed to be
consciously dramatic, for fear, perhaps, of their appearing less real.
But in actual life, in many of those situations in actual life which we
enjoy consciously and keenly, we are at times aware of ourselves in
this way, and these moments are of very great usefulness to dramatic
verse. A very small part of acting is that which takes place on the
stage! Rostand had—whether he had anything else or not—this dramatic sense, and it is what gives life to Cyrano. It is a sense which is
almost a sense of humour (for when anyone is conscious of himself as
acting, something like a sense of humour is present). It gives Rostand's characters—Cyrano at least—a gusto which is uncommon on
the modern stage. No doubt Rostand's people play up to this too
steadily. We recognize that in the love scenes of Cyrano in the garden,
for in *Romeo and Juliet* the profounder dramatist shows his lovers
melting into incoherent unconsciousness of their isolated selves,
shows the human soul in the process of forgetting itself. Rostand
could not do that; but in the particular case of Cyrano on Noses, the
character, the situation, the occasion were perfectly suited and com-
bined. The tirade generated by this combination is not only genuinely
and highly dramatic: it is possibly poetry also. If a writer is incapable
of composing such a scene as this, so much the worse for his poetic
drama.

Cyrano satisfies, as far as scenes like this can satisfy, the require-
ments of poetic drama. It must take genuine and substantial human
emotions, such emotions as observation can confirm, typical emotions, and give them artistic form; the degree of abstraction is a question for the method of each author. In Shakespeare the form is
determined in the unity of the whole, as well as single scenes; it is

something to attain this unity, as Rostand does, in scenes if not the whole play.

—from *The Sacred Wood: Essays on Poetry and Criticism* (1920)

The Nation

Rostand is preeminently a poet of sentiment. He has fancy rather than imagination; delicacy and charm rather than passion. He belongs to that great band of lesser French geniuses, such as Charles d'Orléans, Du Bellay, Voiture, and, among the moderns, Banville, Coppée, and Régnier—the poets of a silver rather than golden Latinity. For him sunlight and shadow flit across the earth's rough surface, and the playful, optimistic mood of the poet is admirably attuned to express them.

On the other hand, what Rostand lacks in originality and depth of thought he possesses in brilliancy and mastery of style. Except for Cyrano, he can scarcely be said to have created a real character; but he can spin a dramatic situation out of a mere physical or moral detail, he can lift his audiences out of themselves by a succession of scintillating images, and in one respect his style is a continuous creation—namely, in the "cliquetis des mots" or the humorous portrayal of moods through the mere clash and jingle of words.

—May 17, 1922

QUESTIONS

1. In literature, improbabilities (such as Polyphemous, the one-eyed giant in the *Odyssey*) often serve as metaphors or allegories for something metaphysical or psychological or moral. What are the improbabilities in *Cyrano*—certainly the character's nose is one— and do you think they work? Why? And what purpose do they serve?

2. One often hears of great men and women whose accomplishments seem to be compensations for some lack or defect: a failed

father, an unloving mother, short stature, poverty. Cyrano's panache is his great achievement. Do you think he has developed this quality in compensation for his unattractive nose? If so, what sort of clues does the play provide?

3. What can be made of the friendship between Christian and Cyrano? Without the goal of wooing Roxane, would they be friends at all? Are they alter egos—that is, is there any Christian in Cyrano or Cyrano in Christian?

4. Is Roxane worth the fuss made over her? Is she a heroic character in any way?

5. Would it be possible for a man like Cyrano to exist and flourish today—with his panache intact? What are some of the things he might set out to do in today's world?

FOR FURTHER READING

OTHER WORKS BY EDMOND ROSTAND

Le Gant rouge (*The Red Glove*), 1889
Les Romanesques (*The Romancers*), 1894
L'Aiglon (*The Eaglet*), 1900
Chantecler (1910)
La Dernière Nuit de Don Juan (*The Last Night of Don Juan*), published
posthumously in 1921

WORKS BY THE HISTORICAL CYRANO DE BERGERAC

La Mort d'Agrippine (*The Death of Agrippine*), 1654
Le Pédant joué (*The Pedant Imitated*), 1654
Histoire comique des états et empires de la lune (*Comical History of the States
and Empires of the Moon*), 1657
Histoire comique des états et empires du soleil (*Comical History of the States
and Empires of the Moon*), 1662

ENGLISH TRANSLATIONS OF *CYRANO DE BERGERAC*

Translated by Lowell Bair. New York: New American Library, 1972.
With an afterword by Henry Hewes. Excellent unrhymed translation; commentary in the afterword on various stage productions
and translations of *Cyrano* into English.
Translated by Anthony Burgess. New York: Applause Theatre and Cinema Books, 1998. This version by the British novelist was used by
Derek Jacobi for the Royal Shakespeare Company's *Cyrano* in

1983, as well as for the subtitles in Jean-Paul Rappeneau's French film version.

Translated by Christopher Fry. Oxford and New York: Oxford University Press, 1996. Introduction and notes by Nicholas Cronk. A rhyming—more precisely, "chiming"—verse translation. The excellent introduction places Rostand in his literary and historical context.

Translated by Brian Hooker. New York: Bantam Classics, 1981. Good verse translation made at the request of American Shakespearean Richard Mansfield; used on stage and in film by such fabled Cyranos as Walter Hampden and José Ferrer.

Translated by Edwin Morgan. Manchester: Carcanet Press, 1992. A verse translation into the native Glaswegian of this talented Scots poet; a tour de force.

Translated by Louis Untermeyer. 1954. Mineola, NY: Dover Publications, 2000. Blank verse translation.

FRENCH EDITIONS OF *CYRANO DE BERGERAC*

Edited by Claude Aziza. Édition revue et augmentée. Paris: Pocket, 1998. Includes a "Dossier Historique et Littéraire" with contemporary reviews of *Cyrano* as well as analyses of the work's structure, characters, etc.

Edited by Patrick Besnier. Paris: Gallimard, 1999. Includes a chronology, well-chosen critical materials, and a fine introduction by Besnier.

Edited by Pierre Citti. Paris: Livre de Poche, 1990. Contains excellent notes and a preface. Le Bret's *Life of Cyrano* is included in the Annexes.

Edited by Patrice Pavis. Paris: Classiques Larousse, 2000. Designed for use by French students, this edition contains many useful lexical and historical footnotes.

Edited by Jacques Truchet. Paris: Imprimerie nationale, 1983. The definitive edition of *Cyrano*, exhaustively researched, contains a wealth of material relating to the play's composition as well as extensive historical information on the historical Cyrano.

CRITICISM IN ENGLISH

Outside of scholarly journals, there is not a great deal of literature in English about Edmond Rostand and *Cyrano*. The play is discussed in the following works:

Amoia, Alba della Fazia. *Edmond Rostand*. Boston: Twayne Publishers, 1978.

Eliot, T. S. "'Rhetoric' and Poetic Drama." In *Selected Essays*. New York: Harcourt, Brace, 1950.

CRITICISM IN FRENCH

Much more is available in French. Readers may consult the following:

Andry, Marc. *Edmond Rostand: Le Panache et la gloire*. Paris: Plon, 1986.

De Margerie, Caroline. *Edmond Rostand; ou, Le baiser de la gloire*. Paris: B. Grasset, 1997. The most thorough biography to date.

Garcia, Carole, and Roland Dargeles. *Edmond Rostand: Panache et Tourments*. Paris: Editions Jean Curutchet, 1997.

Gérard, Rosemonde. *Edmond Rostand*. Paris: Fasquelle, 1935. Memoirs of Rostand's wife, including of the opening night of *Cyrano*.

Ripert, Émile. *Edmond Rostand*. Paris: Hachette, 1968.

Look for the following titles, available now from
BARNES & NOBLE CLASSICS

Visit your local bookstore for these and more fine titles.
Or to order online go to: WWW.BN.COM/CLASSICS

Title	Author	ISBN	Price
Adventures of Huckleberry Finn	Mark Twain	1-59308-112-X	$5.95
The Adventures of Tom Sawyer	Mark Twain	1-59308-139-1	$5.95
The Aeneid	Vergil	1-59308-237-1	$7.95
Aesop's Fables		1-59308-062-X	$5.95
The Age of Innocence	Edith Wharton	1-59308-143-X	$5.95
Agnes Grey	Anne Brontë	1-59308-323-8	$6.95
Alice's Adventures in Wonderland and Through the Looking-Glass	Lewis Carroll	1-59308-015-8	$5.95
The Ambassadors	Henry James	1-59308-378-5	$7.95
Anna Karenina	Leo Tolstoy	1-59308-027-1	$8.95
The Arabian Nights	Anonymous	1-59308-281-9	$9.95
The Art of War	Sun Tzu	1-59308-017-4	$7.95
The Autobiography of an Ex-Colored Man and Other Writings	James Weldon Johnson	1-59308-289-4	$5.95
The Awakening and Selected Short Fiction	Kate Chopin	1-59308-113-8	$6.95
Babbitt	Sinclair Lewis	1-59308-267-3	$7.95
The Beautiful and Damned	F. Scott Fitzgerald	1-59308-245-2	$7.95
Beowulf	Anonymous	1-59308-266-5	$4.95
Billy Budd and The Piazza Tales	Herman Melville	1-59308-253-3	$6.95
Bleak House	Charles Dickens	1-59308-311-4	$9.95
The Bostonians	Henry James	1-59308-297-5	$8.95
The Brothers Karamazov	Fyodor Dostoevsky	1-59308-045-X	$9.95
Bulfinch's Mythology	Thomas Bulfinch	1-59308-273-8	$12.95
The Call of the Wild and White Fang	Jack London	1-59308-200-2	$5.95
Candide	Voltaire	1-59308-028-X	$4.95
The Canterbury Tales	Geoffrey Chaucer	1-59308-080-8	$9.95
A Christmas Carol, The Chimes and The Cricket on the Hearth	Charles Dickens	1-59308-033-6	$5.95
The Collected Oscar Wilde		1-59308-310-6	$9.95
The Collected Poems of Emily Dickinson		1-59308-050-6	$5.95
Common Sense and Other Writings	Thomas Paine	1-59308-209-6	$6.95
The Communist Manifesto and Other Writings	Karl Marx and Friedrich Engels	1-59308-100-6	$5.95
The Complete Sherlock Holmes, Vol. I	Sir Arthur Conan Doyle	1-59308-034-4	$7.95
The Complete Sherlock Holmes, Vol. II	Sir Arthur Conan Doyle	1-59308-040-9	$7.95
Confessions	Saint Augustine	1-59308-259-2	$6.95
A Connecticut Yankee in King Arthur's Court	Mark Twain	1-59308-210-X	$7.95
The Count of Monte Cristo	Alexandre Dumas	1-59308-151-0	$7.95
The Country of the Pointed Firs and Selected Short Fiction	Sarah Orne Jewett	1-59308-262-2	$7.95
Crime and Punishment	Fyodor Dostoevsky	1-59308-081-6	$8.95
Cyrano de Bergerac	Edmond Rostand	1-59308-387-4	$6.95
Daisy Miller and Washington Square	Henry James	1-59308-105-7	$4.95
Daniel Deronda	George Eliot	1-59308-290-8	$9.95

(continued)

Dead Souls	Nikolai Gogol	1-59308-092-1	$8.95
The Deerslayer	James Fenimore Cooper	1-59308-211-8	$9.95
Don Quixote	Miguel de Cervantes	1-59308-046-8	$9.95
Dracula	Bram Stoker	1-59308-114-6	$6.95
Emma	Jane Austen	1-59308-152-9	$6.95
Essays and Poems by Ralph Waldo Emerson		1-59308-076-X	$6.95
Essential Dialogues of Plato		1-59308-269-X	$9.95
The Essential Tales and Poems of Edgar Allan Poe		1-59308-064-6	$7.95
Ethan Frome and Selected Stories	Edith Wharton	1-59308-090-5	$5.95
Fairy Tales	Hans Christian Andersen	1-59308-260-6	$9.95
Far from the Madding Crowd	Thomas Hardy	1-59308-223-1	$7.95
The Federalist	Hamilton, Madison, Jay	1-59308-282-7	$7.95
Founding America: Documents from the Revolution to the Bill of Rights	Jefferson, et al.	1-59308-230-4	$9.95
Frankenstein	Mary Shelley	1-59308-115-4	$4.95
The Good Soldier	Ford Madox Ford	1-59308-268-1	$6.95
Great American Short Stories: From Hawthorne to Hemingway	Various	1-59308-086-7	$7.95
The Great Escapes: Four Slave Narratives	Various	1-59308-294-0	$6.95
Great Expectations	Charles Dickens	1-59308-116-2	$6.95
Grimm's Fairy Tales	Jacob and Wilhelm Grimm	1-59308-056-5	$7.95
Gulliver's Travels	Jonathan Swift	1-59308-132-4	$5.95
Hard Times	Charles Dickens	1-59308-156-1	$5.95
Heart of Darkness and Selected Short Fiction	Joseph Conrad	1-59308-123-5	$5.95
The History of the Peloponnesian War	Thucydides	1-59308-091-3	$10.95
The House of Mirth	Edith Wharton	1-59308-153-7	$6.95
The House of the Dead and Poor Folk	Fyodor Dostoevsky	1-59308-194-4	$7.95
The House of the Seven Gables	Nathaniel Hawthorne	1-59308-231-2	$7.95
The Hunchback of Notre Dame	Victor Hugo	1-59308-140-5	$7.95
The Idiot	Fyodor Dostoevsky	1-59308-058-1	$7.95
The Iliad	Homer	1-59308-232-0	$7.95
The Importance of Being Earnest and Four Other Plays	Oscar Wilde	1-59308-059-X	$6.95
Incidents in the Life of a Slave Girl	Harriet Jacobs	1-59308-283-5	$5.95
The Inferno	Dante Alighieri	1-59308-051-4	$6.95
The Interpretation of Dreams	Sigmund Freud	1-59308-298-3	$8.95
Ivanhoe	Sir Walter Scott	1-59308-246-0	$8.95
Jane Eyre	Charlotte Brontë	1-59308-117-0	$7.95
Journey to the Center of the Earth	Jules Verne	1-59308-252-5	$4.95
Jude the Obscure	Thomas Hardy	1-59308-035-2	$6.95
The Jungle Books	Rudyard Kipling	1-59308-109-X	$5.95
The Jungle	Upton Sinclair	1-59308-118-9	$6.95
King Solomon's Mines	H. Rider Haggard	1-59308-275-4	$5.95
Lady Chatterley's Lover	D. H. Lawrence	1-59308-239-8	$6.95
The Last of the Mohicans	James Fenimore Cooper	1-59308-137-5	$5.95
Leaves of Grass: First and "Death-bed" Editions	Walt Whitman	1-59308-083-2	$9.95
The Legend of Sleepy Hollow and Other Writings	Washington Irving	1-59308-225-8	$6.95
Les Misérables	Victor Hugo	1-59308-066-2	$9.95
Les Liaisons Dangereuses	Pierre Choderlos de Laclos	1-59308-240-1	$7.95
Little Women	Louisa May Alcott	1-59308-108-1	$6.95

(continued)

Title	Author	ISBN	Price
Lost Illusions	Honoré de Balzac	1-59308-315-7	$9.95
Madame Bovary	Gustave Flaubert	1-59308-052-2	$6.95
Maggie: A Girl of the Streets and Other Writings about New York	Stephen Crane	1-59308-248-7	$7.95
The Magnificent Ambersons	Booth Tarkington	1-59308-263-0	$7.95
Main Street	Sinclair Lewis	1-59308-386-6	$8.95
Man and Superman and Three Other Plays	George Bernard Shaw	1-59308-067-0	$7.95
The Man in the Iron Mask	Alexandre Dumas	1-59308-233-9	$9.95
Mansfield Park	Jane Austen	1-59308-154-5	$5.95
The Mayor of Casterbridge	Thomas Hardy	1-59308-309-2	$6.95
The Metamorphoses	Ovid	1-59308-276-2	$7.95
The Metamorphosis and Other Stories	Franz Kafka	1-59308-029-8	$6.95
Moby-Dick	Herman Melville	1-59308-018-2	$9.95
Moll Flanders	Daniel Defoe	1-59308-216-9	$6.95
My Ántonia	Willa Cather	1-59308-202-9	$5.95
My Bondage and My Freedom	Frederick Douglass	1-59308-301-7	$6.95
Narrative of Sojourner Truth		1-59308-293-2	$6.95
Narrative of the Life of Frederick Douglass, an American Slave		1-59308-041-7	$4.95
Nicholas Nickleby	Charles Dickens	1-59308-300-9	$8.95
Night and Day	Virginia Woolf	1-59308-212-6	$7.95
Nostromo	Joseph Conrad	1-59308-193-6	$7.95
Notes from Underground, The Double and Other Stories	Fyodor Dostoevsky	1-59308-124-3	$7.95
O Pioneers!	Willa Cather	1-59308-205-3	$5.95
The Odyssey	Homer	1-59308-009-3	$5.95
Of Human Bondage	W. Somerset Maugham	1-59308-238-X	$9.95
Oliver Twist	Charles Dickens	1-59308-206-1	$6.95
The Origin of Species	Charles Darwin	1-59308-077-8	$7.95
Paradise Lost	John Milton	1-59308-095-6	$7.95
The Paradiso	Dante Alighieri	1-59308-317-3	$8.95
Père Goriot	Honoré de Balzac	1-59308-285-1	$8.95
Persuasion	Jane Austen	1-59308-130-8	$5.95
Peter Pan	J. M. Barrie	1-59308-213-4	$4.95
The Phantom of the Opera	Gaston Leroux	1-59308-249-5	$6.95
The Picture of Dorian Gray	Oscar Wilde	1-59308-025-5	$4.95
The Pilgrim's Progress	John Bunyan	1-59308-254-1	$7.95
A Portrait of the Artist as a Young Man and Dubliners	James Joyce	1-59308-031-X	$6.95
The Possessed	Fyodor Dostoevsky	1-59308-250-9	$9.95
Pride and Prejudice	Jane Austen	1-59308-201-0	$6.95
The Prince and Other Writings	Niccolò Machiavelli	1-59308-060-3	$5.95
The Prince and the Pauper	Mark Twain	1-59308-218-5	$4.95
Pudd'nhead Wilson and Those Extraordinary Twins	Mark Twain	1-59308-255-X	$6.95
The Purgatorio	Dante Alighieri	1-59308-219-3	$8.95
Pygmalion and Three Other Plays	George Bernard Shaw	1-59308-078-6	$7.95
The Red Badge of Courage and Selected Short Fiction	Stephen Crane	1-59308-119-7	$4.95
Republic	Plato	1-59308-097-2	$6.95
The Return of the Native	Thomas Hardy	1-59308-220-7	$7.95
Robinson Crusoe	Daniel Defoe	1-59308-360-2	$5.95
A Room with a View	E. M. Forster	1-59308-288-6	$5.95
Scaramouche	Rafael Sabatini	1-59308-242-8	$7.95
The Scarlet Letter	Nathaniel Hawthorne	1-59308-207-X	$5.95

(continued)

The Scarlet Pimpernel	Baroness Orczy	1-59308-234-7	$5.95
The Secret Agent	Joseph Conrad	1-59308-305-X	$6.95
The Secret Garden	Frances Hodgson Burnett	1-59308-277-0	$5.95
Selected Stories of O. Henry		1-59308-042-5	$5.95
Sense and Sensibility	Jane Austen	1-59308-125-1	$5.95
Siddhartha	Hermann Hesse	1-59308-379-3	$5.95
Silas Marner and Two Short Stories	George Eliot	1-59308-251-7	$6.95
Sister Carrie	Theodore Dreiser	1-59308-226-6	$8.95
The Souls of Black Folk	W. E. B. Du Bois	1-59308-014-X	$5.95
The Strange Case of Dr. Jekyll and Mr. Hyde and Other Stories	Robert Louis Stevenson	1-59308-131-6	$4.95
Swann's Way	Marcel Proust	1-59308-295-9	$8.95
A Tale of Two Cities	Charles Dickens	1-59308-138-3	$5.95
Tarzan of the Apes	Edgar Rice Burroughs	1-59308-227-4	$6.95
Tess of d'Urbervilles	Thomas Hardy	1-59308-228-2	$7.95
This Side of Paradise	F. Scott Fitzgerald	1-59308-243-6	$6.95
Three Theban Plays	Sophocles	1-59308-235-5	$6.95
Thus Spoke Zarathustra	Friedrich Nietzsche	1-59308-278-9	$7.95
The Time Machine and The Invisible Man	H. G. Wells	1-59308-388-2	$6.95
Tom Jones	Henry Fielding	1-59308-070-0	$8.95
Treasure Island	Robert Louis Stevenson	1-59308-247-9	$4.95
The Turn of the Screw, The Aspern Papers and Two Stories	Henry James	1-59308-043-3	$5.95
Twenty Thousand Leagues Under the Sea	Jules Verne	1-59308-302-5	$5.95
Uncle Tom's Cabin	Harriet Beecher Stowe	1-59308-121-9	$7.95
Vanity Fair	William Makepeace Thackeray	1-59308-071-9	$7.95
The Varieties of Religious Experience	William James	1-59308-072-7	$7.95
Villette	Charlotte Brontë	1-59308-316-5	$9.95
The Virginian	Owen Wister	1-59308-236-3	$7.95
Walden and Civil Disobedience	Henry David Thoreau	1-59308-208-8	$5.95
War and Peace	Leo Tolstoy	1-59308-073-5	$12.95
The War of the Worlds	H. G. Wells	1-59308-362-9	$5.95
Ward No. 6 and Other Stories	Anton Chekhov	1-59308-003-4	$7.95
The Waste Land and Other Poems	T. S. Eliot	1-59308-279-7	$4.95
The Way We Live Now	Anthony Trollope	1-59308-304-1	$10.95
The Wind in the Willows	Kenneth Grahame	1-59308-265-7	$5.95
The Wings of the Dove	Henry James	1-59308-296-7	$9.95
Wives and Daughters	Elizabeth Gaskell	1-59308-257-6	$7.95
The Woman in White	Wilkie Collins	1-59308-280-0	$7.95
Women in Love	D. H. Lawrence	1-59308-258-4	$8.95
The Wonderful Wizard of Oz	L. Frank Baum	1-59308-221-5	$6.95
Wuthering Heights	Emily Brontë	1-59308-128-6	$5.95

BARNES & NOBLE CLASSICS

If you are an educator and would like to receive an
Examination or Desk Copy of a Barnes & Noble Classics edition,
please refer to Academic Resources on our website at
WWW.BN.COM/CLASSICS
or contact us at
BNCLASSICS@BN.COM

All prices are subject to change.